Crafting a Tradition of
WiTCHCRaFT

About the Author

Raven Grimassi was a Neopagan scholar and award-winning author of over twelve books on Witchcraft, Wicca, and Neopaganism. He was a member of the American Folklore Society and was co-founder and co-director of the College of the Crossroads.

Raven's background includes training in the Rosicrucian Order as well as the study of the Kabbalah through the First Temple of Tifareth under Lady Sara Cunningham. His early magickal career began in the late 1960s and involved the study of works by Franz Bardon, Éliphas Lévi, William Barrett, Dion Fortune, William Gray, William Butler, and Israel Regardie.

Raven was the directing Elder of the tradition of Arician Witchcraft, and together with his wife, Stephanie Taylor, he developed a complete teaching system known as Ash, Birch, and Willow. This system was the culmination of over thirty-five years of study and practice in the magickal and spiritual traditions of the Indigenous people of pre-Christian Europe.

Foreword by Christopher Penczak

Crafting a Tradition of
WITCHCRAFT

Creating Foundations for Your
Spiritual Beliefs & Practices

RAVEN GRIMASSI

Chicago, IL

Paperback ISBN: 978-1-959883-65-4
Library of Congress Control Number on file.

Disclaimer: Crossed Crow Books, LLC does not participate in, endorse, or have any authority or responsibility concerning private business transactions between our authors and the public. Any internet references contained in this work were found to be valid during the time of publication, however, the publisher cannot guarantee that a specific reference will continue to be maintained. This book's material is not intended to diagnose, treat, cure, or prevent any disease, disorder, ailment, or any physical or psychological condition. The author, publisher, and its associates shall not be held liable for the reader's choices when approaching this book's material. The views and opinions expressed within this book are those of the author alone and do not necessarily reflect the views and opinions of the publisher.

Published by:
Crossed Crow Books, LLC
6934 N Glenwood Ave, Suite C
Chicago, IL 60626
www.crossedcrowbooks.com

Printed in the United States of America.
IBI

Contents

Foreword

Paradox is at the heart of the mysteries, and my beloved friend Raven truly embraced both the mysteries and, in this beautiful book, the paradox embodied in their experience and transmission. How else can you describe the dual mission of preserving past teachings while encouraging one to create new traditions? Is it madness? Can you have both? Are they not at cross purposes?

Raven himself was a bit of a paradox and an enigma to both his beloved readers and critics alike. One side sees him as staunchly traditionalist, never wanting to deviate from anything that was a part of classical Witchcraft and Paganism. The other side thought he was making it all up under a veneer of tradition. For those of us lucky enough to know and befriend him, the truth is more complex. He was passionate about sharing magick in ways he hoped people would understand. Few saw the profoundly loving, humorous, and magickal man behind the role of author, teacher, and academic, demonstrating his integration of the mysteries into his life and his sense of self.

Raven always defended tradition. He was guided by the traditions of his family and the traditions of his teachers and mentors, both of this world and in other worlds. He was gravely concerned with the loss of lore and the wisdom that accompanied it from a new generation with louder voices, for the wisdom was often found in the quiet parts. He balanced oaths and considerations for secrecy with wanting to share as much as he could with as many people who truly wanted to learn. As time goes on, I understand his point more and more, and I grow to have the same concerns. I've learned to follow his example. Advocate for and teach what you feel is important, and the mysteries will be preserved and grow in their own way, even if they are not the most popular. They are often for the eyes of the few, but they will still survive.

While Raven was guided by tradition—truly rooted in the teachings of the past—and considered himself a tender of the roots, this didn't mean he didn't create new things. Much of his later work was born from deep and personal gnosis explored by himself and his wife and magickal partner, Stephanie Taylor, in the formation of a new tradition, Ash, Birch, and Willow. Raven was inspired by the voices of old to create something that would meet the needs of mystery and tradition for the new generation. After many ups and downs in building community around the Italian traditions of Strega, he came to realize those far from a first- or second-generation household experience of an Italian family—those in the general modern American experience—didn't grasp the material as it didn't translate well to their cultural awareness. So he sought the primal roots, beyond the specifics of nation, culture, or ethnicity. He harkened back to our Stone Age ancestors and let the Western occult tradition be his guide.

The first edition of this text, published as *Crafting Wiccan Traditions,* predates a lot of his public unveiling of his own new tradition. As Raven always practiced what he wrote about, writing not only from an academic perspective but the lived experience of the Witch, I can see the principles of this book put into action in own life, knowing some of the ins and outs of his Ash, Birch, and Willow community. Being privy to some personal papers, unreleased writings, and ritual books, I see how he refined this process in his own writings and traditions over many years. While we might want to assume that, through his stories, he inherited a complete and unaltered tradition from his magickal family dating back to antiquity, this is simply not true and something he addressed in his last version of *The Book of the Holy Strega.* He was always deepening his understanding, expanding his knowledge, adding to it, and creating parallel teachings for those outside of the initiatory traditions he taught. He would often talk about, and then share with the world through the creation of his decks, the concept of the Well-Worn Path and the Hidden Path, the one we must trod today and thereby add to the tradition to take the next generation even further.

Never one to assume his way is the only way for all, Raven crafts a text here that encourages us through the same process he used to find our own traditions, whether we are solitary or, ideally, in small community. For in the mysteries, this is the process that is most important: our own personal gnosis of understanding, the "aha" moment that forever changes us for the better.

Like any good mystery tradition, the seeker is challenged at the gate and at many other points of what can often be considered the ordeal before celebration. Through this text, Raven asks us to question our assumptions and the piecemeal traditions we might know. He often challenged what he called the "anything goes" mentality because he was looking for deeper thought and understanding behind our practices, and that was often lacking among those who he would converse (at times, myself included). Raven would ask questions of what I did and why I did it, and even though we might not have always agreed or placed the same emphasis on the same aspects of a teaching or myth, I am a far better Witch because of his teachings, writings, and friendship. Without his support, my own Temple of Witchcraft tradition and community would not be the same, and I am thankful for the amazing support he and Stephanie have always shown us.

Here you will be questioned on your concepts of divinity and cosmology. Does it relate to the roots of anything that has come before you? What are your philosophies? Do the myths you learn and live by support those philosophies and teachings? Not only how do you want to do ritual, but why? What is the pattern to it? Does that align with your ideas of divinity and myth? Raven urges the interweaving of our solar and lunar cycles with our beliefs, practices, and philosophies, rather than have disparate parts unrelated to each other. Are you working in a community or group? If so, how is that organized? How will you transmit teaching and train new members? How will you keep records and pass on lore? Many modern groups fall apart because of a lack of clear roles and organization, and a lack of discussion about how the group wants to operate. Of course Raven will foster some of the traditional structures and hierarchies that have worked well for him, but the very act of asking is an act of magick for us to decide what we want to create, and, more importantly, why.

We live in a time of great change, and while there is so much change, great change is not always *good* change. Raven would remind us that a tree with weak roots will fall down in the next storm. New growth is great when rooted and solid to what was and what is. The changes in our societies, in both greater society, facing the challenges of technology and global economics, and smaller society—our Pagan, Witchcraft, and Wicca groups—can feel much like the metamorphosis of not just the tree of our traditions, but the entire forest. While we have individual transformation, societies transform under a much longer process. We can feel like we were born into a process that is something greater than ourselves, and despite the current speed of society, the collective transformation can take quite a long time. In truth, it never ends. A Witch must be conscious and fully participating in any transformation occurring. That is the essence of magick. We will collectively be on the far end of the process, and we might not see it in our lifetime. A new ecosystem might develop, but it will always have its origin in the patterns of the past. This is the mystery of all things.

If parts of this book seem a little too traditional for you, despite their open-ended nature, keep a vision of Raven Grimassi as a wisdom-keeping hierophant of the Eleusinian Mysteries, a high priest who will offer us the three elements of the mysteries—sacred things said, sacred things done, and sacred things shown. What we do with these mysteries, how they change us, and the ways we in turn convey them in our lives and to the next generation is up to us, but remember to keep our firm roots as we grow high, and thank Raven for the guidance. I know I will.

In Love, Will, and Wisdom,
Christopher Penczak
Summer Solstice 2024

☽ x ☾

Preface

Defining Witchcraft is challenging in modern times. This is because the very nature of contemporary Witchcraft defies the type of structure typically required to present a definitive representation. In essence, Witchcraft is a practice that venerates Nature and sees divinity reflected within all things. Generally speaking, it is a path of personal growth and development that relies upon intuition and self-discernment.

Most modern practitioners view Witchcraft as a personal path that allows for individual interpretation and application of its beliefs and practices. The majority of modern Western Witches do not acknowledge any central authority figure, nor do they rely upon any set doctrines or "Holy Book" that is foundational and directive. Most Witches are self-directed and eclectic in nature.

The basic format of contemporary Western Witchcraft is built upon the beliefs and practices of pre-Christian European religion. Along with this is a blend of elements from Eastern mysticism and various forms of shamanism from different regions of the world. One popular inclusion is the system of chakras (personal energy zones in the body) and the aura, which is an energy field that surrounds the physical body. The basics that comprise Witchcraft today are both ancient and modern. In a real sense, contemporary Witchcraft blends ancestral knowledge and wisdom with the practitioner's needs in modern life.

The contemporary view of Witchcraft is very different from its presentation in the mid-twentieth century, which marked its public appearance. The word "Wicca" was used interchangeably with the word "Witchcraft" during the 1960s and through the early 1980s. For accuracy and respect, it's important to separate the two and view Wicca as a specific system or religion that falls under the umbrella of diverse Witchcraft practices. In other words, the most common modern definition is that Wicca is a religion and Witchcraft is a practice.

History of Wicca in Witchcraft

The word "Wicca" first came to public attention through the writings of Gerald Gardner in the 1950s. Gardner wrote about what he called an "ancient fertility cult," which he claimed had survived into modern times. Wicca, as Gardner depicted it, was reportedly a fragmented system of Witchcraft, which was focused upon a Goddess and God of Nature (as well as being associated with lunar and solar veneration).

If you look up the word *Witch* in most dictionaries, you will find that its root word comes from the Old English word *wicce* or *wicca*. The precise meaning of these words is highly debated, and some people argue that they refer to being wise or having the ability to bend and shape. According to historian Jeffrey Russell, the verb *wiccian* means "to cast a spell," and in such a case, would link *wicca* and *wicce* to the use of magick. Russell notes that the earliest mention of the word Wicca is found in a ninth-century secular trial against a man accused of performing magick. Ironically, some modern Wiccans do not practice magick, nor do they feel that it is even a part of Wicca today.

In the days of Gerald Gardner, Wicca was called "The Old Religion" and "The Craft of the Wise." Gardner claimed that he was initiated into a surviving sect of Witches who traced their lineage to ancient times. Modern scholars reject this claim and argue that what Gardner presented in his books was primarily a modern construction. Others feel that, at the very least, Gardner added modern elements to the material he originally possessed.

During his writing career, Gardner presented Wicca as containing seasonal celebrations based upon the ancient Celtic festivals known as Samhain, Imbolc, Beltane, and Lughnasadh. At a later time, he incorporated the festivals of the Vernal Equinox, Summer Solstice, Autumn Equinox, and Winter Solstice. This provided modern Wicca with the eight seasonal festivals of the year that now comprise the sabbats. While these sabbats are common in Wiccan communities, they are neither limited to that practice nor used by Witches of all creeds. Over time, the names of the sabbats have evolved. In the 1960s and early 1970s, they were commonly known as:

❖ Hallowmas (October 31)
❖ Yule (Winter Solstice, December)
❖ Candlemas (February 2)
❖ Lady Day (Vernal Equinox, March)
❖ Roodmas (May 1)
❖ St. John's Day (Summer Solstice, June)
❖ Lammas (August)
❖ Michaelmas (Autumn Equinox, September)

Note that the date of the solstices and equinoxes vary each year, but generally fall around the twenty-first.

In the 1980s, a Witch named Aidan Kelly renamed the sabbats, which are almost standardized as the non-Christianized and Celtic-oriented titles:

❖ Samhain (October Eve)
❖ Yule (Winter Solstice)
❖ Imbolc (February Eve)
❖ Ostara (Vernal Equinox)
❖ Beltane (May Eve)
❖ Litha (Summer Solstice)
❖ Lughnasadh (August Eve)
❖ Mabon (Autumn Equinox)

During the 1960s and 1970s, Wiccan Witchcraft possessed a definite structure, which included a set of laws. These laws described the roles of the High Priestess and High Priest, as well as codes of conduct for covens and practitioners. Some laws set forth the physical boundaries for covens, and other laws established ethics and protocol regarding the use of magick.

The 1980s saw Witchcraft pass through an intense period of transformation. Innovative authors such as Scott Cunningham pioneered a new vision for Witches and Wiccans, which ultimately transformed the Craft into something new and different from many of its former and foundational concepts. Writers like Cunningham and others removed the traditional structure of Wicca and presented it as a self-styled and self-directed system. This approach has been called the "do whatever feels right" practice of Witchcraft. The majority of authors during the 1980s (and later) followed suit. It was during this period that the bulk of rooted and foundational concepts that originally formed Wicca were no longer passed on in published material. Authors simply stopped writing about them and instead presented their own creative views of Witchcraft, as well as new methods of ritual and magick. The generation born in the 1980s onward naturally inherited this newly transformed Witchcraft, which was constructed through the ideas of a few pioneers.

Only a few of the many facets of the former Wicca were retained in the transformed counterpart. These included the Goddess and God, the roles of High Priestess and High Priest, a system of degrees, eight seasonal celebrations, the use of a ritual circle, four directions and associated Elemental Natures, and a code of ethics known as the Rede. Some of these aspects are also disappearing, or being reinterpreted, as Wiccan-inspired Witchcraft continues to be transformed by a new generation.

The majority of people involved in Witchcraft today are solitary practitioners. They gain most of their information about the Craft from published books and online. The internet features various sites that provide information, and one can also find many social media outlets where discussions can take place. Unfortunately, the internet provides as much misinformation about Witchcraft as it does useful and accurate information. While published books are subject to reviews, which provide insights about the material, there are few reviews of Witchcraft sites that offer discernment regarding their authenticity and accuracy.

In larger cities in the United States, seekers can find classes on Witchcraft that are held in occult shops and bookstores, and more geographically accessible online spaces. These can provide valuable information and opportunities to meet like-minded people. Classes taught synchronously provide a means of asking questions and obtaining immediate clarification, which books and website materials cannot provide.

Witchcraft Today

Modern Witchcraft is comprised of a diversity of beliefs, perceptions, and practices. Therefore, it is difficult to provide definitive descriptions of it as a system, religion, or philosophy. In this section, we will explore the most common elements of Witchcraft that share the basic consensus of agreement. At the same time, we will acknowledge that other views exist and may not conform to what follows here.

The foundation of Witchcraft, when seen as a Western religious practice, is rooted in the concept of divinity being comprised of the archetypal feminine and masculine polarities. These polarities, especially in Western practices, are personified as the Goddess and God. Wicca and Wiccan-inspired Witchcraft possesses a mythology in which the Goddess and God are associated with celestial objects and with seasonal periods on Earth. The Goddess is associated with the Moon and stars and with the cross quarter sabbats (those that fall between the equinox and solstice periods). The God is linked to the Sun and some planetary forces, and with the sabbats that mark the solstice and equinox events.

The ritual practices appearing in Witchcraft are associated with the phases of the Moon and the seasonal tides on Nature (as previously listed). The Moon phases are metaphors for the Goddess, who is often depicted as a triple-image deity that is collectively known as the Maiden, Mother, and Crone. She depicts the stages of life: youth, maturity, and old age. As a goddess linked with the seasons, she is viewed as the Great Mother or Great Goddess. All living things are born from her, and at death return to her womb for rebirth.

The God figure is associated with the Sun and its role throughout the year. He represents the periods of growth and decline as reflected in spring and summer, fall and winter. As a mythical figure, the God is the seed-bearer who impregnates the Goddess of Nature. From their union, the bounty of Nature is born.

The eight sabbats, or festivals, are known as the Wheel of the Year. The Wheel reflects the changing seasons as the cycles of life. The myths associated with the Goddess and God are linked to each sabbat and depict a mated consort pair. Their relationship is reflected in the periods of Nature known as the *waxing and waning times*. The waxing, or growth-oriented period, includes the Vernal Equinox, Beltane, Summer Solstice, and Lughnasadh festivals. The waning, or decline-oriented, period incorporates the Autumn Equinox, Samhain, Winter Solstice, and Imbolc festivals.

In addition to seasonal rituals, modern Witchcraft contains rites called *esbats*, which are linked to the phases of the Moon. The most common rituals are during the New Moon and Full Moon periods, which are observed monthly. While the seasonal rites can be viewed as associated with the phenomena of the material world, the lunar rites are largely linked to mystical or religious themes.

The religious aspects of Wicca and Wiccan-inspired Witchcraft include a belief in an afterlife called the Summerland, which is a temporary realm where the soul awaits rebirth into a new life. This is called *reincarnation*, which is the idea that the flesh body is a temporary vessel used by a soul during many lifetimes. The soul encounters a variety of life experiences from numerous diverse perspectives including different gender identities, socio-economic statuses, and ranges of ability. Through these experiences, a soul learns the fullness of compassion and evolves into a higher order of spiritual being that can serve as a guide for souls still on their journey through mortal life.

As a spiritual path, Wicca and Wiccan-inspirited Witchcraft maintains an ethical philosophy known as the Rede, which is an axiom stating: *"As it harms none, do as you will."* Most Witches interpret this to mean that, as long as no one is harmed by one's actions, one should do whatever feels right at the time. Another tenet in Wicca and related

Craft practices is represented by the "Law of Return" or "Law of Three," which states that every action a person performs (positive or negative) returns to them in triple effect. While popular in some forms of Wicca, these are by no means universal beliefs.

Witchcraft and related religions or philosophies do not present themselves as the "only way" of spiritual enlightenment or evolution. The core philosophy of Western Witchcraft traditions is tolerance, rooted in the acceptance of other beliefs systems and religions as being valid from their own perspective. This philosophy does not condemn different lifestyles and is generally supportive of those outside of mainstream society.

Now that we have looked at some of the basic ideas associated with Western Witchcraft, we can further explore its foundations. Our goal is to build a personal tradition based on a firm foundation, while applying our own unique views and interpretations.

Introduction

This book presents what some people might regard as opposing goals. The primary goal is to demonstrate various methods of creating a Witchcraft system from the ground floor up. The other goal is to preserve the pre-existing foundations of Western Witchcraft. You might think that this is a contradiction, but it is actually a consideration of blending old roots and new growth. This is the formula in Nature—Witchcraft is a Nature-based practice, after all.

The book is partially designed to present various older and more traditional models of Witchcraft as it was known prior to the 1980s. I chose this time period because it marks the beginning of changes that took place in Western Witchcraft, which altered it into a set of practices different in key ways from the Craft I first encountered in the summer of 1969. The book is also designed to suggest methods of creating a personal system that is better suited to the needs of modern practitioners. It is my hope that this book offers the best of both worlds.

In laying out the ideas for this book into chapters, I wanted to provide various models that reflect the time-proven components of Witchcraft and explain why they are important foundational elements. I hoped that, by showing their continued relevance, the resistance to tradition by the new generation might be tempered. In addition to setting out the traditional building blocks, I included ideas on how to fashion a new system creatively.

For those who object to change, please know that my intention is not to encourage a new generation to abandon time-proven ways. For those who object to pre-existing traditions, please know that the intention of this book is not to shackle you to outdated and irrelevant material. Instead, I want to show both sides: that Witchcraft can adapt to a new environment and period while retaining its integrity and momentum from its continuing empowerment from the past.

In addressing the topic of creating traditions, the book is designed for all levels of readers. I felt this was important because of the diversity of modern Witchcraft beliefs about the Craft. I realized that any statement regarding Witchcraft-related beliefs, concepts, and practices would bring disagreement from one faction or another. I also knew that the theme of the phrase "it goes without saying" could not serve the needs of this book. In order to have a common ground for understanding, the basics needed to be stated. I regard the definition of basics as an "agreement of consciousness" between the reader and me.

I selected older foundational views as the starting point, which establishes and defines the basics from which varying views later arose over the course of time. I have added newer views and presented some interpretations and opposing views among these. I did not want to burden the reader with ongoing apologies and endless prefaces on each page that not every Witch believes this and that. Let's have this understanding without repeating it throughout the book. I am hopeful that knowing this ahead of time will save everyone frustration.

For the intermediate and advanced reader, I have woven in the metaphysical aspects that arise and expand once the basics are understood. It is my hope that the well-informed readers will look at them as context for the expanded material. In this way, any misunderstandings of the material can be minimized once the reader understands where I am coming from and what I present.

In the structure of Witchcraft concepts and theology, several key elements apply to different aspects of the religious and magickal systems. In different contexts, the same theme can (and does) enhance the understanding and application. Therefore, a few things are repeated from various chapters in small sections, although not verbatim. Please know there is a good reason for doing so, and it is important not to skip over anything because you feel it's already been discussed. You will find that this is particularly true of material related to the Goddess and God and their seasonal and religious aspects. There are more facets and levels than you may think.

As the chapters continue, you will find that the material becomes more in-depth and addresses the metaphysical aspects of Witchcraft rites, beliefs, and practices that are derived from Wiccan roots. These are important to the spiritual understanding of Western Witchcraft as a whole. In writing at this level, I am assuming that the reader has at least a nodding acquaintance with this type of information. However, so as not to put any reader at a disadvantage, I have included a glossary that contains the concepts that are not as common as others in Witchcraft.

Several chapters of this book are devoted to ritual themes, concepts, techniques, and structure. This will provide you with a great deal of information and examples, so you can formulate your own effective tradition. The keys provided in this book are the same keys used by people in the past to construct their traditions. These vital keys are now offered to you in the pages of this book.

While it's important to acknowledge that many of the concepts outlined in this book are derived from a Wiccan background, this is not a book intended only for Wiccan readers. It can't be stated firmly enough that Western Witchcraft, as it is presented here, is diverse and flexible, suitable for readers from a plethora of different paths and origins. While many core concepts resemble a Wiccan bent, often being drawn from the heritage in which my own practice was raised, they are open and accessible to magickal practitioners to explore or reject as they see fit.

The Enchanted Worldview

Before examining methods of creating your own tradition, it is helpful to look at various foundational elements. This is useful in understanding the inner mechanisms of a tradition and how it interacts and integrates. It is from this understanding that you can draw out the specific components of your tradition, which will support the religious, spiritual, and magickal aspects that bind together whatever you create.

In this chapter, we will review "the enchanted worldview" that is at the core of beliefs related to spirits, deities, magick, and mysticism. Essentially, the enchanted view relates to "supernatural" spirits and forces that operate in the Material Realm. When creating traditions, it is important to have a sound understanding of this view as it relates to non-material realms of existence.

At the most basic level, we find a belief in the activity of spirits that influence human life. However, this can also be indirect, as in the belief that spirits influence crops, animals, weather, and other things important to human life. A direct involvement includes a belief in spirits that intentionally bring luck or misfortune. Direct influences also include haunting and visitations from the dead.

The idea of offerings arose from a perceived need to honor or appease spirits or gods. It was an ancient belief that the dead could bring misfortune if they were unhappy with individuals still among the living. Food and drink were often left to appease them, and this ancient practice resembles the old idea behind Halloween. This was seen as a time when the gateway between the worlds opened, which allowed access between the world of the living and the realm of the afterlife. The trick-or-treat costumes represented the dead returning, and the treats given them were peace offerings.

Among the foundational beliefs, we find the concept of Nature spirits. These are ancient entities involved in the inner mechanism of Nature. For example, one old belief depicts the opening of flowers and the emergence of fruit and grain as the result of the work of spirits. In this view, everything is the result of the activity of one or more spirits. Elemental spirits of Earth, Air, Fire, and Water are also Nature spirits. These Elemental spirits animate and activate the spiritual counterparts of the four physical elements. In essence, they are the creative forces that manifest within the material dimension. In classical occultism, they are represented by gnomes (Earth), sylphs (Air), salamanders (Fire), and undines (Water).

Many "higher level" spirits are found in occult teachings. These are often called spirit guides, spirit helpers, allies, or co-walkers. Traditionally, they are in the Spirit World and once lived mortal lives. Over the course of time, they spiritually evolved beyond the need for material bodies and were released from the Wheel of Rebirth. They now serve the needs of souls still existing in material bodies. In essence, this is a spiritual fellowship devoted to aiding lesser evolved souls.

One unique belief in Western Witchcraft is that of spiritual beings known as the Watchers or the Guardians. These beings are often associated with stars, and, in some teachings, the stars are the eyes of the Watchers. In other teachings, the stars are the campfires of the Watchers in the night sky. Among the oldest associations, the four Watchers are associated with individual stars: Aldebaran, Regulus, Antares, and Fomalhaut. These respectively mark the Vernal Equinox, Summer Solstice, Autumn Equinox, and Winter Solstice. It is the traditional role of the Watchers to guard ritual settings.

At the top of the hierarchy of entities, we find the concept of the Divine Source of All Things, which is personified as the Goddess and God. In essence, they are two halves of the whole. However, in some traditions, a myriad of self-aware deities exist that are not manifestations or aspects of an ultimate source. Whatever view one holds, the teachings simply point to the idea of deities topping the list of known entities.

The Goddess and God

In the mainstream Western Craft, we find the belief in a Goddess and God as mated consorts. The Goddess is most associated with the Moon and the Earth. The God is typically linked to the Sun and the sky. The Goddess and God both possess various aspects, including an association with death and realms of the Otherworld and Underworld.

In Witchcraft, the Goddess commonly possesses three primary aspects that are personified as the Maiden, Mother, and Crone. These represent the three major life stages of the archetypal feminine. The God also possesses various aspects, which include a triformis association. The God can be seen as the Hooded One, the Horned One, and the Old One. These present, respectively, his connection to the plant kingdom, the animal kingdom, and the kingdom of human life. In the latter, the God is often depicted as the Divine King or Slain God. This connects him to agriculture, specifically the harvest, where the grain is cut down and the seeds are saved for the next planting season.

The Goddess and God appear in the Wheel of the Year, which represents the eight seasonal rites known as the *sabbats*. In this structure, they journey together through the year as a mated pair that empowers the forces of Nature. Four of the sabbats mark the two equinoxes and solstices. The other four festivals traditionally fall on the eve of seasonal days that mark the astronomical mid-points between the equinox and solstice days. In this view, the God is associated with the day and the Goddess is associated with the night.

Magickal and Mystical Realms

Ancient myths and legends tell of secret and hidden realms. These can be divided into two categories: the Otherworld and the Underworld. The Otherworld is perceived as the realm of beings such as the Elven and Faery races. This realm is sometimes called the "Eternal Lands" or the "Land of Eternal Youth." Such names as "Avalon" are given to this realm, which is intimately linked to apples. In fact, one of the names for the Otherworld is "The Isle of Apples." In old lore, carrying an apple branch known as the Silver Bough granted safe passage to mortals traveling to and from the Otherworld.

The Underworld is viewed as the realm where the dead dwell while they await rebirth. In some traditions, this is an inner realm within the Otherworld, and in others, it is separate and exists on its own. In some Witchcraft traditions, the Summerland is in the Otherworld, and in others, it is placed in the Underworld. Wherever one places the Summerland, it is believed to be the resting place for souls just crossing from material life (where they await rebirth).

One feature of myths and legends connected to the Otherworld and Underworld is a hidden or lost cauldron. This cauldron possesses mystical powers that can restore life, bestow enlightenment, provide limitless provisions, or transform anything placed within them. A common feature of cauldron tales is the placement of a cauldron in darkness, which is often represented by a secret place in the Underworld or deep within a castle dungeon.

Other realms outside the mortal world include the dwelling places of deities. These are the Heaven Worlds and, in some cases, the Underworld. Two popular examples are Asgard in Northern European lore and Olympus in Southern European lore. Among the oldest of teachings, we find references to Three Great Realms: the Overworld, Middleworld, and Underworld. Often, these are associated with a giant tree, particularly an ash tree. This tree is sometimes called "The World Tree." The branches represent the Overworld, the roots symbolize the Underworld, and the realm of humankind is the Middleworld.

Magick

The belief in the reality of magick is key and central to foundational Witchcraft beliefs. However, it should be noted that some changes have taken place in Witchcraft beliefs over the past several decades, and therefore some followers of Nature-based religions like Wicca do not include magick in their personal beliefs and practices.

Essentially, magick is rooted in the belief that the material world can be influenced by non-material forces. Magick is an esoteric force that can be tapped, drawn, and directed through various means. In Witchcraft, a system of tools, rituals, and spells are used to work with magickal forces.

The ideas of magick helped early humans develop an understanding of the influences of the unseen. To this category, we may add such things as illness, malformations, misfortune, and calamity. Magick provided a means of dealing with unseen forces, which gave humans a sense of control. The ability to exert some degree of control within the enchanted world created a class of healers, magicians, Witches, shamans, and cunning folk.

In modern Witchcraft, magick is often viewed as a metaphysical science. It is frequently defined as the ability to manifest desire in accord with personal will power. This suggests a departure from the ancient view of magick as a non-material substance. In modern times, magick is often viewed as generated and controlled by the mind. However, an earlier view within Witchcraft groups involved the belief in two types of magick: raised power and drawn power. The former came from within the practitioner; it was their personal and developed powers. The latter came from another realm outside the material world.

The Astral Realm

A common occult teaching is the existence of a realm where thoughts can literally be transformed into material forms. The idea is that this realm consists of an etheric substance that can bind to the energy of thoughts. Such a bound energy becomes what is called a *thought-form*. Here, a strong will empowered with a vivid visualization draws the astral substance to itself. The substance then forms around the envisioned desire and creates an image of it. You can picture this as melted wax forming on an object dipped into it. In this analogy, the wax is the astral substance, and the object is the thought.

Once a thought-form is created, the process of manifestation begins because the astral nature has become dense and no longer in harmony with the astral plane. The thought-form is drawn to the material plane, where density is natural to the dimension. The book you are holding was once a collection of my thoughts that I desired to manifest in material form. The book is a solidified thought-form. This is the essential principle behind the Astral Realm. It should be noted, however, that daydreams lack the cohesion and intensity required to effectively create thought-forms. They do not attain a sufficient density, and this is why they remain dream-like instead of becoming a material reality.

As you work to create your own tradition, you will be establishing thought-forms. With dedication, you will be able to draw power into your system and create links to pre-existing sources of energy.

The Elemental Realm

Among occult teachings, we find the inclusion of a realm containing the non-material counterparts of the creative forces known as Earth, Air, Fire, and Water. These occult properties are the building blocks of the Material Realm. They also influence the mind, body, and spirit of all living things. In this sense, the Elemental Natures have a profound effect on emotions.

In essence, each Element contributes a quality towards manifestation: Earth provides substance, Air applies transmission, Fire brings about transformation, and Water gives movement or motion. Another set of correspondences presents Earth as giving stability, Air providing expansion, Fire lending vitality, and Water allowing for adaptation.

The Elemental Forces work in conjunction with the astral substance to transform thought-forms into material realities. As an active force, the Elemental Realm can be viewed as a river that flows to and from the material dimension. Thought-forms leave the material world through the current of this river and pass into the Elemental Realm. They are then bathed in the Elemental Natures that best match the desired manifestation (as contained in the generated thought-form). Once the thought-form absorbs the Elemental Natures, it is then passed into the astral fabric. Here, it draws a coating of astral material, establishing a cohesive representation of the desire.

When a thought-form appears completed within the astral dimension, its vibration changes, causing the thought-form to move off and away from the astral levels. It then slips back into the Elemental Realm, which in turn passes the thought-form into the material dimension. This is because the Elemental Realm has already contributed its qualities, and so the thought-form moves to a dimension in which it can manifest its impregnated imagery. This dimension is, of course, the material world.

The Material Realm

In mainstream Witchcraft, the Earth is considered a living, sentient being. It births, nurtures, and hosts all living things. The Material Realm allows non-material beings (such as souls) to experience this dimension. Living a material existence is believed to educate the soul and teach it greater compassion.

According to occult tradition, the material world provides the experience of distinct cycles and phases. These are observed and learned through the changing of seasons as well as the life passages of birth, maturity, old age, and death. Nature is said to be the Great Teacher, for it reflects the workings of Divine Consciousness within it. This concept can be likened to how the nature of the artist resides within the artwork. Likewise, Nature contains the imprint of divine hands. This is one of the reasons why many Witchcraft practices involve veneration of the seasons and cycles of Nature.

From a metaphysical perspective, the Material Realm is the lowest in energy vibration. The vibration is so slow that certain forms of energy become cohesive and visible. In other words, they look and behave as material objects. If we consider the fact that material objects are comprised of atoms and molecules, which are energy versus matter, then the teaching takes on scientific credibility. Another aspect of this teaching is rooted in quantum theories, which are too complex for the scope of this text.

In the teaching of reincarnation, it is said that souls become attached to the Wheel of Rebirth, which causes them to return and dwell in physical bodies. As these souls evolve, they eventually increase their spiritual vibration to such a degree that they can no longer be bound to material existence. In other words, the vibration is too high to become cohesive and visible in the material dimension. Thus, the soul sheds the density of material existence by attaining a vibration that is too etheric to maintain physical attachments. This is when it passes into the spiritual realms that are harmonious to the soul's higher and refined vibration.

Between the Worlds

Among the many beliefs of occult tradition, we find the concept of a place between the worlds. This realm is like a corridor or anteroom that exists between the Material Realm and the Spiritual Realm. In this sense, it exists in neither realm, but resides in-between.

In occult tradition, the in-between places are the most magickal of all. In addition to being assigned its own realm, such things as doorways and crossroads are said to be in-between places. It is at such places that spirits can reside and be encountered.

In Witchcraft traditions, magickal or ritual circles are often established "between the worlds" to operate in a mystical realm. Such a placement does not allow the laws of mundane physics to constrain the magickal and ritual designs of the participant's intentions. The classic reference to the in-between realm defines it as a place without a place in a time without a time.

A common traditional belief in many Witchcraft traditions is that the ritual or magickal circle, once cast between the worlds, is enveloped by an energy sphere. The circle "floats" in the center and is shielded on all sides, above, and below. The placement of the circle between the worlds allows the energy of the ritual or magickal operation to pass directly into the Elemental and Astral Realms (uncontaminated by the dense vibration of the Material Realm).

Sacred Space

The idea of a ritual setting as "sacred space" is not a new concept, but its use within rites of the Craft is most likely a modern interpretation. Sacred space in ritual is often where a circle is created for a community gathering and left "open but unbroken" during the event. In this light, sacred space is a blessing and a containment of energy that protects and unites all within its influence.

The basic concept of sacred space in its modern rendering is rooted in changes in Witchcraft communities during the mid-1970s and early 1980s. During these periods, the idea of a less structured ritual arose. Previously, the ritual circle was deemed a protective barrier and sphere that contained the energy generated by the people within it. Such a ritual circle required that an opening be made to release energy or to allow a person to enter or exit the circle. A modern view arose in which people could enter or leave a circle at will without creating an opening. This evolved into a concept that did not include the traditional understanding of the "cast circle" as it appeared in the older Craft understanding.

The concept of sacred space still incorporates certain aspects of traditional circle casting. Among these, we find the evocation of the Four Elements, the call to the quarter Guardians, and the evocation of the God and Goddess. Most people who use sacred space still formally release the "circle" after the rite is complete.

Now that we have reviewed the basics of Witchcraft's enchanted worldview, we can move to the next chapter and begin our examination into crafting Witchcraft traditions.

Building Your Own Tradition

In this chapter, we will explore ways of creating your own tradition or system of Witchcraft. The information and material provided here can help you decide how you wish to construct your own tradition of the Craft. You may want to go with a more traditional approach or blend in your own views. Perhaps you may decide to create something entirely unique that matches your personal needs outside of a formal structure. In any case, this chapter will provide you with suggested guidelines and tips.

Before we continue our exploration, it may be helpful to first define what we mean by a tradition. Essentially, it is a system based upon foundational beliefs and practices. It is a collection of cohesive and connected concepts that allow for the construction of powerful ritual formations, which will be covered in Chapter Five, "Creating Rituals." The thing to remember is that a tradition expresses the foundation of your beliefs and practices. It is your view of inner reality and a map of how your mini-universe operates.

One of the values of a tradition is that it preserves and transmits the time-proven practices and alignments of the people who created the system. A well-established tradition uses training stages that are designed to present concepts in a practical and functional order. This allows members of the tradition to receive teachings and techniques in a logical manner.

When a student is acclimated to the foundational concepts, their consciousness is directed in essential and beneficial ways. Naturally, this improves their understanding and experience of the teachings, beliefs, and practices of the tradition. Therefore, it is helpful to map out the key elements of a tradition.

There are several foundational elements to consider when creating your own tradition. Let's look at each one and consider its importance.

- ❖ Concept of Deity
- ❖ Myths or Legends
- ❖ Ritual Purpose
- ❖ Ritual Structure
- ❖ Religious or Philosophical Views
- ❖ Training Format
- ❖ Hierarchy and Degrees
- ❖ Magickal Practices
- ❖ Coven or Social Structures
- ❖ Laws and Codes of Conduct

Look over the list and consider the information about each aspect. You may find that you want to use all of them, or perhaps you may prefer to select or modify in accord with your own preferences and views. Once you have an idea of how each one works and contributes to the formation of a tradition, it should be easier to make informed decisions. Each of the following is covered in more depth in other chapters.

Concept of Deity

We will assume that you have a belief in the existence of the Divine Source, whatever your view of it may be. It is useful to consider what you believe and how you might picture this and reflect it within the rituals and beliefs of your tradition. The easiest approach is to depict the Divine Source as comprised of a Great Goddess and a Great God, who personify the polarity contained within the Source. While it is not necessary to pair deities, it is a common practice in modern Witchcraft. In Chapter Three, "Finding Your Pantheon," we will explore how to choose a pantheon of specific deities. But for now, the goal is to first apply your core beliefs about the Divine and consider how you will work this into a tradition.

You may feel that you want to express deity only as the feminine. This theme is found in such systems as the Dianic Tradition, which views Divinity as a Goddess that contains masculine and feminine polarities. The possibility also exists that you may not want to express gender in any personified form. You can explore this more in Chapter Five, "Creating Rituals."

Another factor to consider is how you see Divinity reflected within Creation. For example, some traditions personify Divine Consciousness as the Moon Goddess and the Sun God. Other traditions take the view of an Earth Mother and Sky Father. You may wish to consider how you want to express and personify the indwelling consciousness of the Divine.

An easy way to express Divinity within your tradition is using titles instead of names. For example, you can use the "Lady of Nature" instead of a specific name for a goddess. In the same way, you can use "Lord of Light" in place of a specific name for a god. Chapter Three, "Finding Your Pantheon," will help guide you in considering a deity structure or presentation.

Myths and Legends

In modern Witchcraft, there are myths and legends associated with the seasons of the year. These myths reflect the operation of Divine Consciousness within any given season of the year. For example, in the spring, when life appears renewed in the return of budding plants, we find the story of the Goddess returning from the Underworld or Otherworld to the mortal world. When life appears to be slipping away in the falling of leaves from the trees, we find the tale of the God who dies and enters the Realm of Shadows.

You may wish to incorporate the myths that exist in Witchcraft, or you may want to create your own. If your tradition will embrace the eight seasonal sabbats, then you will find it easiest to use myths related to the changing seasons. One effective way is to think of a mated goddess and god pair who share a relationship as they move through the year. Here, the myths depict them meeting, courting, mating, and producing offspring. Death is also a theme and is typically depicted as a dying god instead of a goddess. The God as the seed-bearer dies and falls into the

Earth, but the Goddess as the divine womb of the Earth never dies in traditional Witchcraft myths.

If you desire a full and complete mythical structure, you can compile a creation myth as well as the myths that comprise the seasonal foundation. You might find it helpful to explore the myths and legends of various cultures to get a good sense of the common elements. The commonality will assist you in understanding what our ancestors felt was important in myth and legend. Once the overall theme is apparent, you can easily create your own mythical system if you desire.

Ritual Purpose

When considering what rituals to create, it is helpful to contemplate the purpose or intent of a ritual. Do you want your rituals to be ceremonial, magickal, mystical, or celebratory? What purpose or goal will be served? These are some of the ideas to think about when creating the rituals of your tradition.

You might also want to consider whether to incorporate transformational aspects, which is something found in the old Mystery Traditions of ancient times. This can be as simple as a sacred meal that represents union with deity or as involved as fasting and using methods of trance inducement.

An easier approach to ritual is the use of a basic rite of veneration or celebration. This type of ritual is less structured and allows for greater spontaneity and intuition. Here, you can offer grain and fruit to your deities while singing and chanting. You may even wish to perform a dance or play a musical instrument as an offering. In a loosely structured ritual, intuition is the key and spontaneity is the directing force.

Ritual Structure

When creating your own rituals, think of having a beginning, middle, and end. To begin a ritual, it is beneficial to state the reason for performing the rite. For example, in a group ritual, the rite can begin with words such as: *"We gather here, on this first day of spring, to honor and venerate the forces of rebirth and renewal. Today, we welcome the Goddess of Nature who returns to us now in this season."*

Part of beginning any Witches' ritual is the casting of the ritual circle or the creation of sacred space. This establishes the physical area where the ritual will be performed, and it aligns the participants to the spiritual quarters that mark the boundaries. In traditional terminology, this creates what is known as "the world between the worlds." This is a realm that is neither fully in the physical realm nor the magickal dimension.

The middle portion of a ritual can be seen as the evocation of deity or spirits. During this portion, you can include a symbolic drama or involve the ritualists in raising energy through such things as drumming, chanting, dance, and so on. It is typically at this stage that any act of magick or spell casting is performed.

The ending of a ritual should include releasing the energy and thanking the spirits and deities. During this stage, the ritual circle is dissolved, or the sacred space is released from mundane containment. Offerings and libations can also be performed during the end phase of your ritual.

Modern ritual structure commonly incorporates the four directional quarters of North, East, South, and West. Each is given a nature or characteristic, which differs according to tradition. It is also customary to assign an Elemental Nature to each directional quarter. See Chapter Nine, "The Correspondences," for more information.

Another common feature in many traditions is the inclusion of mystical guardians known as the Watchers or Guardians. These beings have been described as evolved spiritual beings, angels, karmic agents, Faery or Elven spirits, and stellar-beings. Their role is to guard the ritual circle against the intrusion of unwanted spirits and protect the integrity of the sacred space surrounding the ritual circle. Traditionally, each Watcher is assigned an Elemental Nature and or directional quarter. Various names have been used for the Watchers, including Boreas (North), Eurus (East), Notus (South), and Zephyrus (West).

Religious or Philosophical Views

You will find it useful to consider the basic belief system for your tradition. Some things to consider are your concepts of deity, the sacredness of life, reincarnation, the afterlife, codes of ethics and behavior, and community. These can be organized and written into a blank book, often called a Book of Shadows. This book is a traditional record of rituals, spells, recipes, and mystical experiences.

Over the course of time, your views may change on any given subject. Therefore, you may want your Book of Shadows to be a binder so pages can be added or removed. When you feel ready, you can set the beliefs and practices of your tradition into a permanent Book of Shadows. Traditionally, students copy from their teacher's book during their training. If you desire to incorporate this into your tradition, think about how you want to organize your book. You can find some guidelines in Chapter Eight, "Book of Shadows."

When establishing the beliefs and practices of your tradition, decide on what kind of system you want. Will the tradition be founded upon pre-existing systems, or will it be innovative, and, if so, to what degree? Is the material comprising your tradition an eclectic gathering, or will it be rooted in a particular cultural expression such as Celtic, Germanic, or Italian? These are important decisions to make, as they will influence everything within your traditions from ritual formats to deity forms.

Before deciding upon the beliefs or views for your tradition, research a variety of tenets and philosophies from various regions of the world (ancient and modern). Being well-read and well-informed will make things operate more smoothly as your tradition grows. New members will naturally bring their own perspectives and backgrounds when they join. You will encounter fewer conflicts when your tradition's beliefs and practices share similar core beliefs with other religions and philosophies.

I am not suggesting that you abandon any contrary views, but I merely point out that a blend will help others easily acclimate to your tradition. However, a tradition will contain its own unique elements, and the views of its founders will naturally be central to its identity. What is unique about a tradition is what often attracts others, and what is comfortable helps people remain within the system. Uniqueness is attraction and familiarity is comfort.

Training Format

One important element within a tradition is the training and experience it offers. There are several key areas to consider: deities, myths and legends, ritual structure, magickal training, arts of the Craft, core tenets and practices, codes or rules, and levels of advancement. Your tradition can contain them all or focus on specific ones.

When creating a training program, think in terms of what you want members of the tradition to achieve in the long run. An easy way to break this down is to examine what areas of knowledge a teacher should possess. Do you want them to have a command of some form of divination, and, if so, which methods? Should they have a practical knowledge of herbs, the preparation of potions, or the healing arts? Do you want your teachers to have magickal and ritual knowledge and experience? You will need a plan to teach them such things at various stages of their training.

There are other areas of knowledge that you may want your teachers to address. These include historical and anthropological information to support any claims you might make about the roots, origins, and foundations of your tradition. Unfortunately, there will always be people who desire to discredit the work of others, and you will find it less frustrating if you confirm your facts as you organize your tradition.

One final tip is to provide opportunities for your clergy to attend workshops on management, relationship counseling, positive thinking, and other areas that develop good people skills. At the very least, your clergy should be encouraged to read self-help books in these areas. A time will come when members of your tradition will need to turn to someone for help and support. You will want the best of your people available at such times.

Hierarchy or Degrees

When formulating your tradition, you may want to consider levels or degrees for members. This also includes any roles or positions that people may hold or fulfill. Some traditional roles include Priestess and Priest, High Priestess and High Priest, Coven Crone, Coven Maiden, Summoner, and so on. For further information, see Chapter Seven, "Initiation and Metaphysical Aspects of Witchcraft."

An element worthy of serious consideration is whether you prefer a Socratic or democratic foundation and system. The Socratic approach consists of direction given by a leader, while the democratic approach is directed by consensus. There are pros and cons to each system. In addition, you will need to decide how rituals are presided. Will there be an established High Priestess and High Priest, or do you want to rotate who presides so that everyone has an opportunity?

Common to most traditions is a degree system, which typically consists of three degrees. The first degree marks the beginning of priesthood, the second degree is the phase of the Priestess or Priest, and the third degree denotes the role of High Priestess or High Priest. While the degrees are common in earlier forms of Wiccan-inspired Witchcraft, many traditions exist without this structure and recognize a single initiation. When considering a degree system, you will want to also think about whether to create initiation rituals for each degree. If so, you will find helpful guidelines for initiation rituals in Chapter Seven, "Initiation and Metaphysical Aspects of Witchcraft."

Magickal Practices

While magick and spell work is important to many traditions, you will need to decide whether to incorporate them into your tradition. If so, you will want to consider the type of magickal system. Will you focus on simple folk magick, or draw upon Ceremonial Magickal systems that appear in traditional grimoires? Perhaps a blend of the two might appeal to you more.

If you use magick in your tradition, there are some considerations that you will want to explore. Bear in mind that the source of power for your magick is directly linked to your beliefs. Therefore, it is advisable to examine what it is that you believe. For example, do you believe in the inherent power of herbs and minerals? Do you believe in spirits of Nature and the Otherworld? What is your connection to the forces that you believe can empower your magick? Once you decide where the power of your magick comes from, you are in a better position to construct your magickal system.

As previously noted, a traditional aspect of Witchcraft is creative forces called Elements, which are considered to be the universal building blocks for manifestation. The energies of Earth, Air, Fire, and Water are the non-material expressions of their material counterparts. In other words, the Elements are the energies associated with the earth, air, fire, and water in everyday life. It can be said that the Elements are also spiritual or emotional, as reflected in our personality and character. In the same way that people are said to be like their zodiac sign, so too can an Elemental Nature be a part of our makeup.

Elemental Natures are an important part of the Witche's philosophy. In Wiccan-inspired Witchcraft, we find four traditional ritual tools linked to an Elemental Force. These tools are the pentacle, wand, athame, and chalice. There are two main systems related to the Elemental Nature of any given tool, both rooted in Ceremonial Magick.

System One:
- ❖ Pentacle is linked to Earth and the North quarter of ritual circle.
- ❖ Wand is linked to Air and the East quarter of ritual circle.
- ❖ Athame is linked to Fire and the South quarter of ritual circle.
- ❖ Chalice is linked to Water and the West quarter of ritual circle.

System Two:
- ❖ Pentacle is linked to Earth and the North quarter of ritual circle.
- ❖ Athame is linked to Air and the East quarter of ritual circle.
- ❖ Wand is linked to Fire and the South quarter of ritual circle.
- ❖ Chalice is linked to Water and the West quarter of ritual circle.

When designing a ritual circle for magickal purposes, there are a variety of systems to draw upon. You may wish to create your own based on your surroundings. Is a large lake to your north? Perhaps you feel the Element of Water and the chalice more strongly from that direction. Is there a forest to your south? Consider associating the Element of Earth and the pentacle with the South. The suggested reading list at the back of this book provides helpful signposts.

Coven or Social Structure

A tradition typically contains a social structure of some sort such as a coven. Generally, a coven is a group comprised of three to thirteen members. Some people prefer to use the term "Fellowship" or "Grove" instead of coven. When forming a group, there are some basic things to consider, such as whether your coven will require a rite of initiation for a person to become a member. Another consideration is an oath of secrecy or privacy so that everyone feels safe in the intimate setting of a coven.

It is customary for a coven to perform ritual either dressed in ritual attire like robes or nude (also known as "skyclad"). Whatever your preference may be, it is advisable for the coven to dress (or undress) specifically for ritual, as this creates a sense of the special nature and bond of the group. You may want to name the group after something symbolic, such as mythical creature, a constellation, or a sacred place. One example is Stonehenge Coven, and another is Coven of the North Star.

As previously mentioned, you will want to consider how the directing roles will function. Do you want to have a specific High Priestess and High Priest facilitate ritual, or do you prefer rotating coven members as facilitators?

Another element related to the coven is the process by which members are added. Traditionally, this is done by a unanimous vote and any dissenting vote negates the proposed member. This approach ensures complete acceptance and harmony within the coven membership. Another aspect to consider is whether attendance at a ritual or celebration is mandatory. All these things influence mental and emotional health and are therefore important considerations for the well-being of the coven.

Laws or Code of Conduct

Consider whether your tradition will have formal laws or some system of guidelines. You may ultimately decide that it will not include anything of this nature, but it is wise to have an established plan. It has been my experience that providing expectations related to the behavior of the members within your tradition works best. This way, everyone knows in advance what is expected from them.

It is wise to not only write out what the law states but also include what the law is intended to accomplish or prevent. This will help future members understand the spirit of the law versus what the wording appears to indicate. In this way, there will be less argument over the need for the laws and less misinterpretation when applying the law to whatever circumstances arise.

If you choose to have a system of laws, then consider what consequences apply when these laws are broken. Think about intent: will it matter why the law was broken, or will the letter of the law prevail? Bear in mind that, when a law is broken for even the best of intentions, the impact upon other people can still be a negative experience. However, laws that are strictly enforced as written without any personal consideration can result in people leaving your tradition because it appears too harsh.

It has been my experience that a beneficial system outlines the expectations for attending rituals and establishes simple codes of conduct that do not intrude on the members' personal lives. Will everyone be required to attend all the yearly sabbats? What about the monthly lunar rites? In my experience, the healthiest covens had members who were able to build strong personal bonds. These bonds came from being together as a family for all the rituals. However, I have also discovered that some people are not happy in a system that requires them to do anything. You will want to give the matter serious thought. In the end, I believe you will find that the needs of the many outweigh the needs of the one.

Now that we have looked at the framework for a tradition, it is time to turn our attention to the concept of deity. How you view and wish to interact with deity will determine the divine connection to your tradition. Therefore, it will be beneficial to explore this aspect of creating your tradition. In the following chapter, we will explore the concept of deity within Witchcraft and methods of incorporating a working relationship with the divine in your system.

Finding Your
Pantheon

The concept of deity in most traditions consists of a mated goddess and god. Many traditions also include a host of other deities, which is called the *pantheon* of the tradition. It is important to explore the myths and legends of any deities that you want to include in your pantheon. It is advisable to have deity pairings that are harmonious or are balanced polarities to one another. In this way, you can avoid internal conflicts that arise when creating corresponding rituals, myths, and legends.

Many people prefer to work with deities that are connected to their roots, such as Celtic, Germanic, Hungarian, Greek, Italian, and so on. One of the advantages of this approach is that it connects the tradition to ancestral origins. Something stirs in the blood when we link to the ancestral current of knowledge and wisdom.

Some people are drawn to pantheons that have no direct link to their roots. This may be due to unfinished business from a past life, or it may be a call to experience new teachings. The concept of reincarnation includes experiencing many different lives, connections, and conditions that allow for the full and complete education of the soul. Therefore, you do not need to be concerned if you aren't drawn to the deities of your bloodline.

Reading the myths and legends of various cultures is a good way to explore and get acquainted with a variety of deities. In addition, stories are a useful means of conveying metaphors related to the nature of specific gods and goddesses. The ancient models depicted deities as being pleased by certain offerings and offended by others. Each goddess and god had likes and dislikes, emotions, pet peeves, and relatively predictable responses within any given matter.

One way to view such myths is like a "blueprint of energy" that maps out the inner mechanism of how a specific deity operates. This demonstrates the interplay once the Divine Consciousness is stimulated. In other words, myths provide a working model of the nature and character of a deity as viewed from a human perspective, which can be used when constructing rituals.

Getting to know a deity is like getting to know another person. When we meet someone at any given stage of life, what we encounter is the culmination of things that made this person who and what they are today. But the person in front of us today is only a specific reflection of the entire being. The future may bring changes of any kind. Therefore, to really know the person, we must ask questions about where they are from, how they grew up, what events shaped their life, what the person's aspirations are, and so on. Getting to know a deity calls for the same exploration. Without this, we can only know what we are currently looking at, which is only part of the totality.

Whenever you read an ancient myth or legend, you are essentially looking at how our predecessors related to various gods and goddesses. Some of the things within a myth or legend are warnings about what angers the deity. Such tales no doubt arose from a perceived "cause and effect" observation, and it can be helpful to consider the assessment of our ancestors when we work with any deity.

If you desire to work within the customary structure of the Craft, then you will want to select deities that align with seasonal and celestial themes. It is helpful to examine these themes in connection with a goddess and god figure. Once you know and understand the customary themes, then you can select deities that fit the model.

Agricultural Theme

One of the early concepts in Western Witchcraft was the idea of an Earth Mother Goddess and her son, both associated with agriculture. The Goddess is the deep rich soil, and her son is the seed-bearing plant that arises from the Earth's body. Together, they assure the cycles of Nature.

When exploring which goddess to incorporate into your tradition, it is best to think in terms of a fertile deity as opposed to a chaste or virginal goddess. A goddess associated with grain, fertility, or the harvest is a good choice. For a deeper level of connection, you may wish to consider incorporating a goddess associated with journeys or events linked to the Underworld. This relationship ties together the theme of the planted seed and the darkness within the Earth, where the seed awaits birth.

The seed is the metaphorical Son of the Goddess. It is birthed from beneath the soil, rises a stalk, and eventually progresses to bud, leaf, and flower. The last stage is the appearance of the seed. This seed will fall as the plant declines or dies and then sink into the Earth. Here, we find the cycle of life and the mythical theme associated with the God through legend.

The classic mythological theme depicts the rise and fall of the Sun God, who is both the Seed of Light and the physical seed of plant renewal. We see the birth, rise, and death of the plant as a representation of the cycle of our own bodies. The cycles of the Sun (seemingly rising from the Earth and falling back into its depths) reflect the soul descending into a physical body over a series of lifetimes.

The Pagan theme of the Dying and Rising God is also found in Christian theology. The original theme was a personal alignment with the God for the soul to be carried through his passages. The soul is believed to resurrect through this intimate connection.

In the classical mythology of the Goddess, we find her as the Great Mother from whom the God is born into the mortal world. Unlike the God, the Goddess never dies. Instead, she withdraws from the Mortal Realm in a conscious act to retrieve the God from the Underworld. This is a metaphor for the life force stirring beneath the soil, which awakens the buried seed. In the myth of the Goddess, she follows the Dying

God into the Underworld, magickally rebirths him, and then returns to the Mortal Realm. These events are marked by the sabbats known as Samhain, Yule, and Ostara.

Celestial Theme

In mainstream Witchcraft, we find the customary association of the Goddess with the Moon and the stars. Through these associations, she is often called the Queen of Heaven and linked to the phases of the Moon and certain stars and constellations. The celestial nature of the Goddess demonstrates her "higher self," distinguishing her from the Goddess as the Earth Mother.

Her lunar nature represents the Goddess as a transformer and shapeshifter. Through the parallels of the Moon's phases, we can view the Goddess as manifesting various natures. When the Moon is new, we see the Maiden. The Full Moon represents the ripe Mother, and the waning phase symbolizes the Wise Woman. The stars connect the Goddess to the Otherworld, which exists in the depths of the Universe.

The God is commonly associated with the Sun and the sky. He is viewed as physically above the Goddess in her earthly manifestation. This holds fertile symbolism as the impregnator of the Goddess, who is the Soul of Nature. The setting of the Sun can be seen as engaging the Goddess in sexual union. The rising of the Sun can be viewed as being birthed from the womb of the Goddess.

The association of the sky with the God represents his "higher self," distinguishing him from the God of the Sun. The sky connects the God to the Heaven Worlds that are immediate in nature for the souls crossing over from mortal life. These are the human constructions that appear in various religions as temporary abodes (although most religions do not view them this way).

Otherworld Theme

In modern Witchcraft, we find the theme of the "Otherworld," which is a realm unlike the Afterlife or Underworld commonly depicted in most religions. In older myths and legends, the Otherworld is a place where both the living and the dead may enter. It is intimately linked to magickal kingdoms, Elven or Faery Realms, and enchanted lands.

The Otherworld is connected to teaching opportunities, spirit guides, and ascended masters. If you desire an Otherworld component to your tradition, you may wish to use legendary figures associated with this theme. They can serve as co-walkers who may assist you in Otherworld contact and work. You can choose classic figures such as Merlin, or you can work with various forms like the "Crone of the Cottage" or the "Walker in the Woods" (see glossary).

One popular way is to use the Elven or Faery connection and work with these forms as contacts to the Otherworld. Statues, figurines, or paintings of these figures can be used as a meditation portal. You may even want to learn their names as a means of interfacing.

Triformis Goddess Theme

The idea of a goddess depicted in three forms or aspects is central to mainstream Witchcraft. In modern Craft, they are called the Maiden, Mother, and Crone. Here, we can see the ancient model of the Three Fates, who, in ancient art, are depicted as a young woman, a mature woman, and an elderly woman.

One theme that appears in the triformis nature is the idea of the ancient Three Worlds: Overworld, Middleworld, and Underworld. We can see a goddess of the Heavens, the Earth, and the Underworld. When considering a triformis deity, you will want to bear these connections in mind. This is because the Three Worlds have an association with the eight sabbats, which contain the mythos of the God and Goddess. The more the aspects of your tradition connect and agree with one another, the more solid and productive your system will be.

As previously mentioned, the Triformis Goddess is intimately connected to the phases of the Moon. The cycles of the Moon are reflected in the menstrual cycle, and here we find an intimate connection between the Goddess and fertility. This is one of the reasons why the triple nature of the Goddess is divided into Maiden, Mother, and Crone. These are cycles of fertility marked by menstrual bleeding and its cessation.

On a more universal level, the Triformis Goddess relates to magickal and mundane themes. The Maiden is seen as the innovator and the renewer of vitality. New beginnings and new ventures are associated with her. The Mother is viewed as the birther and nurturer, bringing things to fullness. Protecting, caring, and sustaining are associated with the Mother. The Crone is seen as the preserver and reflector upon inner nature, for she is wisdom gained from experience.

Triformis God Theme

In modern Witchcraft, we can divide the God into three aspects that complement the Triformis Goddess. These aspects are the Horned One, the Hooded One, and the Old One. In mainstream modern Witchcraft, the God is typically viewed as having dual nature, a god of both light and shadow. In this regard, he represents the waxing and waning periods of Nature.

The Horned One is most depicted as a "stag-horned" god of fertility. The stag symbolism relates to protection of the herd. The nature of the dominant stag to fend off competitors creates a link to the maiden goddess form. Here, we see the Horned One as the consort of the Maiden.

The Hooded One is symbolized by the classic Green Man imagery and also by a man of the forest wearing a hooded cloak. The Oak King and Holly King are forms of this aspect, although they are not typically viewed in Witchcraft as gods. The lush growth of field and forest creates a link to the mother goddess form. Here, we see the Hooded One as the consort of the Mother.

The Old One is symbolized by the wise sage figure, the great elder carrying his staff. He is the most human of forms and yet is the meeting place between the Mortal and Divine Realms. Unlike the other forms that are connected to the animal and plant kingdoms, the Old One represents the union between human and Divine Consciousness. Here, we see wise-man imagery, which creates a connection to the Crone goddess form. In this, we find the Old One as the consort of the Crone.

Cultural Expressions

When we look at the myths and legends of various cultures, we find a commonality of how our ancestors viewed gods and goddesses. The stories that appear in various cultures are flavored by regional differences, including climate, terrain, and animal life. For example, the colder regions of Northern Europe have different depictions of the gods than Southern Europe. Another example is a culture that is nomadic versus one that settled in rich agricultural regions. Here, we find differences in the tales of gods and goddesses. However, when looking at all these cultures, we find more similarities than we do differences.

It is interesting to note that, in the character of the deities depicted in myth and legend, we find the nature of the people that worship them. Where resources are more limited and weather is harsh, we find deities that are seemingly stern and aggressive. In regions where the weather is mild and resources are plentiful, we find deities that appear refined and joyful in comparison. It is only natural that our ancestors saw the gods in the same way that they saw their own lives. The deities express the needs, desires, and fears of the people who worship them.

When selecting a pantheon, it is advisable to think about your own nature and how you might want to strengthen or enhance it. There are two primary approaches to consider. If you tend to be passive but want to be more assertive, then active and strong deities can help transform your nature. However, if you are comfortable with being passive, then you may wish to connect with deities that reflect that nature. So, in this context, you can complement or transform your nature.

A Word of Caution

Many people in modern Witchcraft prefer an eclectic approach when selecting a pantheon. The eclectic view is that just about anything is okay if it works for the individual or group. Over the years, I have seen people use a pantheon comprised of a goddess of love and a god of war, for example, Venus and Ares. I have also seen people match deities such as Athena and Ares as a consort pair. But is it wise to create consorts who are not mates in the myths and legends of our ancestors? Is there a practical and noteworthy reason why our ancestors matched and mated certain deities and not others?

Some Witches go outside of specific cultures and create consort pairs that are not from the same region. One example is creating a consort pair with an Aegean or Mediterranean goddess and a Celtic god, or vice versa. In choosing this approach, care should be given to understand the myths and legends of each deity and their culture before pairing them. This includes looking at the animal familiars associated with each to be certain that neither deity is offended (remember, gods and goddesses have their own likes and dislikes). But you do not need to be concerned about the compatibility of the animal familiars, such as a goddess associated with cats and a god associated with wolves. The primary concern is not to include animal familiars that are referenced as offensive in the myth of any specific deity.

Pairing deities from other cultures is especially challenging. For example, creating a consort pair with an African god and Celtic goddess can be problematic because their natures are rooted in different social consciousnesses. They may not integrate in the same way that deities from different regions might. It is important to respect and value deities that may come from traditions and cultures that are not our own and to respect them if they choose not to work with us (or with the pairings we have chosen for them). Likewise, we must respect fellow practitioners with different backgrounds from our own.

I recall several years ago when I was given a Ganesh statue (the Hindu elephant-headed god). I was looking for a place to set it in my bedroom, and to free my hands to prepare an area, I temporarily placed Ganesh on the table where my shrine to Hecate is established. I immediately felt an unpleasant jolt of energy go through me, and an inner voice sharply spoke: "Get that thing off my shrine!" It was the voice of Hecate.

This example strongly suggests that it may be more practical and respectful to pair gods with the same cultural roots. Cultural pantheons are energy forms that blend and work well together because they were created in that regard. Mixing and matching pantheons from different cultures can be like mixing chemicals of different and unrelated compositions. Education and caution are highly recommended in both ventures.

Patron Deities

A patron deity is one that assists and inspires you in some specific way or for a particular venture. In most cases, a patron deity involves a less formal relationship than the primary deity of a tradition. The connection made to your patron deity, however, is just as powerful. A patron deity may not even require a pre-established schedule for veneration and offerings. It can be as simple as providing an offering whenever you invoke or evoke the deity.

There are several ways to discover your patron deity. One method is to find a festival day that honors a particular deity and coincides with your birthday. Explore mythology books and look for deities whose nature calls to you. For example, I was born on the festival day of the goddess Ceres, who is the patron of the Mysteries. Long before I discovered this fact, I had already been drawn to studying the ancient Mystery Traditions of Greece and Rome. Upon discovering the date connection, I realized that Ceres was my patroness.

Another method is to look for connections to your natural talents. For example, if you have always been strongly drawn to music, art, or literature, you may connect with deities of the arts. A list can be found in Chapter Nine, "Correspondences."

In many cases, you will find that a patron deity seeks you, as opposed to you searching one out. This can manifest in several ways. One common experience is continually encountering tokens or totems associated with a deity. For example, you may continually come across things connected to owls and then later discover an attraction to a deity represented by an owl. Another way of encountering your patron deity is through a dream, meditation, guided pathworking, or trance state.

A patron deity is not necessary to your tradition or craft, even if it is a popular topic in modern Witchcraft. If you don't feel called to a deity, do not feel required to establish a relationship with one. Likewise, you may seek to connect with a deity even if signs have yet to manifest. It is important to remember that, however you connect with deity, you must do so with respect and veneration.

Nameless Gods and Goddesses

A final consideration is the use of deity titles as opposed to actual names. In medieval Witch mythos, you will find many gods associated with Witchcraft that had no names. For example, in Italy you find *La Signora del Gioco*, or "The Lady of the Game," who met in secret with Witches. In American folklore, you may meet "the Man in Black" at the crossroads, ready to bestow magickal powers. The benefit of nameless deities is that you will not be tied to any specific cultural pantheon. This universal appeal may be helpful for a tradition with diverse views concerning deities and the cultures from which they originated.

In this section, I will present a working model drawn from my previous book, *Witchcraft: A Mystery Tradition*. The basic format includes a mated pair that journeys together in a common mythology marked by the eight sabbats. The following is a list of deity titles associated with the eight sabbats.

- ❖ **Samhain:** Lady of Shadows and Lord of Shadows
- ❖ **Yule:** Lady of the Womb and Lord of Rebirth
- ❖ **Imbolc:** Lady of Fire and Lord of Ice
- ❖ **Ostara:** Lady of the Lake and Lord of the Reeds
- ❖ **Beltane:** Lady of the Green and Lord of the Green
- ❖ **Litha:** Lady of the Flowers and Lord of the Woods
- ❖ **Lughnasadh:** Lady of the Fields and Lord of the Barley
- ❖ **Mabon:** Lady of the Harvest and Lord of the Sheaf

Let's look at the titles and the themes they express.

The idea of deities within shadows is linked to chthonic nature and to a concept beyond the typical classifications of gods and goddesses. For example, in Etruscan mythology, a race of beings existed known as the *Involuti*. These beings were above the so-called "High Gods" who appear in rulership roles. Another example is the Fates, who were above the Olympic gods. In Celtic myths, we can include the Tuatha Dé Danann as deities within the Realm of Shadows.

In the mainstream view shared by many Witches, the year begins on Samhain. Here, we begin in the darkness of the late autumn season. In essence, this is the dark womb from which the waxing year will arise. The Lady and Lord of Shadows rule this time of the year. Therefore, we can assign this season to mysterious and magickal deities associated with hidden or secret realms.

The following season is marked by the celebration of Yule. At this time, the deity titles are the Lady of the Womb and the Lord of Rebirth. Within this mythos, we find the idea of light being born from the darkness. In one sense, this is the ancestral view of the Sun and the Moon rising in the East (seemingly from beneath the Earth). In this season, the deities of birth and regeneration rule.

Next, we arrive at the season of Imbolc. The deity titles for this season are the Lady of Fire and the Lord of Ice. Here, we find the world frozen in the grip of winter. The most noticeable aspect of winter is the loss or reduction of vegetation, as well as the appearance of ice and snow. The God, typically associated with vegetation, is frozen away. It is the Goddess whose passionate flame can thaw and release the God. In this season, the ruling deities are associated with potential and the power of forging and fire.

The next season is Ostara. The deity titles for this season are the Lady of the Lake and the Lord of the Reeds. The ice and snow have melted away with the warmth of the fire of the Goddess. The God is released from bondage within winter's grasp. In this mythos, we find the return of warmth and the transformation of ice and snow into water. Deities of liberation, release, fertility, and planting are associated with this season.

The following season is Beltane. The deity titles for this season are the Lady and the Lord of the Green. The combination of warmth and water has brought forth lush vegetation. The Goddess is the Green Lady, and the God is the Green Lord. In this mythos, we find deities associated with return, regrowth, and renewal.

Next, we arrive at Litha. The deity titles for this season are the Lady of Flowers and the Lord of the Woods. The greenery of the last season has grown to enhance the fields and forests. In this mythos, the Lady brings forth the beauty of Nature in the flowers and colors of summer.

The God is within the animals, trees, and plants of the woodlands. Deities associated with wildlife and botanicals rule at this season.

The following season is Lughnasadh. The deity names for this season are the Lady of the Fields and the Lord of the Barley. The bounty of Nature now looms in ripeness, and the anticipation of the harvest is at hand. In this mythos, the deities of abundance, maturity, and ripeness now rule the season.

Finally, we arrive at the last season, Mabon. The deity titles for this season are the Lady of the Harvest and the Lord of the Sheaf. This season marks the harvesting of nature's bounty and the collecting of seeds for the planting season. At this time, the deities of descent, decline, transformation, and mystical journey rule.

Now that we have looked at the general themes of the sabbats, you have a template for deity natures. By engaging with deities whose nature coincide with any given mythos or seasonal theme, you can create a sound pantheon that empowers your Wheel of the Year. With this understanding in hand, let us now examine the Wheel of the Year itself.

Weaving the
Wheel of the Year

In mainstream Witchcraft, there are eight celebrations or festivals collectively known as the Wheel of the Year. As a symbol, they are often depicted on an eight-spoke wagon wheel, with each spoke representing one of the eight seasonal rites. The Wheel of the Year is symbolic of the natural sequence of the seasons, which is often referred to as the "turning of the year."

Many Witchcraft traditions include seasonal themes that incorporate the myths and legends of the associated deities. These themes appear in the eight seasonal celebrations, which are also known as the sabbats. The ritual of each sabbat is built upon the myth or legend of the deities associated with that season. This is known as a *mythos*, which is a cohesive and interconnected collection that serves as the foundation for the celebrations of the year.

A well-constructed and blended Wheel of the Year structure will provide a rich connection to the Momentum of the Past. The Momentum of the Past is a spiritual current that flows from past generations into contemporary times. This will help vitalize your rituals in ways that will intensify the ritual experience. Therefore, it is beneficial to consider the Wheel of the Year as both a "whole" and a "series" of connective parts.

For the purposes of this chapter, we will think of the Wheel as a complete story. Each of the sabbats is a chapter in that story. The story is about a mated Goddess and God. Their relationship and their lives are played out in the unfolding of the seasons. Once you know the theme of each sabbat (as an expression of the whole), you can then work your deities into the Wheel of the Year to suit your tradition.

In the mainstream view of modern Witchcraft, the mythological theme of the Wheel of the Year can be sorted into the topics listed below. Note that the first listed month reflects the northern hemisphere, while the second listed month reflects the southern.

* **October or May:** Samhain, the beginning of the year, awaiting birth in the Realm of Shadows.
* **December or June:** Yule (Winter Solstice), the birth of new light.
* **February or August:** Imbolc, the time of purification and preparation.
* **March or September:** Ostara (Vernal Equinox), the stirring of fertility, the awakening of the seed.
* **May or October:** Beltane, the mating of the feminine and masculine forces, the impregnation of Nature.
* **June or December:** Litha (Summer Solstice), the fullness of Nature's bounty.
* **August or February:** Lughnasadh, the harvest or birth of abundance.
* **September or March:** Mabon (Autumn Equinox), the decline of the life force into Shadow.

Most modern traditions incorporate two central themes into the Wheel of the Year. The first is a mated Goddess and God pair that represents the fertilizing and life-giving forces of Nature. The second theme integrates personifications of the waxing (growing) and waning (declining) forces of Nature, which divide the year into two halves. One half is the season of growth and gain, and the other is the season of decline and loss. One personification is found in the Holly King and Oak King figures. Another example is the Stag (waxing) and Wolf (declining) figures, which are primal forces versus human imagery.

The God and Goddess Theme

One of the most popular mythical themes in modern Witchcraft is that of a Goddess and God who meet, court, fall in love, and produce an offspring. The Goddess is connected to the Moon and the Earth. The God is connected to the Sun and the Earth (although, in many traditions, he is also the "Sky Father" as opposed to being specifically the Sun). These themes are further explored in other chapters.

The God is born at Yule and represents the new Sun for the coming year. This theme is quite ancient and reflects the concept of rebirth and renewal. At Yule, a time when daylight has dwindled, the newborn Sun symbolizes the new light that will save the world from darkness. The mother of the newborn Sun God is the Earth Goddess who dwells in the Underworld during this season. Just as the Sun seems to rise from below the Earth and the seed rises from below the soil, so too is the Sun God birthed from the Earth Mother.

At the time of Imbolc, the Sun God is bound to winter's hold. The Goddess is the flame that begins to thaw and allure the God. At the Vernal Equinox (Ostara), the Goddess returns youthful to the Mortal Realm from the Underworld, bringing the promise of renewed life. Beltane then marks the courtship of the young Sun God with the Divine Maiden.

At the Summer Solstice (Litha), the Goddess and God wed. The seasonal rite of Lughnasadh marks the ripened harvest. The Autumn Equinox (Mabon) features the death of the Sun God as the Harvest Lord, at which time the Goddess descends into the Underworld to retrieve her lover. With the onset of Samhain, the Goddess and God are reunited in the Underworld, and then the celebration of the Winter Solstice (Yule) marks the renewal of the Wheel of the Year mythos once again.

The God and Goddess in the Wheel of the Year

Over the past few decades, many eclectic systems have altered the pre-existing mythos or have modified it to create something new. This has resulted in many different themes and can lead to confusion when researching deities and their role in the Wheel of the Year mythos. In this section, we will explore some approaches to creating a cohesive storyline upon which to build your own Wheel of the Year deity assignments.

In order to construct a Wheel mythos, you will first need to decide in which season to begin your story. As previously mentioned, most modern traditions place the meeting of the Goddess and God at the Vernal Equinox. Their courtship begins in May, and the Goddess is visibly pregnant by the Summer Solstice. The God dies in autumn (in some traditions, this occurs at Lughnasadh, and in others at Mabon). The Goddess and God are reunited in the Underworld at Samhain (November Eve), and the Goddess gives birth to their son on the Winter Solstice.

Some confusion exists because most contemporary traditions begin the year with the season of Samhain at the close of October or beginning of November. In contrast, the Goddess and God meet in spring. The problem here is that, at the time of Samhain, she is already with child. Therefore, the year apparently begins in the middle of the relationship between the Goddess and God. This is only a problem if the chronology bothers your sense of logic. Keep in mind that the mythos and stories are there to point to greater truths about Nature and the Goddess and God themselves.

One way to resolve this is to begin the year in your tradition at the Vernal Equinox. Another way is to simply view the year as non-linear, a circle with no beginning or end. Here, Samhain can be viewed as a point within the shadow of the year, a moment to begin the mythos in procreative darkness, which moves toward the birth of light at the Winter Solstice.

Another potential storyline problem exists in assigning the Crone to the season of Samhain. In most traditions, the Goddess is pregnant at this time of year, which seems to conflict the nature of an elderly deity. When we look at the Wheel of the Year, the deities age rapidly compared to humans. Typically, the God is born at Yule, an adolescent by Imbolc, and a young man by Beltane.

The confusion regarding a pregnant deity, who is also the Crone aspect of the Goddess, is rooted in eclectic creativity. The earlier structure depicted a patroness of the Samhain who escorted the dead but is now viewed as the Crone aspect of the Goddess. Behind this appearance, there also existed the larger mythos, which reflects the Wheel of the Year (as opposed to a singular festival association). But, in the earliest forms of this mythos, the Goddess is not described as any specific age.

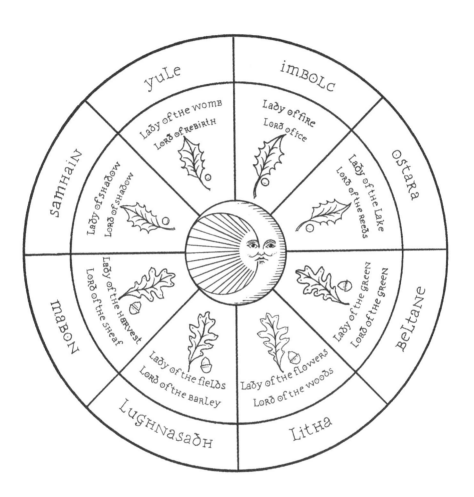

When we look at the contemporary construction of Witchcraft, we often find overlapping myths and legends that originally stood separate and independent from one another. It is helpful to note the parallel mythos that mark a sabbat, along with the mythos that turn the Wheel of the Year. One example is the appearance of the Oak King and Holly King at the Summer Solstice and Winter Solstice. They do not appear elsewhere in the Wheel of the Year and are mentioned only on these two sabbats. Therefore, they are independent tales that do not require reconciliation with the overall mythos of the sabbats.

The singular appearance of a deity or character signifies the outer layer of a mythos as it relates to the Wheel of the Year. You can picture this like a circle with a ring in the center. The circle represents the sabbats, and the ring symbolizes the inner mythos of the Wheel of the Year. On the circle, each sabbat is associated with a deity or mystical character. On the ring, the mated pair of deities who travel together throughout the year appears.

In effect, there are two stories being told. One is the tale of individual deities or figures as they appear at different points of the year. The other story presents the Goddess and God as a couple continually depicted together.

While the Wheel of the Year is often a foundation to many contemporary Witchcraft traditions, you may choose not to incorporate it. In these cases, it is ideal to research the myths and legends of your deities to build a mythos in accord with the roots of your tradition.

In Shadow and In Light

When we look at the sabbats from a traditional perspective, a distinct pattern emerges. This pattern depicts the celebration of the sabbats on dates that alternate between day and night. What we note first is that solar festivals fall on either an equinox or a solstice. These clearly belong to the Sun God and his unique mythos.

The second thing we note is that four of the sabbats traditionally fall in the evening. For example, May Eve (Beltane) and October Eve (Samhain) are night festivals.

Imbolc was traditionally celebrated on the eve of February, and Lughnasadh was traditionally celebrated on August Eve. In modern times, this has changed to daytime celebrations, with Imbolc on or near February 2, and Lughnasadh on August 1. Many modern traditions also celebrate Beltane on May 1, while most traditions still celebrate Samhain at night. If you choose to create your tradition in accord with an older view, then you will want to set your sabbat dates to reflect day and night.

In the mythos of shadow and light, the Goddess represents all that is associated with the night. Naturally, this includes the Moon and the stars. Because night obscures our sight, it is associated with the hidden, secret, and mystical. Night also represents potentiality, the idea that anything is possible before it can be seen. This is, in part, the notion of magick. In this regard, we can view the eve celebrations as spiritual and conceptual.

In contrast, the solar rites are performed beneath the Sun. Therefore, the God represents all that is associated with daylight, including the Sun, blue skies, and clouds. Because daylight reveals everything to our sight, it is associated with the tangible, practical, and commonplace. Daytime also represents safety, protection, and the idea that we are forewarned and alerted because of increased visibility. In this regard, we can view the daytime celebrations as worldly and detail oriented.

By focusing on the alternating role of the Goddess and God through the year, you can separately honor each deity. If you choose to adopt this approach, it is beneficial to highlight the Goddess or God in some special way on the appropriate sabbat. This can be as simple as decorating the altar statue or incorporating a play in your ritual in which the deity is given offerings or special attention.

To select offerings or create rituals to honor the deities, you can research and study the myths and legends of your deity pair. Look for mentions of any food, flowers, or settings that appear in myth. This will help you select appropriate offerings and learn the likes and dislikes of any particular deity. It is also beneficial to note any adventures and special achievements in a myth or legend. This will give you ritual text to include, so you can "sing the praises" of the deity. The deities enjoy a little flattery.

The Waxing and Waning Theme

In modern Witchcraft, the year is divided into two halves. As mentioned earlier, one half is called the waxing year, which refers to the seasons of growth and gain. The other half is called the waning year, which refers to decline and loss. Some traditions mark these shifts at the Summer Solstice and Winter Solstice. Other traditions mark them on the Vernal Equinox and Autumn Equinox.

In many systems of the Craft, the Holly King assumes power at the Summer Solstice, and his reign brings the decline of Nature into fall and winter. The Oak King assumes power at the Winter Solstice, and his reign ushers in the season of growth and abundance of Nature in spring and summer. In some systems, the stag assumes power at the Vernal Equinox, and the wolf does the same at the Autumn Equinox. Like the Oak King and Holly King, these entities initiate the changing of the seasons that mark the waxing and waning periods.

If you want to include the theme of the waxing and waning halves of the year, then you can add the personifications of your choice into your ritual. This can be as simple as decorating the altar or ritual area with images of the Holly and Oak King, or the Stag and the Wolf. The old-fashioned Santa figures at Christmas time are ideal, and you can select them according to the objects and seasonal foliage carried by any given figure. The dark clothed Santa figures (greens and browns) can serve as the Oak King, and the lighter clothed figures (reds and whites) make a nice Holly King. Figurines of a stag and a wolf can be found throughout the year.

Another way of acknowledging the waxing and waning forces is to perform a ritual drama in costume. Decide whether to mark the waxing and waning periods on the equinox or solstice celebrations. In accord, you can choose the figures you want to represent the waxing and waning forces (and, of course, the drama includes the resulting victory of one over the other).

Mock battles have been part of ritual traditions for many centuries. This is the classic struggle of "good" and "evil" as perceived by humankind. However, in Nature, such things do not exist, and there is only the cycle of birth, growth, maturity, decline, and death. The interpretations of "good" and "evil" are subjective.

The Altar and the Wheel of the Year

The altar is the focal point of ritual proceedings and may be decorated to represent the central themes of a season. In addition to the décor, it is advisable to set the icons and symbols connected to the essence of your tradition. This is where your tradition will come together in symbolism and representation, allowing the participants to connect on deeper levels with what is displayed on the altar.

Ideally, the altar is placed in the center of the ritual circle. In this way, the directional points of North, East, South, and West cross and meet at the center of the altar. This becomes the sacred area of the altar, and you will want to think about setting something special in this place. In my tradition, we place the "spirit flame," which is a lighted bowl of high-grade alcohol (such as 180 proof). The flame represents the living and non-personified presence of divinity. For yourself, you may instead want to place a special crystal to catch and focus the quarters' emanations.

Upon the altar, place a statue or representation of the Goddess and God. Think about what position on the altar is most symbolic. In my tradition, we place the Goddess on the left and the God on the right. These positions represent magnetic (left) and electrical (right). They are symbolic of the archetypal masculine and feminine polarities in Western occultism. You can use symbolic placement or not as you wish.

To complete the altar as an operative center, set representations of the four creative Elements: Earth, Air, Fire, and Water. In my tradition, we use small bowls that contain a representation of each. You can place soil in the Earth bowl, incense in the Air bowl, a votive candle for Fire, and some spring water in the Water bowl. These representations are the "battery" for the creative forces that aid you in casting your ritual or magickal circle.

Now that you have the core established, the next step is to place the operative tools. These include your candles, incense holder, snuffer, cutting blade, cords, and whatever else you may need. To complete the altar's functionality, you will want to set your ritual tools in place as well. Traditionally, these are the pentacle, wand, athame, and chalice.

If appropriate, you may include representations of spirits or ancestors associated with your tradition. For example, you may place a skull to represent your ancestors, personal sigils given to you by spirit allies, or statuettes of animals important to your practice. Including your own symbols and representations will infuse your tradition with currents unique to your practice and capture the essence of the spirits.

The final stage is to decorate the altar with seasonal themes. In this regard, think of the plants, fruits, grains, and flowers that are indicative of the season. For example, pumpkins and gourds are typical for the fall season. Flowers can be used for the summer, and seeds and bulbs are ideal for spring. For winter, the traditional holly and pinecones are good choices. As a final touch, add colored candles to symbolize the "feel" of the season.

Now that we have looked at the Wheel of Year and its essential aspects, we can turn our attention to constructing the rituals of a tradition. In the next chapter, we will explore creating rituals and look at some functional models to consider. Turn to the next chapter, and let's move deeper into crafting a tradition of Witchcraft.

Creating Rituals

In previous chapters, we have looked at the aspects of creating a tradition and selecting a pantheon. In this chapter, we will examine the process of creating rituals that express the connection of the pantheon to the tradition. A ritual structure built around a pantheon brings a cohesive and empowering component to the rites of the tradition.

Within most traditions, there are two primary types of ritual. One is of a religious or spiritual nature, and the other is of a magickal nature. The primary purpose of a religious rite is to participate in the relationship with the pantheon, which includes veneration and offerings. Magickal rites are typically designed to request aid in a variety of matters or to raise energy for protection, healing, and resolving conflicts.

One ancient idea is that what happens to the deity eventually happens to its followers. In the ancient Mystery Traditions, this included the idea of death and resurrection. This is also an aspect of Christianity, as seen in the mythos of Jesus dying and rising from the dead, which is a very old Pagan theme. Ritual can help create alignments to deity that unite us with its essence. Through this, the soul is carried in the cycle or flowing stream of the Divine Emanation. In other words, aligning with a god who is born, dies, and returns places the soul in the same pattern and current of energy.

Ritual magick is the idea that non-material forces can create changes or manifestations in the material world. This type of magick requires a formula with specific procedures, techniques, and applications. Such a system is believed to attract or raise energy that can be condensed, contained, and directed in accord with the desired effect. This energy is attracted, amplified, and directed through means of a ritual or magickal circle large enough to contain the practitioners.

Let's look at a couple of models for creating a ritual circle. From these, you can get an idea about the type of circle you want and what you need to create one for your tradition.

Circle Models

The role of the circle is to map out the ritual area, to contain the energy raised within, and to protect the participants from contrary forces that might appear. The traditional model for a Witches' ritual circle is a marked-out area at least eighteen feet in diameter. In the center, an altar is placed, upon which sit the ritual tools and required items for the rite. Along the edge of the circle, a candle or torch is set at the cardinal points to mark the North, East, South, and West quarters.

The four creative Elemental Forces of Earth, Air, Fire, and Water are evoked to establish a sphere of energy that will enclose the entire circle (including the top and bottom). In essence, the Elemental Forces maintain the integrity of the sphere during the ritual. In order to dissolve the sphere, the Elemental Forces must be released to their natural and separate states of existence. The withdrawal of the Elements will automatically dissolve the energy sphere.

In mainstream Witchcraft, it is common to evoke circle guardians to the four quarters. This is usually done after the circle is established with the Elemental Forces. Many traditions call upon guardians, beginning at the East quarter and then moving clockwise around to the East again. In some traditions, the evocations begin at the North, continuing in a clockwise manner. Traditionally, the guardians are released in a counterclockwise fashion.

Customarily, the circle is declared cast following its ritual establishment. Once the ritual is completed, the circle is released and declared dissolved. This affirms the circle's status in both the Material Realms and Astral Realms. In this way, no undesired residual energy is left behind from the ritual.

Now that we have reviewed the basic idea of constructing a circle, let's turn our attention to a couple of functional models.

Model One: Circle Casting

1. On your altar, consecrate the salt and water by mixing in a pinch of salt to a small container of purified water, saying:

   "I consecrate this water with salt and thereby cast out all that is negative and contrary to my intent."

2. Sprinkle the consecrated salt water around the ritual area where the circle will be cast.

3. Mark out the ritual area for the circle on the ground with rope, stones, or candles.

4. To evoke the Elements, place representations of the Four Elements on the altar (for example, soil for Earth, incense smoke for Air, a votive candle for Fire, and a cup of water for Water): Earth is in the North, Air in the East, Fire in the South, and Water in the West. Place the palm of your left hand over each of the bowls (beginning with Earth and moving clockwise) and say:

   "I call between the worlds and evoke the Element of _____ to be present in this time and place."

5. Charge your athame (or sword). Touch the tip of the blade to each Elemental substance (beginning with Earth and moving clockwise) and say:

   "I charge this blade with the creative Element of _____, that it may be a tool through which I establish my will and intent."

6. Trace over the circle with the athame (or sword) and say:

> *"I conjure this circle to be a place between the worlds, which shall contain the power raised within. I consecrate this circle as a barrier and a protection against all that is contrary to my will and intent."*

7. Return to the altar and affirm:

> *"In the name of the Goddess and God, I declare the circle has been established."*

8. Evoke the Guardians by going to each of the directional quarters (beginning East and moving clockwise) and presenting the pentagram of evocation.

EVOKING   BANISHING

Trace the pentagram in the air, saying:

> *"Please hear me Old Ones, Guardians of the circle between the worlds. I summon, stir, and call you forth to be witness to the rites performed herein."*

9. Return to the altar and declare the circle to be fully cast.

10. Once the ritual is complete, bid farewell to the Guardians in reverse order, and then release the Elements at the altar bowls (also in reverse order of the evocation). To do so, thank the entities for attending the ritual, bow, and say something as simple as:

> *"Fare thee well."*

In this model, we are looking at the basic structure of establishing or casting a circle. As demonstrated in the ritual, the Four Elements are evoked to provide the building materials of creation. These Elemental qualities are drawn into the athame, which is then used to direct the Elemental Forces into the creation of a ritual or magickal circle. The presence of the Elemental Forces (temporarily bound to their representations on the altar) feed the Elemental energy fields that comprise the circle. They form and maintain a sphere of energy that encloses the ritual area, with the altar sealed inside.

The magnetic properties that bind the Elemental Forces together also "record" the spoken, visualized, and willed intent of the ritualist who cast the circle. This is like the principles that allow magnetic strips of tape to record voices and music on a cassette, or data that becomes stored on a magnetic disk. This is at work in the ritual as the evocational calls are sounded to conjure the intent of the circle. In the first model, the intent is to contain energy and protect from any energy contrary to the nature of the ritual.

Once cast, the circle is declared established in the name of the Goddess and God. This is, in essence, the invocation of deity, which breathes life into the circle and brings the Elements into harmony. This is reflected in the occult principle that the fifth Element of Spirit governs the interaction of the Four Elements of Earth, Air, Fire, and Water.

The final stage of casting the circle in Model One depicted the evocation of the Guardians or Watchers. As previously noted, the Watchers fall into the category of stellar beings that exert influence upon the Earth. This is a very old concept seen in the astral magick systems of ancient Mesopotamia. In the Babylonian system, there were four stars known as the Royal Watchers. It is an old belief that stars influence the nature and destiny of humans. Today, we see this principle operate in astrology and horoscopes. In this sense, we can say that the Watchers exert influence over the ritual circle and the proceedings within it.

As seen in the first model, once a ritual is completed, then the Guardians or Watchers and Elementals need to be released back to their domains. In addition to being sound ritual and magick, it is also simple courtesy. With the withdrawal of these entities, the sphere dissolves, and the circle shifts back from between the worlds.

The following model for circle casting is very similar, except that it incorporates the Elemental Forces more deeply. Look it over and see which model you prefer. As always, you can modify the material in this book or create something entirely different. The value of what is presented lies in its foundational material, which you can build upon.

Model Two: Circle Casting

1. Mark out the ritual area for the circle on the ground with rope, stones, or candles.

2. Light altar candles and each of the circle quarters: North, East, South, and West.

3. On your altar, consecrate the salt and water by mixing in a pinch of salt to a small container of purified water, saying:

   "I exorcise thee, O' creature of Water, that thou cast out from thee all impurities and uncleanliness of the spirits of the world of the phantasm. In the name of the Goddess and God, so mote it be."

4. To evoke the Elements, place representations of the Four Elements on the altar (for example, soil for Earth, incense smoke for Air, a votive candle for Fire, and a cup of water for Water). Earth is in the North, Air in the East, Fire in the South, and Water in the West. Place the palm of your left hand over each of the bowls (beginning with Earth and moving clockwise) and say:

   "I call between the worlds and evoke the Element of _____ to be present in this time and place."

5. To draw the Elements, take each of the Elemental representations around the circle, starting at the associated quarter (returning to the quarter and then moving to the altar).

Air: Starting at the East, carry smoking incense and say:

"In the beginning, the thought moved out into nothingness and filled the void..."

Fire: Starting at the South, carry a lighted candle and say:

"And into the misty void burned the desire for creation..."

Water: Starting at the West, carry a container of water and say:

"Then, from within the flame of desire, poured forth movement and direction..."

Earth: Starting at the North, carry the soil and say:

"And from movement and direction, there arose substance and so did manifestation take root."

Return to altar.

6. Charge your athame (or sword). Touch the tip of the blade to each Elemental substance (beginning with Earth and moving clockwise), saying:

    "I charge this blade with the creative Element of _____, that it may be a tool through which I establish my will and intent."

7. Trace over the circle with the athame (or sword), saying:

    "I conjure this circle to be a place between the worlds, which shall contain the power raised within. I consecrate this circle as a barrier and a protection against all that is contrary to my will and intent."

8. Return to the altar and affirm:

> *"In the name of the Goddess and God, I declare the circle has been established."*

9. Evoke the Guardians by going to each of the directional quarters (beginning East and moving clockwise) and presenting the pentagram of evocation. After tracing the pentagram in the air, say:

> *"Please hear me Old Ones, Guardians of the circle between the worlds. I summon, stir, and call you forth to be witness to the rites performed herein."*

10. Return to the altar and declare the circle to be fully cast.

11. Once the ritual is complete, bid farewell to the Guardians in reverse order and then release the Elements at the altar bowls (also in reverse order of the evocation). To do so, thank the entities for attending the ritual, bow, and say something as simple as:

> *"I fare thee well."*

In addition to the circle models, there are other models to consider. The three primary models to explore are the lunar, solar, and sabbat models. These will help you decide how to structure your ritual themes in order to create the most effective alignments to your tradition.

Lunar Models

The role of the Moon is both magickal and spiritual. Rituals associated with the Moon are designed to align with its various phases. Each phase emanates a specific type of energy that can enhance a work of magick or ritual intent. There are four basic lunar models: Dark Moon, Waxing Moon, Full Moon, and Waning Moon.

Traditionally, the Dark Moon is the three days when the Moon cannot be seen. To this phase belong chthonic themes, shamanic journeys, ancestral veneration, and things of an occult nature. When we read tales of cauldrons hidden in a dungeon or in the depths of the Underworld (or Otherworld), this is the time of the Dark Moon. When working with Dark Moon energy, it's effective to include ritual items such as jet and amber, black candles, black clothing, earthy incense, and dark wine.

The Waxing Moon is beneficial for rituals of gain, prosperity, increase, improved health, and general good fortune. Traditionally, the waxing period begins after the last night of the Dark Moon (with the first appearance of the crescent). Waxing Moon rituals are well served by incorporating green candles, sweet incense, light-colored clothing (if any), and white wine.

The night of the Full Moon is traditionally the time of magick and mystical events. Works of magick and ritual intentions are amplified by its energy. The Full Moon is also among the highly favored times to venerate ancestors and deities of the Moon and stars. For good results, include silver and white colored items, camphor-based incense, and offerings of red wine and grain cakes or cookies.

A classic lunar ritual is "Drawing Down the Moon." In mainstream Witchcraft, this refers to invoking the consciousness of the Goddess into the body of a coven member. In some traditions, the Goddess is invoked into a Priestess or Priest, but the Goddess can descend into whoever she pleases. It is believed that this makes it possible for the Goddess to speak directly through the human vessel. Drawing Down the Moon is most often performed at the time of the Full Moon.

A variant of Drawing Down the Moon involves directing the light and energy of the Moon into an object. The light and energy are considered magickal. It can be condensed and amplified once it is drawn and collected. This is often performed by using a mirror to reflect the light of the Moon onto or into an object. The Moon's light can be used to bless or charge ritual items, charms, or even the ritual participants.

The purpose of lunar rites is to incorporate the spiritual associations of the Moon with the subtle energies of its radiance. When incorporating lunar elements, think of ways to use the Moon's light. One very old tradition used a mirror to direct the light, and another used a bowl of water to catch the reflection of the Moon.

When incorporating spiritual elements into your ritual, think in terms of Goddess imagery. Symbols such as white shells, round cakes, ripe fruit, and silver decorations are ideal for lunar associations. The inclusion of a cauldron to represent the womb of the Goddess is a very useful tool. Offerings can be set around it, and petitions on small pieces of parchment can be placed into the cauldron. For an example of the religious, mystical, and sacred aspects of ritual construction, see Chapter Seven, "Initiation and Metaphysical Aspects of Witchcraft."

Solar Models

While much of Witchcraft is lunar-based, it does indeed possess significant solar aspects. The God in Witchcraft is represented and symbolized by the Sun. The journey of the Sun throughout the year is personified in the seasonal mythos of the God. As noted previously, the solar rites are highlighted by the equinoxes, solstices, and the midpoints of the year that fall exactly between them. These comprise the eight sabbats of the Wheel of the Year.

The year is divided into two halves: waxing and waning. These can represent the Lord of Light and the Lord of Darkness, which are the duality of the God's nature. In this respect, he is the Sky Father of the bright day and the Underworld Lord when his light descends beneath the Earth, leaving darkness to cover the land.

Solar-based rituals include items such as yellow candles, grain, stag antlers, and gold-colored objects to represent the Sun. Musical instruments such as the flute and harp can be incorporated into the rites. These types of items enhance the solar vibration and help create the required magickal and spiritual alignments that evoke and invoke solar energy.

The purpose of the solar elements is to bring balance and support to the lunar connections. This complimentary energy creates a stable polarity, which enhances the energy for practitioners of any gender in the circle. Incense made with frankincense and cinnamon is ideal for solar alignments. During the waning half of the year, add myrrh, which symbolizes the death of the Lord of Light.

Sabbat Models

The role of the sabbat is celebratory and serves to align us with the energy of Nature at any given season. The sabbat tells a story of the Goddess and God and follows them throughout the year. In this story, their relationship reflects the process of Nature as well as the journey of the soul through life and death within the Material Realm. It is ideal to create or establish a story that flows without interruptions to the plot or disappearances of key characters.

Other chapters of this book deal with the sabbats in greater detail, and, for this reason, I will only touch on a few important elements here. Remember that there are two parallel stories taking place in the Wheel of the Year. The stories alternate back and forth like two people singing a duet. Continuing with the metaphor, two songs are sung together as one. This is noted in the fact that the festivals aligned to the God are marked by daytime celebrations on the equinoxes and solstices. The festivals aligned to the Goddess are celebrated on the eve of the dates that fall exactly in-between each of the equinoxes and solstices.

The central theme of the Wheel of the Year is the idea that the God is the life force and the energy of creation. He is intimately linked to the Sun and to its light. He is also connected to the agricultural year, which is dependent upon the Sun's light. By contrast, the Goddess is the vessel of life and the energy of regeneration. She is intimately linked to the Moon and its light. She is likewise connected to the phases of the Moon, the fertile essence, and death and rebirth (for which the changing form of the Moon is strongly linked).

The courtship of the Sun and the Moon appears in many old tales. In essence, this focuses on the rising and setting of the two lights at different times. The Moon, more mysterious in nature, is an alluring figure. The Sun, less complicated in nature, is often the figure that is attracted to and pursues the Moon.

Because the light and warmth of the Sun diminish during the year, the God is depicted as declining in strength and passing away. The Moon, however, remains the same throughout the year in each month's appearance. Therefore, in her myths, she never dies. However, she does journey into the Underworld to retrieve the descended God and return his vitality through rebirth. These two primary themes should be maintained and incorporated into your tradition's mythos for the Wheel of the Year. Let's look at an overview of the separate yet related stories of the Goddess and God in the Wheel of the Year.

Her Story

In the mythos of the Goddess, we find two stories. In one, the Goddess is connected to the Moon, and in the other, she is connected to the Earth. These are the Moon Goddess Cycle and the Earth Goddess Cycle. Each of them expresses the presence and interaction of the divine feminine.

In the Moon Cycle, we see the Goddess comprised of four natures, each one associated with the phases of the Moon: Dark Moon, Waxing Moon, Full Moon, and Waning Moon.

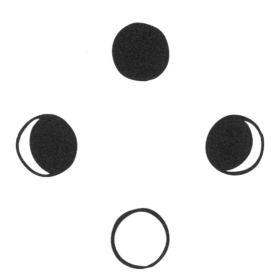

In the Dark Moon, she is the Goddess of Shadows and the Otherworld or Underworld. She is the essence of magick itself and sometimes called the Enchantress. Because she is unseen during the three nights the Moon is not visible, this aspect of the Goddess is often not noted in modern Witchcraft. Instead, the mainstream traditions view the Goddess as comprised only of three aspects related to the Waxing Moon,

Full Moon, and Waning Moon. We know these aspects as the classic Maiden, Mother, and Crone.

The general story of the Moon Goddess tells us that she dwells in the Underworld. She rises nightly on the eastern horizon from her abode into the world of humankind. In the night sky, she drifts gently overhead and then returns to the Underworld through the western horizon. The Moon Goddess gives light to the darkness and emanates her fertile energies, which regulate the menstrual cycle. She breathes the essence of magick from the light that falls upon the Earth. Through the repeating cycles of the Moon, the Goddess teaches us that all life exists within a cycle of birth, maturity, decline, and death. But death is not the end; instead, it is the beginning of the next repeating cycle of life. In this teaching, we find the connection to Fate.

In ancient times, the Fates were depicted as three people. One was a young maiden, another was a mature woman, and the third was elderly. In essence, they depicted the three stages of life: youth, maturity, and old age. It is easy to see here the concept of the Maiden, Mother, and Crone. The symbols of the Fates included a spindle, a spinning wheel, and a pair of scissors. The Fates were the daughters of Nox, the goddess of night. In the book *Pantologia: New Cyclopaedia* by John Mason Good, we read this verse: *"Them the Fates shall summon, of whom this beauteous maiden, the Moon, is one."* (p. 1913)

The ancient philosopher Plutarch wrote in his essay *The Face in the Orb of the Moon* that the souls of the departed abide for a time in the paradise of the Moon. It is in such themes that we encounter the spiritual role of the Moon Goddess and her connection as the birth-giver of souls. The connection between departed souls and a Witch goddess is reflected also in the role of Hecate at the crossroads. In ancient times, the crossroads were believed to be the gathering place of souls unable to find rest or their way to the Otherworld or Underworld.

When constructing rituals with lunar themes, think in terms of the mysteries of birth, life, death, and rebirth. Incorporating lunar themes and imagery into initiation rituals is also effective. This is covered in Chapter Seven, "Initiation and Metaphysical Aspects of Witchcraft."

The second model of the Goddess to consider is the Earth Goddess Cycle. In this model, the Goddess is more tangible and less esoteric than she appears in the Moon Goddess Cycle. The primary festivals that mark the Goddess are Samhain, Imbolc, Beltane, and Lughnasadh.

At Samhain, she descends into the Underworld or parts the veil and enters the Otherworld in search of her departed mate. At Imbolc, she liberates him from the frozen embrace of winter. By Beltane, the Goddess appears renewed as a young maiden. She is pregnant during Lughnasadh and gives birth to fruit and grain.

When we look at the entire Wheel of the Year mythos, we note the addition of the solar story in relationship to the solar festivals, which unite the Goddess to the God on deeper levels. The Earth Goddess Cycle tells the story of a maiden who appears in the spring. She rises from the Underworld or Otherworld and enters the realm of humankind, bringing with her the emanation of new life.

As the story continues, the Goddess arrives at May Day, which marks her courtship with the fertile young Lord of Nature. It is through their courtship that the bounty of life returns and is sustained for another year. This theme is dramatically marked by the marriage and impregnation of the Goddess, which manifests with the Summer Solstice. Here, the Earth Goddess is ripe with the bounty of Nature.

At Lughnasadh, the Goddess is visibly pregnant, and she gives birth to the harvest gathered at Mabon. The festival of Mabon marks the death of the Harvest Lord and his descent into the Underworld or Otherworld. As previously noted, the Goddess departs the Mortal Realm and journeys to find him. They meet in the Realm of Shadows on Samhain when the Goddess is once again impregnated. The fruit of this union is the newborn Sun God (the Child of Promise), who is born on the Winter Solstice. At this time, the Earth Goddess becomes the Great Mother in the divine sense, as opposed to the Great Mother of Nature at Lughnasadh.

When constructing rituals with Earth Goddess themes, think in terms of the seasonal shifts and agricultural symbolism. Incorporating themes associated with fertility and imagery associated with seeds, fruits, and general bounty is important to a cohesive ritual structure related to the Earth Goddess Cycle.

His Story

In the mythos of the God, we find two related stories. These stories fall into the Sun God Cycle and the Harvest Lord Cycle. In the first, the God is connected to the Sun, and in the other, he is connected to the Earth. Each cycle expresses the presence and interaction of the divine masculine.

In the Sun God Cycle, we see the God with two natures, each one associated with the two phases of the year. These are the waxing and waning halves marked by the equinoxes and solstices. In the Sun God story, he is the light and warmth that encourages and sustains growth and life in the mortal world. It is for this reason that his myths pivot on the equinox and solstice days, as these are the clearest markers of the solar changes of the year.

Upon examining the Sun God Cycle, we note that it begins with the birth of the God at the Winter Solstice. At this time of diminished light and warmth, the newborn deity is the promise of renewal and return. As the myth continues, the God appears as a youthful man at the Vernal Equinox, where he begins his courtship with the Spring Goddess. With the arrival of the Summer Solstice, we find the God wed and his wife with child. On the Autumn Equinox, the God begins his journey into the Underworld or Otherworld, leaving behind the cooling season and the coming increase of darkness.

When we blend this model with the Earth Goddess Cycle, the entire story unfolds a grander view. It is here that we better understand the Goddess and God as a mated pair that interact throughout the Wheel of the Year. There is but one other aspect to add to see the whole picture, and this is the story of the Harvest Lord.

The Harvest Lord is a solar-based deity with a mythos related to the Earth as opposed to the sky. In this model, the Harvest Lord reflects the cycle of plant life. This became an important element of life for humankind as it shifted from a hunter-gatherer society to an agrarian society dependent upon cultivated crops.

The agricultural model of the God begins with the seed, which is the God in the Underworld, waiting in the darkness of procreation. His birth is signaled by the first sprouts that break the surface of the soil. Here is the fragile infant whose inner power is yet to shine forth in its greatness. The first appearance of leaves is the symbolic herald of the Harvest Lord of the cultivated lands.

The presentation of buds on the plants and trees signals the growing powers of the Harvest Lord. The display of flowers that follows depict him in the full array of his vitality. With the appearance of fruit and grain, the Harvest Lord is at the peak of his full power. This is followed by his decline and death, as symbolized by the gathered sheaf. The seeds are collected from the harvest for the next season, which becomes the first and last symbols of the Harvest Lord, his birth, and his death in the endless cycle. You can also use fall leaves on the altar to symbolize decline.

When incorporating elements of the Harvest Lord Cycle into your ritual, think in terms of symbols that represent life phases. Select the phase that best suits the intent or theme of your ritual and use the representations (like seeds, flowers, sheaves) on the altar as decorations or focal points. For the Sun God Cycle, do the same and take note of the symbolism appropriate to the waxing and waning forces. An incense of frankincense is ideal for the Waxing Lord, while myrrh is ideal for the Waning Lord.

Yule/Winter Solstice

Mabon/Autumn equinox

Ostara/Spring Equinox

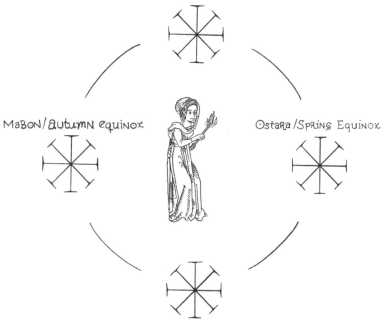

Litha/Summer Solstic

Ritual Components and Structure

Now that we have looked at various models for constructing rituals, let us examine the practical elements of creating and empowering rituals. To understand this better, we need to consider two primary aspects: the ritual tools and the steps to create a cohesive and functional ritual. In Chapter Seven, "Initiation and Metaphysical Aspects of Witchcraft," we will explore other metaphysical aspects that require discernment.

Let's begin with a look at ritual circles. In essence, a circle represents the cosmology of the tradition. In other words, it is constructed and understood along the lines of the internal beliefs and concepts. Therefore, within the circle casting, we should expect to find ideas of divinity, sacred directions, Elemental Energies, Guardians, and so forth. This is often represented on the altar and at the four directional quarters. For example, the altar is set with deity statues, representations of the Four Elements, and tools that focus and direct divinity and the Elemental Forces. The most common tools are the traditional pentacle, wand, athame, and chalice.

The use of ritual tools helps arouse altered states of consciousness. Altered states are required for the most effective rituals. In ancient times, this was accomplished through "round dances" and the ingestion of an intoxicating drink or substance. In modern circles, the most common method is through the personal will and mental imagery.

The process of altering consciousness within a ritual often begins with chanting. The participating members are led in a chant by a central figure at the altar. The members move around the circle as the chant continues, gradually speeding up. The members do not know when the chant will cease, which frees the mind to the experience itself. The end of the chant will be signaled abruptly by the director at the altar. This act releases the energy raised through dance and chant into the circle.

Moving within a circular motion (in essence, through the Earth's magnetic field) causes subtle shifts of electrical energy within the physical bodies of the dancers. This intensifies the aura of each member, and as energy is raised through dance, each person passes through the accumulative energy field of the coven. You can imagine this as a vapor trail through which all members move together. This unites each person and joins them to the group mind of the coven.

Among the most effective way to raise energy through dancing is to have the members hold hands and equally distance themselves. To increase the raised energy, the dance rhythm includes shuffling feet across the ground, which is then followed by a stomping action (and then the shuffling is repeated, and so on). Create your own rhythms and tempos through experimentation. One suggestion is:

shuffle, shuffle, shuffle, shuffle, stomp, stomp, stomp, stomp,
stomp, stomp, shuffle, shuffle, shuffle, shuffle, stomp, stomp, stomp.

Another effective method is to slip-slide across the ground instead of shuffling. This is similar to how kids "skate" with socks on a slippery floor, but with shorter movements. Naturally, you will want to fashion a dance step that is more appropriate to the dignity of a ritual setting.

While dancing, the members need to maintain the chant, which is directed by the person at the altar. Any changes or additions to the chant are called out by the director as one chorus nears its end. This allows the dancers to prepare and join in on the new or added verse. For example, if a chant includes a series of goddess names, the director can call out another name to chant as the original verse draws close to being repeated. This will then change the following verse to the new goddess name in the chant without breaking the tempo.

The dancers need to retain awareness of the perimeter of the ritual circle. There are two reasons to honor these boundaries. The first reason is that doing so breaks the connection with the inner cosmos of the circle and spins the person away from the center of what empowers the ritual. This severs the intimate connection between coven members, which affects the group mind. In essence, the circle is like a solar system, and the members are like planets in orbit around the Sun. When one leaves orbit, all the gravitational fields are affected.

The second reason is the energy field itself. The circle is an astral barrier. Passing your astral body (which is attached to your physical body) through an astral barrier is like jumping through a glass window.

Injuries are likely, and, in the case of the astral body, may not show up for several days or weeks. When it does, it can manifest as illness.

There are two ways to avoid damage when exiting a circle. One is to not cast a circle but instead create sacred space. This is a blessed and consecrated area as opposed to a formally established ritual circle. The second way to avoid damage is to create a doorway in the circle. While this eliminates injury, it still separates the person leaving from the centrifugal force at the center of the circle.

We should bear in mind that a "properly" constructed ritual circle crosses between the worlds. In other words, it meshes with other dimensions, and, in this regard, it is like an environmental sphere that supports our needs as living beings. It is wise not to leave the deep-sea diving suit while in the depths of the sea. Sacred space is more of a personal agreement about the ritual setting and therefore does not present the metaphysical constraints of a cast circle. However, it also does not provide the same protections and occult benefits.

Another component of the ritual circle is the altar. We have already addressed the altar in this chapter, but it is important to note its central theme. The altar is, in essence, the hub of the circle. It is the direct spiritual center where we meet and interface with divinity. Traditionally, coven members bow at the altar as a gesture of veneration as they enter the ritual circle. Another tradition is to place a kiss upon the altar or upon an agreed symbol placed upon the altar. The importance of the ritual kiss is described in Chapter Seven, "Initiation and Metaphysical Aspects of Witchcraft." You may wish to consider whether the altar is devotional or operative. I highly recommend the former choice.

When setting the altar, you can create its layout in accord with the traditional occult mythos of creation. To do so, place a black cloth over the altar to represent the darkness of procreation from which all things issue forth. In this darkness of outer space, set a candle to represent the presence of divinity, burning at the center of the void. Next, place candles or statues to represent the Goddess and God as personifications of the Divinity (the central light). At this stage, you will have depicted the Goddess and God overseeing the process of creation.

The next stage is to establish the Four Elements of Creation, which in ancient myth were in chaos within the void. According to the tale, Spirit (the fifth Element) brought the Elements into harmony so that creation could take place through their joined properties. You can serve as the hand of harmonizing Spirit by arranging the Elemental representations of Earth, Air, Fire, and Water on your altar. Pass your hand over the center candle flame to connect with the purity of the divine, and then set the Elemental representations in place according to their quarterly associations of North, East, South, and West. You can, of course, choose not to adhere to this tradition, in which case you will want to think about what the altar represents or means to you. From there, you can set the altar up as is most appropriate.

As noted earlier, casting a circle begins with the Elemental connections from the altar. What we need to consider next is the invocation of an altered state of consciousness as we create the ritual circle. One effective method is to shift your consciousness as you walk the circle, aligning to each of the four quarters as you approach and pass them.

One method of creating alignments is to visualize the Guardian of the directional quarter as you approach it. For example, at the North, you can visualize an earthy grotto, inwardly feeling the cool rock and the smell of primal Earth. As you take this imagery into your spirit, you can then visualize the appearance of a Guardian that is appropriate to such a setting. Ideally, you should speak or chant the name of the Guardian at this stage. This will help evoke its presence to the circle and within your consciousness as well.

It is effective to create a drawing or painting for each Guardian so that a group mind visualization exists for the members of your tradition. This imagery will help feed and strengthen the presence of the Guardians, creating a powerful group consciousness. But bear in mind that such images are not fantasy characters of the imagination. They become vessels in which sentient beings of the Otherworld can manifest in the Material Realm.

As you walk the circle, repeat an alignment specific to the Guardian of each quarter. In this way, you establish the inner and outer cosmos of your ritual circle, which is a mini-universe that represents your tradition's view of creation and its intelligent forces. A circle constructed in this way will enhance the group mind and bring powerful energy to your rituals.

In an altered state of consciousness, it is effective to affirm the visualized sphere of the ritual circle. To do this, you can use incense smoke. Simply tread the circle and affirm the boundary lines by stating them out loud. Be sure to include above and below along with the edge of the circle itself. For example, as you pass along the perimeter of the circle, you can say:

"Here, I mark the boundary of the circle's edge."

As you lift the censer up to pass the smoke upward, you can say:

"Here, I mark the boundary of that which is above."

Next, you can lower the censer and say:

"Here, I mark the boundary of that which is below."

For your review, here is a brief outline of creating a ritual circle:

1. Prepare your altar.

2. Mark out the ritual circle with rope, stones, votive candles, or other objects.

3. Activate the altar by calling upon the Elemental Forces.

4. Cast the ritual circle with the ritual tools.

5. Evoke and invoke the quarter Guardians.

6. Affirm the sphere of the ritual circle.

7. Declare the work complete in the names of your goddess and god.

Now that we have looked at the process of establishing a ritual circle, let us examine the components of ritual techniques and structure.

There are five components that comprise the art of creating successful rituals. You can adapt them or arrange them according to your own needs, but I strongly recommend that you incorporate them all in your ritual design. They are as follows:

- ❖ Personal Will
- ❖ Timing
- ❖ Imagery
- ❖ Direction
- ❖ Balance

Let's look at each one separately.

Personal Will

This can also be thought of as motivation, temptation, or persuasion. You must be sufficiently motivated to perform a ritual or work of magick to establish enough power for your goal. If you care little about the results or put only a small amount of energy into your desire, you are unlikely to see any real results. The stronger the need or desire, the more likely you will raise the energy required to bring about the change you seek. But desire or need is not enough by itself.

Timing

In the performance of ritual magick, timing can mean success or failure. The best time to cast a spell or create a work of magick is when the target is most receptive. Receptivity is usually assured when the target is passive. Therefore, choose a time when the target of your intent is not active but is passive and receptive. Consider the phase of the Moon, which should be waxing for gainful intents and waning for dissolving intentions. In essence, you want to work with Nature and not against it. Generally speaking, 4 a.m. in the target's time zone is the most effective time to cast a spell, because this is generally a passive and receptive time in Western society.

Imagery

The success of any work also depends upon images created by the mind. This is where the imagery enters the formula. Anything that intensifies emotions will help generate images with vitality and therefore add to a successful outcome. Any drawing, statue, photo, scent, article of clothing, sound, or situation that helps you merge with your desire will greatly contribute to your success. Imagery is a constant reminder of what you wish to attract or accomplish. It serves as a homing device in its role as a representation of the object, person, or situation that is your target or ritual intention. Imagery can be shaped and directed according to your will. This becomes the pattern or formula that leads to the realization of desire. Surround yourself with images of your desire and the vibrations will resonate, magnetically attracting your intention.

Direction

Once enough energy has been raised, you must direct it toward your desire. Do not be anxious concerning the results, because anxiety will draw the energy back before it can take effect. Reflecting upon the spell tends to ground the energy because it draws the images and concepts back. Try to give the matter no more thought so as not to deplete its effectiveness. After your ritual, mark seven days on your calendar and evaluate the results after this period passes. It usually takes about one week (one lunar quarter) for magick to manifest.

Balance

The last aspect of magick to take into account is personal balance. This means that one must consider the need for the work of magick and the consequences upon the spell caster and the target. If anger motivates your magickal work, then wait a few hours or sleep on it. While anger can be a useful propellant for a ritual intent, it can be detrimental and cloud your thinking. If possible, make sure you have exhausted the normal means of dealing with something before you move to a magickal solution. Make sure you are feeling well enough to work magick and plan to rest afterwards. Magick requires a portion of your vital living essence, which is drawn from your aura and body energy centers. Replenish this with rest, even if you do not feel tired. Health problems can begin long before you are aware of them.

Having looked at the mechanics of ritual, it is time now to consider the nature and roles of ritual tools in your tradition. There are two different schools of thought related to the tools. The primary differences center on the assignment of the Elemental Forces to the wand and athame. The ones listed below are most common in Wiccan-inspired Witchcraft, but keep in mind that other traditions may have their own tools. A general review of each tool will help you decide on how to organize this within your tradition.

The Pentacle

Traditionally, this tool is assigned the Element of Earth. As such, it is most appropriately constructed from clay or metal. Bronze, brass, or iron is a very common substance for a pentacle. Ceramic pentacles are also popular. The pentacle is the least mystical of the four tools and is often used in relatively mundane contexts. Many traditions use it as a platter to place and bless or consecrate ritual objects.

On a magickal level, the pentacle can ground or stabilize energy and provide protection in the form of a shield. As such, it can be placed to temporarily seal a breech in the circle (as in the case of opening a doorway to the outside). It can also be used to protect against unwanted energy directed towards your ritual setting. The pentacle can also shield against unruly spirits by holding it out against them within the circle. The design of the pentagram on the pentacle's surface is very effective for such uses.

On a spiritual level, the pentacle represents valor and bravery. In this light, it is the shield of the spiritual warrior. On an occult level, the pentacle is assigned to the material body of the ritualist.

The Wand

The wand has two different Elemental assignments, so you will want to select one that works best for you. One Elemental assignment is Fire, and the other is Air. For simplicity, I will deal here with the assignment of Air. For the assignment of Fire, see the section on the athame and simply make the switch of representations.

The wand is traditionally made of wood, and we find mention of the oak, willow, and beech among the oldest references. Air represents the mind and mental communication. When assigned to the wand, Air is a gentle but powerful force. The wand is compelling in contrast to the athame, which is exacting. It is for this reason why deity is called with a wand rather than an athame. Spirit allies are also called with the wand. One exception is the Guardians, who are traditionally summoned with the athame.

The wand is also used to direct and bestow blessings. In initiation ceremonies, the wand is used to bless the initiate by touching various areas of the body. In lunar rites, the wand is used to Draw Down the Moon upon the High Priestess.

On a spiritual level, the wand represents intuition and foresight. In this light, it is the far-reaching lance of the spiritual warrior. On an occult level, the wand is assigned to the mental intention of the ritualist.

The Athame

Like the wand, the athame has two different elemental assignments. One is Fire, and the other is Air. For the purposes of this section, I will deal with the athame as a tool of Elemental Fire. If you prefer the Air assignment, then use the alignments in the preceding wand section.

As a tool of Fire, the athame represents the raw energy or force of the Element in which the metal blade was forged. It is a tool of emotions as opposed to a tool of the mind (the latter being the nature of the wand). The athame is traditionally used to cast a ritual circle, and through its actions, a protective sphere of Elemental Fire is established. Fire is the force of transformation and is required to change mundane reality into a mystical event.

In some traditions, the athame is used to challenge new initiates seeking initiation. The blade is typically pressed against the chest, and the initiate is admonished not to continue unless they are prepared to fully accept what lies ahead. The athame is also used to banish unwanted spirits and entities from the ritual setting.

On a spiritual level, the athame represents controlled and directed emotions. In this light, it is the sword of the spiritual warrior. On an occult level, the athame is assigned to the emotional energy of the ritualist.

The Chalice

Traditionally, the chalice is made of silver and contains the ritual wine. Like the pentacle, the chalice serves a more practical nature in a ritual setting. However, because it contains the sacred wine and provides spiritual nourishment, the chalice cannot be assigned to the mundane. It is featured in the Rite of Cakes and Wine.

In essence, the chalice symbolizes receptivity, and, like the cauldron, can symbolize the womb of the Goddess. It's paired with the wand, a tool intimately linked to the God. Together, they enact the Great Rite, which is the divine union of Goddess and God nature.

On a spiritual level, the chalice represents compassion and acceptance. In this light, it is the heart of the spiritual warrior. On an occult level, the chalice is assigned to the spiritual awareness of the ritualist.

The Four Elements in Ritual and Magick

An integral part of any ritual or work of magick is the inclusion of the Four Elements. These vital forces are the building blocks of creation and manifestation. When incorporating them into a ritual, it is helpful to understand their natures and how they influence the energy and intent of the ritual's design. Let's break each one down:

❖ **Earth:** The quality of this Element stabilizes, strengthens, and gives foundation. It is used to encourage manifestation and balance the Element of Water, which is formless. It is also used to reduce the over-activity of the Element of Fire and slow the abundance of the Element of Air. The evocational and invocational tonal of Earth is the vowel sound of the letter A, elongated into a deep tonal chant: *"Aaaaaaaaaaaaaaaaaaaaaaaa!"*

❖ **Air:** The quality of this Element transmits, conveys, and communicates. It is used to carry images, scents, and sounds in an astral manner. It is also used to stimulate Earth and Water, and to revitalize Fire. The evocational and invocational tonal of Air is the vowel sound of the letter E, elongated into a deep tonal chant: *"Eeeeeeeeeeeeeeeeeeeee!"*

❖ **Fire:** The quality of this Element energizes, radiates, and transforms. It is used to alter forms, whether material or astral. It is also used to stimulate or diminish inactive Water (as in boiling), reduce overabundance of Air, and change the composition of Earth. Fire is the preferred Element to cast circles because of its transformational properties and natural quality as a barrier. The evocational and invocational tonal of Fire is the vowel sound of the letter I, elongated into a deep tonal chant: *"Iiiiiiiiiiiiiiiiiiiiiiiiiiiiiiiiii!"*

❖ **Water:** The quality of this Element creates movement, liquifies, and purifies. It is used to create motion, adaptability, and dissolve substances. It is also used to diminish the over-activity of Fire, alter the solidity of Earth, and slow the activity of Air. The evocational and invocational tonal of Water is the vowel sound of the letter O, elongated into a deep tonal chant: *"Oooooooooooooooooo!"*

In circle casting, the tonal of each Element can be sounded at each quarter to evoke the presence of its corresponding Elemental Nature. While the circle is being cast with the athame, the tonal of Fire can be chanted. This is particularly effective when the coven members chant the tonal as someone casts the circle. This person can join in and recite the words for evoking the circle, which are prescribed by the tradition.

Rituals Signs and Gestures

There are many signs and gestures to choose from in your tradition. The use of signs and gestures can enhance the ritual experience and draw upon Otherworld energies. These are presented in Chapter Eight, "The Book of Shadows."

Symbols in Witchcraft

There are a variety of symbols that can be incorporated into your tradition. They can be used to mark sacred objects, enhance the texts of your tradition, or keep things hidden from prying eyes. These symbols are depicted in Chapter Eight, "The Book of Shadows."

Now that we have explored the components and themes associated with constructing rituals, let's turn to the next chapter and examine ritual patterns.

Ritual Patterns

Rituals within a religious system contain the theology of the tradition. In modern Witchcraft, these themes are found in the mythos of the Goddess and God. Witchcraft incorporates the Wheel of the Year into its rituals and other secondary themes of a religious or mystical nature. The latter includes the Oak King, Holly King, the Green Man, and the Harvest Lord.

In this chapter, we will examine the religious, magickal, and mystical natures of the figures that appear in the rites of the Craft. We will also look at examples of ritual structures. In this way, you can consider how to incorporate these vital aspects of theology and ritual. Let's begin with a review of the secondary figures in legend and lore found in Witchcraft's history.

In the tale of the Oak King and Holly King, we find two brothers who compete for reign over the waxing and waning seasons of the year. As we noted earlier in this book, the Oak King rules from the Winter Solstice to the Summer Solstice, while the Holly King rules from the Summer Solstice to the Winter Solstice. In the general mythos, we find them competing for the favor of the White Goddess. The figures appear to be connected to the Oak Knight and Holly Knight, and the Winter King and Summer King, who can all be found in old lore. Their appearance is brief and their legends vague and obscure, but despite this, they persist in Witchcraft through their connection with the solstice periods. The importance of the Oak King and Holly King is that we can use their images and symbolism to mark the waxing and waning periods and keep pace with them. This helps keep us in balance, internally and externally, with the forces of Nature.

The Green Man is a figure who, like the Oak King and Holly King, is associated with seasons through plant life. Although the history of the Green Man is unclear and widely debated, he is the personification of the Plant Kingdom in modern Witchcraft. In this light, we can also associate or equate him with the Woodland Lord, also known as the Hooded One. In essence, the Green Man represents the tenacity of the life force. This theme is also reflected in the Harvest Lord. The Green Man's imagery serves as an umbilical cord to the vitality of Nature. By using his imagery, we can maintain a healthy flow of Nature's energy into our lives.

The Harvest Lord is an old figure that also appears in folklore and folk ballads, such as John Barleycorn. Like the Green Man, he is associated with the Plant Kingdom. However, the Harvest Lord is specifically connected to cultivated crops, unlike the Green Man, who is the Spirit of the Wild Woods. In much of Witchcraft's lore, the Harvest Lord presents the cycles of life from seed to sheaf and back again. His imagery and its meaning unite the pattern of our lives to the promise of renewed life.

The Harvest Lord is a slain god figure, the willing sacrifice, the sacred king, and the sacred seed. He is cut down and his seeds plant into the earth so that life may continue and be ever more abundant. This mythos symbolizes the planted seed nourished beneath the soil and the ascending sprout that becomes the harvested plant by the Autumn Equinox.

This mystical theme of transformation associated with agriculture is found in many European folk tales. The mythos of the Harvest Lord is preserved in ancient texts dating back to Homer and Hesiod and into modern folklore. It is perhaps best preserved in the story of the Passion of the Flax and the Dying God. In ancient Greece, he was Linos; in Lithuania, he was Vaizgantas; and, in Scotland, he was Barleycorn.

It is interesting to note that the common word for flax in European languages unites Old Europe with Celtic Europe. In Greek, it is *linon;* in Latin, *linum;* and in Old Irish and Old German, it is *lin.* This general mythos is also reflected in the Hans Christian Andersen story of the flax, and in the Danish tale of Rye's Pain (Rugen's Pine).

Essentially, such tales address the planting of the seed and its struggle to sprout from the Earth, followed by it having to endure the elements. Then, in its prime, the flax is pulled out of the ground and subjected to thrashing, soaking, and roasting. Eventually, it is combed with hacklecombs and thorns, spun into thread, and woven into linen. Finally, it is cut and pierced with needles and sown into a shirt. In all of this, we find the sacrifice of the Harvest Lord for the welfare of his people.

In a Greek myth, Dionysos is slain and dismembered. He is then boiled, roasted, and then devoured. The Orphic myth of Dionysos includes the same sequence but adds the re-composition and resurrection of his bones. Ancient writers, such as Heraclitus, remark that Dionysos and Hades are one and the same, thus associating Dionysos with the Underworld (a classic Witchcraft mythos, the Lord of Shadows). Further evidence of this connection comes from the labyrinth tale of the Minotaur, Dionysos, and Ariadne. The Labyrinth symbolizes the Underworld, and Ariadne (mistress of the Labyrinth) symbolizes the funerary goddess. The marriage of Dionysos and Ariadne, celebrated during the Anthesteria (an ancient springtime festival), coincided with the return of the souls of the dead, which connects Dionysos with them and the Underworld.

The Slain God is rooted in the early hunter and warrior cults that existed prior to the formation of agrarian societies. In the early tribal states, hunters and warriors held a prominent place in the social structure. The bravest and most cunning hunter or warrior was honored and looked upon as a leader. The well-being of this individual affected the well-being of the tribe. We find this theme in the King Arthur mythos of Northern Europe, where the land and the king are one. It is also reflected in the Southern European mythos of Rex Nemorensis, who was the King of the Woods in the sacred grove of Diana of Lake Nemi.

Before the invention of farming and herding, the hunt was essential to the preservation of life. Without successful hunters, the tribe would perish. Hunting was dangerous because early weapons required them to be close to their prey. Bodily injuries were common, and many hunters lost their lives or became disabled as a result. The hunter was also the tribal warrior, risking their life for the sake of their people.

The needs of the tribe, whether for food or defense, required sending out the best that the tribe offered.

This idea evolved along with religious and spiritual consciousness. The concept of deity and its role in life and death took shape within ritual and dogma. The idea arose of sending the best member of the tribe directly to the gods to secure the tribe's needs. This was the birth of human sacrifice, and those who went willingly were believed to become gods.

Offerings were nothing new to our ancestors; many times, food, flowers, or game were laid out before the gods. To offer one of your own was considered the highest offering the tribe could make. Among human offerings, the sacrifice of a willing individual was the greatest gift—the gods would surely grant the tribe anything if someone willingly offered their life.

The blood and flesh of the sacrifice were distributed among the clan and given into the soil. Parts of the body were buried in cultivated fields to ensure the harvest. Small portions of the body and blood were added to the ceremonial feast. This ancient practice was symbolically incorporated in Christianity as the body and blood of Christ in the Rite of Communion.

In the Slain God mythos, sacrifice is only part of the story. The sacrificial offering must be returned to the tribe. To accomplish this, rituals were said to have been designed to resurrect the Slain God. Special maidens were prepared to bring about their birth (usually virgins who were artificially inseminated so that no human could be pointed to as the father). Bloodlines were carefully traced from the pregnant maiden, and the returning soul was looked for among her children.

As human consciousness matured and evolved, human sacrifice was replaced entirely by animal sacrifice and eventually by plant sacrifice as the harvest festival. The same ancient mythos applied to both animal and plant sacrifice. In the Mystery Tradition of Witchcraft, we find the theme of "eating" deity or consuming the Harvest Lord through the celebration of cakes and wine (flesh and blood) ritual.

In the ancient tradition, it was through the connection of the body and blood of the Slain God that the people became one with deity. This is essentially the concept of the Christian rite of Communion or Eucharistic Celebration. At the "Last Supper," Jesus declares to his followers that the bread and wine are his body. He then declares that he will lay down his life for his people and bids them to eat of his flesh and drink of his blood (the bread and the wine). Blood was believed to contain the essence of the life force. The death of the king freed the sacred inner spirit. By distributing his flesh and blood, Heaven and Earth were united, and his vital energy renewed the Kingdom.

The Slain God appears throughout the ages. His image can be seen in the Jack-in-the-Green, the Hooded One, the Green Man, and the Hanged Man of the Tarot. He is the Lord of Vegetation, the harvest, and in his free, untamed aspect, the forest. In the Green Man image, the Slain God is the Spirit of the Land manifesting in all plant forms. He is the procreative power and the Seed of Life.

The Slain God a bridge between the worlds. This is why he is often depicted as either tied to or hung from a tree. The tree bridges the gap between the Underworld and the Heavens, for it is rooted in the Earth and its branches reach into the sky. The Slain God is one with Heaven and Earth—to be one with him is to be one with the Source of All Things.

Ritual Formats

The sabbat rituals are constructed around the seasons and the veneration of deities associated with different times of the year. Incorporated into each sabbat is a portion or reflection of the myths connected to the deities. This unites all elements together and establishes the necessary alignments for the ritual celebrants.

The format for each sabbat is also intended to bring the celebrants awareness of life stages, which are symbolized by the myths of the deities and the general themes of the season. The ideas of planting, nurturing, harvesting, and preserving are metaphors for the resilience of human life. Even though most Witches are not farmers, the seasonal themes still speak to family, career, lifetime goals, and old age.

Woven into the structure of Witchcraft rites is the principle of giving something back in exchange for what is received. This is reflected in offerings to deities in exchange for aid or favor. Through this, we acknowledge that all things are connected and in relationship with one another.

Fertility is the underlying principle in the seasonal rites of the Craft. The rites are not only a means of replenishing what we have drawn from the Earth but also about the fruitfulness of our lives. This relates to all facets, including children, career, creativity, prosperity, and health.

In the winter, we ask: what can renew our lives? What calls for rebirth in our relationships, work, goals, and dreams? What plans do we need to bring renewal and rebirth? What is our Child of Promise?

When spring arrives, we ask: what are the symbolic seeds we need to plant in order to achieve our desired harvest? What symbolic weeds have spoiled the garden of our relationships, career, goals, and dreams? What actions can we take to remove these weeds and clear our garden? When is the best time to prepare and plant the garden?

In summer, we ask: what have we achieved in our lives that we feel good about? What is good about us as individuals? In what area of our lives is there abundance and prosperity? In what area of our lives is there growth?

With the arrival of fall, we ask: what in our lives no longer serves us or others? What do we need to shed or rid ourselves of? What in our lives taps our energy and drains us? What can we do without? What must be cut away that will allow new growth in our lives? What seeds do we retain for a new season of life? These are the questions the rites of Witchcraft can lead us to ponder in mind, body, and spirit.

When we break down the groupings of these rites, the eight sabbats fall into two sets of four rituals: one in the waxing half of the year and the other in the waning. Within each half of the year, the four rituals alternate between an evening celebration and a daytime festival.

The Winter Solstice, or Yule, reflects the Sun as a divine image focused on renewal and rebirth. Here, we find the metaphor of the survival and return of the light, which we can liken to the journey of the soul from lifetime to lifetime. In a religious sense, the Winter Solstice is the promise of the undying soul and its covenant with the Divine Source. This covenant marks the promise that we shall never be abandoned by the Source from which we were created.

In the Mystery Tradition, the Winter Solstice celebrates the birth of the Sun God as the Child of Promise for the coming year of new light. Our ancestors created a mythos that began with birth because it is the natural entry into the material world. This core concept connects fertility and the Mother Goddess, which is the foundation of many Western nature-based religions like Wicca.

The ancient veneration of a tree as a dwelling place for a god also appears as the Yule tree. The tree, as a Yule log, has long been associated with the Winter Solstice. In some traditions, the Yule log is burned, and in other traditions, a lit candle is set upon it. It is interesting to note that, in ancient times, fire had to be drawn or "birthed" from wood. This involved using a wooden drill to create friction. In effect, this wooden rod or shaft penetrated the log, and from this act, a flame was generated. Here, we can see the log giving birth to the flame, which is the divine light.

The traditions associated with Yule are rooted in Pagan concepts and imagery. When we picture a hearth with stockings hung upon it and a fire burning within it, we are looking at the ancient grotto of the Goddess. The woven stockings are symbols of the Fates who weave the patterns of life and death. The log and the fire are a mated pair, aspects of the Divine Source that manifest as the archetypal masculine and feminine polarities.

It is easy to confuse the concepts related to fire regarding what polarity is assigned to its manifestation. In early writings of Western literature, fire is the goddess Hestia, later known to the Romans as Vesta. This can cause us to consider fire as feminine. However, if we consider that all things issue forth from the Mother Goddess, it is easy to reconcile a flame (generated from the Goddess) as the masculine part of the feminine whole.

We know from ancient times that fire was believed to dwell within wood. This belief arose from the fact that fire could seemingly draw out of the wood by rapid rubbing. In later times, a glass lens was used, much in the same way a magnifying glass is used to burn wood by focusing sunlight. An ancient custom required fire to be drawn from a piece of the sacred tree of a grove sanctuary, which called for the flame to be passed to a torch. The torch carried the divine fire to the new grove, where it was ritually and magickally passed into the new sanctuary.

In the mythos of the Mystery Tradition, the Sun God guards the sacred coven. He protects the Divine Source, concentrated in the sacred tree, which is the Great Goddess. In this aspect, he appears as the Stag-Horned God and Lord of the Woods. But the focal point of the Winter Solstice is not upon this older form of the Sun God; instead, it is upon his birth as the Child of Promise who brings new light.

This light renews the material and spiritual essence within and without. The Child of Promise is the seed of new hope, renewal, and new growth.

The festival of Imbolc celebrates the coming of spring and the release of winter's hold upon the land. In Celtic lands, the festival marked the Day of Bride, which is another name for the goddess Brighid (also known as Brigit). One old legend features Bride as a captive in the realm of winter, where she is held for three days. She escapes and emerges at Imbolc as a youthful maiden after drinking from the Well of Youth. Here, we find the theme of transformation associated with Imbolc.

In another legend, Bride bears a magickal wand. One touch of her wand turns the land green and brings forth the white and yellow flowers of spring. The wand symbolizes the fertilizing and impregnating forces of the Goddess.

In Scotland, an old folk custom featured the construction of a bundled sheaf of grain into the image of a woman. This image symbolized the youthful and pure maiden, who shall later become the May Queen. The sheaf was typically saved from the last harvest before the winter season that preceded Imbolc. Here, we find the connection between the Earth Mother and the Harvest Lord, for it is into the body of the Goddess that the slain Harvest Lord returns. He is reborn and later dies as the Straw Man, the harvested sheaf representing the Sun God.

At Imbolc, the Goddess is the Lady of Fire and the God is the Lord of Ice. Folk traditions associate a female figure wearing a crown of candles with the Imbolc season. Here, we see the Goddess of Fire as the reigning queen. It is she who raises the passion and enflames the energy of the God (note symbolism of Bride's wand). The God has been bound in the Underworld since he entered as the Harvest Lord. The ice represents the "stillness" of the Underworld water on which the God lays in his reed basket boat. The passion of the God is awakened by the Goddess's flame of desire, which frees him from bondage and allows the Underworld river to flow back into the world of the living. Water is an important element in spring, where we find the Goddess as the Lady of Lake and the God as the Lord of the Reeds.

The Vernal Equinox marks the renewal of the life force within the land. The seeds that slept beneath the blanket of winter begin to feel the quickening of energy. In the Mystery Tradition, we find the tale of the Goddess ascending from the Underworld (like the Moon rising from beneath the horizon). The God rises also and follows her in a ritual of courtship. Here, we find myths attached to the cycles of the Sun following the Moon and the Moon following the Sun through the sky.

Fertility was the essence of the season and the focal theme of ancient rites. The plowing of furrows and the planting of seeds symbolized human sexuality, associated with the adolescent phase of life and the preparation for the growing season and harvest. This was expressed in myth as a young maiden goddess and a young lord.

With the melting of winter ice and warming weather, water appears in lakes and wetlands. Lakes have long been associated with the Underworld and Otherworld. Ancient beliefs held that they were gateways to these other realms. The ancient mystical figure known as the Lady of the Lake is rooted in this old belief.

Around the lakes and in the wetlands, reeds grow quickly. They were used to make harvest baskets, and such baskets appeared as cradles in the birth myths of various Sun gods. For example, the god Dionysos (the Divine Child) is set adrift in a harvest basket. In another myth, Llew is cast adrift by his mother, who places him in a basket made of weed and sedge. Here, we find that water and the seed within the harvest basket join, uniting the cycles of life and death.

The Goddess, as a maiden figure at spring, represents the new fertile season, an allegory for the maturation of the reproductive system. The God, as the young woodland lord in spring, symbolizes the mating drive. The maiden quickens his energy with her allure, and fertility awakens in the plant and animal kingdoms.

The festival of Beltane celebrates the renewal of life as the forces of spring begin to manifest the buds, flowers, and greenery of Nature. The Goddess now appears on the Earth as a young maiden and the God appears as a young man. In this season, the courtship begins and leads to abundant crops and herds as the blessings of the union of the Goddess and God spread throughout all of Nature.

In ancient times, bonfires were lit on hilltops in a custom that included a belief that the light of the fire attracted the Sun. Following a long cold winter, such an act held great importance. Beltane also included fertility rites, such as lovemaking in freshly plowed furrows of the planting fields. Customs included the crowning of a May Queen and May King who oversaw games of competition and reward. Folkloric figures such as the hobbyhorse and Green Man were featured during the festival of Beltane.

In Northern Europe, the hawthorn is among the first trees to blossom near Beltane. It has a long association with the Elven and Faery race. In ancient legend, the hawthorn is a guardian tree that protects the entrance to magickal realms. One ancient belief held that an oak and ash tree flanked the pillars of portals to the Faery Realm. The hawthorn tree guarded access to the oak and ash portal. In this sense, the hawthorn became a symbol of initiation and passage, as well as guardianship.

As we have previously seen, the tree is a gateway and bridge between the realms that we call the Overworld, Middleworld, and Underworld. A May Day custom involved gathering bundles of wood from the field and forest. These branches were separated and tied together into small bundles, which were hung over doorways to protect the household. A long pole called the maypole was decorated with ribbons and placed in the center of the town or village. Dancers would hold the ends of the ribbons and intertwine them in a crisscross and weaving dance that led them inward towards the pole.

The maypole represented, among other things, the phallus that impregnates Nature. The colored ribbons were intended to revitalize the fertile essence by binding renewal to the maypole phallus. The maypole colors varied throughout Europe. The most common colors were white (renewal of the bone with new life) and red (the vital blood of life). Other colors included green, blue, yellow, and additional hues associated with love and spring.

Various folk magick customs are connected to the maypole dance. A primary custom involved people of the community dancing in an alternating circle around the Maypole. Traditionally, the men would take the white ribbons and the women would take the red. The men turn to face their left and take one step out from the pole. This creates two circles of dancers facing one another. The music begins, and the dancers start a weaving dance, moving their ribbon over the first person they meet and under the next. The dance continues, over and under, until the wound ribbons are too short to continue. The dancers would then embrace and begin the celebration.

The Summer Solstice marks the celebration of growth and the fertility of Nature. In the Aegean and Mediterranean regions, fireflies swarm and mate at this time. In folklore, the glowing light of the firefly connected midsummer's eve to the faery legends. The yellow blossom of St. John's Wort resembled the color of the firefly. Thus, the herb was believed to possess magickal powers when harvested on the morning of the Summer Solstice.

In many European traditions, this season is intimately linked to faery lore. The popular play *A Midsummer Night's Dream* is rooted in such lore. In ancient times, it was believed that Faeries brought about the flowers, fruits, and the abundance of Nature. Therefore, summer was the peak of their power and a time of celebration and revelry.

In the Mystery Tradition, the Summer Solstice also marked the wedding of the Goddess and God. Here, they reigned as the Lord of the Plant and Animal Kingdom and the Queen of Nature. Because the Summer Solstice is the longest day of the year, the God was at the height of his prowess. His power and vitality radiate into the land, and before his strength fails, he must be taken in his prime.

There is an ancient theme that the well-being of the king and the well-being of the land (and the Kingdom) are tied together. In this mythos, what becomes of the king then befalls the land and the people. At the core of this mythos is the "Sacrificial King," who is also known as the Slain God. These figures are part of the character known as the Harvest Lord. Summer marks the beginning of the harvest season, which concludes with the onset of autumn.

The festival of Lughnasadh celebrates the beginning of the harvest season in Northern Europe. It is technically the gathering of the first fruits of Nature's bounty. It is here that the mythos turns to the theme of the "whole" and the "parts." An ancient concept held that the Earth was the mother, which made seed crops their offspring. Since it is the seed that impregnates the Earth (from an ancient perspective), the seed is both the lover and the son of the Great Mother. In this sense the season of Lughnasadh reflects the separation of mother and child so that the expansion of life may continue.

In the Mystery Tradition, the season known in modern times as Lughnasadh finds the Goddess as the Lady of the Fields and the God as the Lord of the Barley. This demonstrates the relationship between the two deity forms, with the Goddess as the fertile field and the God as the ripened grain that issues forth from within her. Here, we clearly see the whole and parts of the whole manifest within Nature.

In Northern Europe, Lughnasadh was popular for handfasting ceremonies (marriages). This may have been related to the seasonal theme of the separation of parent and child, and so the couple joins together as independent from parental reign. This season was also favored for the observation of omens, which is rooted in the awakening of the Underworld forces during the act of harvesting the planted fields. The Underworld forces have long been considered vital to foretelling the future.

As a ritual celebration, Lughnasadh is a time of anticipation for abundant crops in the cultivated fields at this season. This is the "offspring" of the Goddess, the fruit of her womb issued forth from the rich fertile soil. Within the bounty of Nature, the "god seed" is contained in the grain, fruit, and vegetables, which shall ensure the future harvest crops of yet another season to come.

The Autumn Equinox marks the period of the final harvest and the last gathering. This season celebrates the bounty of Nature. Here, the Earth Mother has given birth to all the fruits of the Earth. Therein reside the seeds of her son, the Lord of the Harvest.

In one mythos, we find a tale assigning the Spirit of the Land to the Harvest Lord figure. In this belief, the Spirit of the Land is drawn into the sheaves of grain as they are cut and gathered. Here, the Harvest Lord leaps from bale to bale as the threshers harvest the field. When the last sheaf is gathered and bound, the Lord of the Harvest remains fixed to the field. In a time-honored ritual, the Spirit of the Land is then returned to the Earth.

The Autumn Equinox also marks the beginning of the descent of the Goddess into the Underworld. In this mythos, she journeys to find and retrieve her lost lover. This is a metaphor for the harvested fields that now lay void of summer's abundance. The gathered seeds of the Sun God are stored away, and the renewal of life is asleep within the Spirit of the Land.

Samhain marks the parting of the fabric that separates the world of the living from the Otherworld realm. Here, we find the Goddess in her aspect as the Lady of Shadows and the God as the Lord of Shadows. In a related mythos, they are viewed as the King and Queen of the Faery Kingdom and as the Lord and Lady of the Underworld, who oversee the Ancestral Realm. This relates to an ancient belief in the spirits of the dead and the use of primitive burial mounds. Over time, such mounds became associated with Faery hills in folklore and folk magick.

In the Mystery Tradition, the Otherworld and Underworld are intimately associated with the ancestral spirit. This is imagined as a collective consciousness that contains and preserves the memories of all who came before us. In the Italian system, this is depicted as an entity known as the *Lar*. The skull represents what remains after death: the memory and experience of those who once lived in the material world. It is honored as a guardian, preserver, and escort who stands at the threshold between this world and the next.

The well-known image of the skull and crossbones appears in the oldest forms of the Mysteries. The crossed bones symbolize guardianship over the gateway into the Otherworld, and the skull represents ancestral knowledge, wisdom, and oracular power. In the Mystery Tradition, a candle is placed on top of the skull, and when lighted, symbolizes communication between the worlds.

It was an ancient belief that blood vitalized the spirits of the dead and granted them the ability to speak to the living. A few drops of blood were offered to the ancestral spirits to establish direct and reliable communication. In modern Witchcraft Mysteries, this is often symbolized by placing a red candle on the skull. Red represents blood and vitality and is therefore a symbol of the living ancestral spirit.

The Halloween tradition of bobbing for apples is rooted in the mysteries of this ancient seasonal celebration. The apple has long been associated with the Faery Realm and, in ancient legend, served as a food for those who journeyed into the Otherworld. Since legend held that eating any food from the Faery Realm prohibited anyone from leaving, taking apples into the Faery Realm allowed one to eat and still return. Water was intimately connected to the Otherworld and Underworld, and sacred lakes and wells were often considered to be entrances into the Hidden Realms. In this view, bobbing for apples symbolizes the initiatory journey into the Otherworld and the ability to return by eating the sacred fruit.

Many ancient legends in Northern Europe speak of the "silver bough" that allowed mortals safe passage to and from the Faery Realm. The bough was said to bear apples (usually nine in number) sacred to the Faery Queen, who protected all who bore it. In Southern Europe, the "golden bough" served the same purpose and appears in the tale of

Aeneas, who is guided into the Underworld by a sybil that secures the golden bough for him to bear on his journey.

Now that we have looked at ritual formats and their Inner Mystery themes, you can better understand the levels within the sabbat rituals (and how they function together). In the appendices, you will find examples of each sabbat rite for group or solitary practice. These rituals are based upon the Mystery Tradition rites and can be easily modified for other types of Witchcraft ritual themes. Use them as templates or ideas for creating your own rites. The signs, postures, and gestures mentioned in these rituals can be found in Chapter Eight, "The Book of Shadows."

Add coven songs and chants to the rites where you feel they are appropriate. It is beneficial to fill parts of the ritual with song or chant whenever coven members are waiting. This helps keep life within the ritual. Remember that these rituals are templates, and it is expected that people will bring their intuition and spontaneity to the otherwise structured rituals.

Initiation and Metaphysical Aspects of Witchcraft

Initiation may very well be the most controversial topic in modern Witchcraft. There are those who question its place in the tradition. Be that as it may, there are two types of initiation that we encounter in the Craft. One is a simple, light-hearted welcoming rite, similar to joining a mundane club or organization. The other type is a formalized ritual, serious in nature, and performed by individuals who were initiated by others in a chain of experienced initiators and teachers.

In modern Witchcraft, we also find two other types of ceremonies. One is the rite of dedication in which a person formally declares their intention to study Witchcraft for a certain period. The usual length is a year and a day, though it varies by practitioner and tradition. The other type of ceremony is called *self-initiation*, which is the notion that a person can initiate themself. Before we examine the different types of initiation, it can be helpful to consider the meaning of the word.

The English word initiation comes from the Latin *initiare*, which itself is derived from the Latin *initium*. The basic meaning is "to begin" or "beginning." The literal meaning of the word is little more than a formality. However, in a mystical or occult sense, initiation is something more complex. We will examine this later in the chapter, but for now, let's look at the basic forms of initiation in modern Witchcraft.

Dedication

The dedication period is for a person to study and explore the Craft to decide whether this is the religion or practice that will be right for them. The traditional period is a year and day, a theme commonly found in old Celtic tales of mystical journeys. During this time, the seeker commits to study and instruction. Typically, this involves reading and training assignments. The goal is to familiarize the seeker with the tradition's core elements and provide various indications of what it's like to live as a Witch.

In modern Witchcraft, this can be a personal commitment to oneself or a formal contract between student and teacher. The period exists to allow enough time to understand the path of Witchcraft and work out any concerns or personal issues. One of the primary challenges many people face is breaking through the erroneous stereotypes about paths like Witchcraft in Judeo-Christian-dominated Western culture.

When joining a group or coven, it is not uncommon for the seeker to be asked to discuss past events and issues related to training that may present challenges to embracing Witchcraft as a spiritual or religious path. In this regard, think about topics such as ritual nudity, intimacy, and other things that you may or may not want to include in your tradition. If you do, then it is wise to have a long heart-to-heart discussion with any seeker during the dedication stage. You may want to create a questionnaire similar to a job application, customized to address various feelings and past experiences. Knowing if someone experienced abuse, trauma, or incarceration in the past may be important in determining whether that individual will fit in with a specific group's dynamics. This can help avoid triggers, disagreements, or upset in the future.

When the seeker is ready to commit to a dedication, then a simple rite is beneficial. It can include the lighting of a candle and some incense in a quiet setting. The seeker can anoint themselves with a pleasant oil fragrance and then speak words to this effect:

> "I hereby dedicate myself to a period of one year and day, during which time I will commit to a serious and thoughtful study of Witchcraft. I will approach this with an open mind and open heart. By the honor of my word, I do so swear to undertake and complete this journey of dedication."

There is one last word of advice I have to offer: make sure that you and the seeker have the same understanding of what it means to give one's word or to swear an oath. I have unfortunately discovered that, to some people, a sworn oath holds only while it is convenient. You will want to avoid discovering this too late and wasting much of your time, energy, and trust.

Initiation

Once a decision has been made to practice Witchcraft, a rite of initiation traditionally follows. Typically, this is performed on the night of a New Moon or Full Moon. As previously mentioned, there are two basic types of initiation in modern Witchcraft. Let's begin with self-initiation as a concept. Here, a person can initiate themself into the Craft. Some conclude that the Goddess and God will bestow initiation upon the sincere seeker when simply asked to do so. There is a fair amount of controversy regarding the authenticity of such a non-traditional approach. If you decide upon using self-initiation in your tradition, you will want to understand the arguments for and against.

In essence, the argument against self-initiation is that a person cannot give themself something they do not possess. This argument can only be understood by knowing that traditional initiation is bestowed by an initiator with the knowledge, experience, and the current of power the initiate seeks. Therefore, such a person can pass the essence of this energy to the initiate and align them with the forces that the initiator is already in contact with. This is sometimes referred to as "passing the power."

The counterargument against needing an initiator is that the first initiate in history had no initiator. The return argument is that the first initiate was taught by Otherworld contacts. Then, in time, this person brought others to this same contact, and from this was born the occult tradition of initiation. Another counterargument is that the same self-discovery and connection should also work today. While this is true, we need to understand two things. First, in the case of the "first initiate," the work of connection was accomplished first and the stage of being an initiate came after the experience. Therefore, if equated to traditional initiation, self-initiation cannot be the starting point through a personal rite. It would come after the experience and training; thus, the self-initiation ritual would mark a perceived achievement of gaining the traditional initiate level. Fortunately, the means for creating the old Otherworld connections still exist and can be accomplished through the ritual and magickal techniques presented in this book.

Finally, self-initiation is not a means through which you can become part of an established tradition. One example would be the Gardnerian Tradition. To be a Gardnerian, the person would need an initiation done by a valid Gardnerian initiate; a person is unable to self-initiate into the tradition. However, it is important to note that this does not make your tradition any less valid. As already stated, the means to create Otherworld connections are still available to this day.

Now that we have looked at the concept of self-initiation, let's explore traditional initiation. We have already looked at the idea of Otherworld contact and its connection to traditional initiation. Let's explore this a little further by journeying back in time to our distant ancestors.

In our early tribal phase, there were individuals who possessed the ability to connect with spirits and the Otherworld. These were the shamans, medicine people, and witch doctors common to so-called "primitive" societies. Many of these people possessed a deep knowledge of plants and their chemical uses. Among them were the Witches and the cunning folk.

Old myths and legends tell us of beings, often called Faerie or Elves, who contacted humans. In the deep quiet woods and the silence of the dark night, relationships were formed. Sometimes, according to various tales, an object was given to a human by one of the Faerie or Elven beings. This object possessed magickal abilities, allowing the human to accomplish things they could not previously do.

Over the course of time, the human was either taught or stumbled upon a variety of magickal techniques. These enhanced their ability and manifested as oracular powers, creating a seer. At some point, the human taught select others. Through this, a connective lineage of initiation was established, the essence of which still exists today. It is often referred to as the living chain of memory associations.

The idea of memory-chains is that connected ideas carry consciousness across dimensional planes by using an association-chain linked to the vibrations and entities within each dimension. Occult initiation aligns the initiate with these memory-chains, they become connected to the chain of associated ideas, and awareness is brought through to the subconscious mind of the initiate. This awareness draws the memory of what resides in other dimensions, and the mind connects with the memory-chain associations. The consciousness and memory begin to share a relationship. However, this is different from the type of memory function through which the mind holds a record of an event. Instead, it is linked to the living memory of the chain of connections that lead through the non-material dimensions. Once connected, the inner awareness will allow you to perceive things you have not before. You will see things differently because you realize the connection of all things (realization and knowledge are two different things). At this point, the "shroud of unawareness" that you inherited from societal constraints is lifted, and your vision is then opened to new expansive vistas.

The living memory-chain is used by non-material spirits, ascended masters, spirit guides, and other beings for communication between the planes. The psychic art of channeling uses the memory-chain and connects with beings within non-material realms. However, this type of connection is temporary and does not create the sustained connection initiation brings. The concept and use of the memory-chain will become clearer as the chapter continues. For now, let us continue on the subject of degrees.

Degree System

There are different models of the initiate degree system in some formalized groups practicing Witchcraft. The most popular model is the three-degree system, which is used largely in Wicca and Wiccan-based traditions. In essence, the degrees mark basic, intermediary, and advanced training periods. In addition, this often includes a religious "office" association. For example, a second degree designates a more seasoned Priestess or Priest, and a third degree level notes a High Priestess or High Priest. Not all systems adhere to a standard, and I am not sure we can argue that there is one in this eclectic age of modern Witchcraft.

In some traditions of Witchcraft, each degree also bestows certain Mysteries and privileges to the initiate. One example could be the ability to perform certain rituals. Another example would be that a second degree initiate might have access to certain material not available to a first degree.

If you choose to have a degree system in your tradition, it is useful to create training materials. One model is to establish "first degree" as the stage in which initiates learn how to set the altar, cast a circle, and gain a basic understanding of magick and spell casting. Second degree can be set up as an in-depth study period for the theology of your tradition. In addition, the initiates learn more of the ritual and magickal arts. In this way, they can conduct or help conduct the rites of your tradition. The third degree level can be established as the mastery of the ritual and magickal arts. In addition, it can be the most significant "religious office," marked by the Great Rite, which is the divine marriage in some Wiccan traditions. For more information, see the section on the Great Rite in this chapter.

When considering the structure of degrees, think about whether you want to have the initiation level begin the period of training or mark its completion. In other words, will a second degree initiate already be accomplished or just beginning to attain second degree training? I liken this to martial arts, where a white belt is a novice with no knowledge or experience when they begin. However, the next color belt is achieved by first learning the techniques required for the next level and demonstrating them in a practical display. In this example, a second level belt means that the person can already perform at this level and is training to meet the requirements of the third level.

Coven Offices

If you want to have a coven structure in your tradition, then you will find it beneficial to establish offices. All organizations have offices and officers, and a smoothly run system requires people working together at different supporting levels. Decide whether the officers are voted in or appointed, and whether there is a set term of service. You may even want to rotate officers so that everyone can share in the experience. Here are the most common:

❖ High Priestess or High Priest
❖ Priestess or Priest
❖ Maiden
❖ Guardian
❖ Mediator
❖ Scribe (Secretary)
❖ Treasurer
❖ Summoner

The High Priestess and High Priest are traditionally the directors of the coven or tradition. They oversee the operation of the system and are responsible for providing training and support. In effect, they are held responsible for everything that goes on in a coven setting. Outside of this role, they are the spiritual channels that help keep the soul of the coven or tradition alive and integrated.

The Priestess and Priest traditionally aid the High Priestess and High Priest with teaching and training. They also perform or assist in various rituals of the tradition. Outside of these roles, the Priestess and Priest are the religious channels that help maintain connection with the deity forms of the tradition. This includes a thorough study of the myths and legends, the care of statues, and observation of the days sacred to the tradition's deities (a responsibility shared with the High Priestess and High Priest).

The Maiden is, in essence, the High Priestess's aid. She is traditionally training to become the High Priestess. She typically tends the altar during ritual and ensures that supplies are furnished, candles and incense stay lighted, and that the High Priestess has what she needs at various stages of the ritual.

The Guardian is, in essence, the High Priest's aid. He is traditionally in training to become a High Priest. He typically helps maintain order during the ritual, keeps watch on safety factors, and helps move people around during initiation rituals. The Guardian also ensures that the High Priest has everything he needs at various points of the ritual.

The mediator of the coven is a trusted and respected person that coven members can go to when problems occur between members. They can serve as go-betweens to resolve issues or sit neutral and keep the peace during talks while directing the discussion in healthy ways. It is vital that the mediator never take sides but instead helps opposing parties hear and understand one another.

The scribe or secretary is responsible for recording minute meetings, agreements, rules, laws, and anything requiring recollection or written record. This should be someone with good writing skills who can also help create ritual text and other material that will be set to paper, disc, or hard drive.

The treasurer is responsible for keeping an account of any money that the coven or tradition acquires. Typically, a fund is collected for ritual supplies and other needed items. This keeps the financial burden

Raven Grimassi

from falling upon any single individual in the coven or tradition. While covens do not charge for membership, members should share common expenses to support the needs of the coven.

The summoner is responsible for letting people know the time and place of coven meetings and rituals. The summoner should communicate with everyone to coordinate attendance and who is bringing what. The High Priestess and High Priest should be able to know from the summoner exactly who is coming and that everything is in order for a gathering.

The Eightfold Path

In traditional Wicca, we find methods of raising energy for initiates of the Mystery Tradition. The Eightfold Path is one of the teachings dropped from mainstream books on Witchcraft during the 1980s as authors presented self-styled teachings versus time-honored and traditional ones. In essence, the Eightfold Path presents techniques for Witches to enhance ritual work and achieve higher levels of consciousness. Let's examine each of the techniques and methods:

1. Mental discipline through fasting and physical disciplines

2. Development of the will through mental imagery, visualization, and meditation

3. Proper controlled use of drugs that alter the state of consciousness

4. Personal power, thought-projection, raising, and drawing power

5. Ritual knowledge and practice. The use of enchantments, spells, symbols, sigils, and charms

6. Psychic development and dream control

7. Rising upon the Planes. Astral projection and mental projection

8. Sex magick, sensuality, and eroticism

Mental discipline is an important aspect of magickal training. It strengthens the will and sharpens the mind of the initiate. The importance of the phrase "as my will, so mote it be" stems from the benefits of mental fortitude, concentration, and determination. When a trained and accomplished person brings self-discipline and strong will to a ritual or magickal intent, then "as my will, so mote it be" generates a powerful force that seals the intent.

There are a variety of mundane methods that can help a person develop self-discipline. These include such things as yoga, martial arts, dietary regiment, and a routine of physical exercise. Once discipline is achieved, then the personal will of the individual can be further strengthened through a practice of visualization and meditation. One effective exercise involves creating mental images in the mind. For example, you can think of an airplane whose shape and size you are familiar with. Once you have it in your mind, begin to look at the details of your image. In what direction is the nose of the plane facing? What color is it? How big is it? Look further into its design and note the contours and curves. Can you see the texture of the materials of the plane? Performing this exercise with a variety of envisioned objects will help develop your ability to visualize thought-forms, which are essential for creating astral images that can manifest in the material dimension.

The use of drugs and alcohol is very controversial. There is little doubt that, in ancient times, alkaloid plants were used by our ancestors with ergot mold to induce trance and altered states of consciousness. In modern Witchcraft, we still find the presence of ritual wine, which was used as an intoxicant in the ancient Mystery Cult of Dionysos. Ritual cakes once contained intoxicating herbal ingredients designed to alter and enhance the mental faculties of the coven members. This may have induced trance states for astral projection, which allowed the coven to experience "Otherworld" journeys and astral sabbats. If you so choose to incorporate herbal intoxicants, build a relationship with the spirit of the plant itself. The spirit may help you on your journeys to the Otherworld. As with all things in modern Witchcraft, the individual must decide what is personally appropriate and what is not.

Personal power to draw and raise energy is an integral part of magickal and ritual training. It is attained through several traditional methods, including celebrating the eight sabbats and the Full Moon rituals. Such participation aligns individuals to lunar and earthly currents, which create an energy charge within the aura. The flow of these energies becomes concentrated within a ritual circle, surrounding coven members in a pool of forces swirling in a ritual circle on occasions such as an equinox or solstice. Through these practices, the coven can raise energy for a cone of power (see Glossary). By attracting and directing power with the wand or athame, the initiate becomes proficient at working with energy fields to accomplish a variety of magickal and ritual goals.

Learning the various correspondences employed in magick is important to the ritual and magickal art. The knowledge of various herbs, enchantments, charms, and spells helps fine tune the Witch's ability to direct energy. A working knowledge of how a ritual functions helps the Witch focus and draw upon the momentum of past concepts. Like anything in life, practice is required to become skillful. You can only be as skilled in the arts as the time and energy you invest in your training.

Psychic development is a very useful tool for the initiate and helps discern things of a non-physical nature. This is important because, when a person practices magick and ritual, their will eventually encounters non-physical entities. The psychic senses help perceive the presence and actions of various spirits and Elemental creatures. Breathing camphor fumes and drinking rosemary tea (with temperance) when the Moon is full will aid in the development of psychic abilities. Dream control is another method that can train the psychic mind. This involves developing the ability to become conscious in the dream state and then to knowingly control and direct the dream as desired.

Astral projection and "rising upon the planes" are aspects of Witchcraft designed to allow the Witch to access non-physical realms and states of consciousness. In the ancient Mystery sects, it was used to negate the fear of death by proving to the initiate that they still exist outside of the flesh. The projection of the astral body is something that everyone does while they sleep. It is the dream body that we see in dreams, and its senses allow us to see and feel while in the dream state. This stage of training aims to project the mind into the astral body, allowing you to operate in a conscious manner while exploring astral dimensions. In this way, you can operate in a conscious manner while exploring astral dimensions. See suggested reading list for a personal study.

The use of sex magick in many traditions of Witchcraft is perhaps an even more controversial subject than the use of drugs and alcohol. Sexuality and sensuality were once part of traditional Pagan rites intended to ensure a bountiful harvest or a successful hunt. To that end, various levels were incorporated as a means of raising energy. In this way, sexual energy served as the battery that empowered the old rites. It typically followed erotic dancing and provocative chants. In modern Witchcraft, many practitioners employ symbolic acts with ritual tools to mimic sexual union. This typically involves the wand (or athame) and chalice. Thus, it is common in Witches' circles to insert the wand or blade into the chalice, replacing what was once a rite of sexual union. Though these acts are symbolic, they do not have less power than physical sexuality. It is everyone's responsibility to communicate expectations surrounding divine sexuality, gender polarities, and consent; maintain proper boundaries; and uphold those agreements in any contemporary Craft practice.

With the Eightfold Path, you have a guideline for fields of study and practice that can lead you to a mastery of the arts. A personal study of each path will provide the tools to obtain deeper levels of magickal and ritual knowledge. Through this, you will possess the keys of a very old and time-proven tradition.

Preserving Tradition

However you decide to structure your tradition, it is important to factor in things already preserved in traditional systems. To that end, it is important to know and understand what value such things possess. Once you know this, you can better understand why they are included. However, in the end, only you can decide what will and will not comprise your tradition.

The value of a cohesive tradition is that it preserves what is connective, functional, and transformative. It teaches time-proven methods that allow an individual to access spiritual energy for personal growth. Its structure provides measured levels of training that weave connections together in the necessary order to lead to the fullness of comprehension. By contrast, eclectic systems shift according to self-directed modes and have no lasting fibers or threads that maintain connective patterns.

If you want to create an eclectic tradition, I recommend you create lasting fibers and threads to anchor your system to a sound foundation. Once the foundation is in place, you can build what you like with little concern for instability. I liken this to saying that you must build a house in accord with proven methods of sound construction, but no one can tell you how to live your life inside the house. Likewise, how you decorate your home and what you do with the interior is entirely up to you.

A sound tradition contains an established theology, practical understanding of magick, a view of the other dimensions, and the knowledge of practical and functional ritual. It connects its members with the Momentum of the Past and links them to the vital memory-chain of its predecessors. This chain is the core concept upon which religion, ritual, and magick are founded.

An effective tradition teaches the differences between religion and spirituality. Religion is the system, mechanism, structure, and process. For example, establishing a shrine, setting an altar, making offers, and reciting prayers are all religious actions. By contrast, spirituality is the personal connection to divinity; it is the reason why we do religious things. Examples of spirituality include feeling the presence of deity, experiencing inner connections, and interfacing with the divine through song, chant, and prayer.

We find the core memory-chains in Witchcraft as a Mystery Tradition and the principles that are foundational and vital to the initiate's ways. A Mystery Tradition is a means of preserving key and connective elements, leading to functional levels of enlightenment. Enlightenment leads to far vision, leading to a glimpse of the world as it is rather than as we imagined it.

The Mystery Tradition

Each Mystery Tradition is built around its own inner view of the cosmos, which is the microcosm reflecting the higher in the lower. This microcosm contains the connections to higher levels of understanding, and one can include greater evolved beings in this definition. Each Mystery Tradition creates its own symbols, fashioned from streams of consciousness that communicate between dimensions.

In Witchcraft as a Mystery Tradition, the myths and legends (along with the hierarchy of deities and spirits) form the setting to make memory-chain accessible. To accomplish this within your own tradition, be clear about the roles and relationships with your deities, spirits, and Elementals. This is one reason why it is risky to blend deities from different cultures. Such pairings may not connect to pre-established memory-chains and possibly short-circuit.

Once you have your deities, Guardians, Elements, and other spirits matched and cohesive, you will need to establish symbols. Your symbols will be important forms of communication. They maintain the Mysteries within a tradition, and no system can sustain itself without them. For example, the pentagram symbolizes the harmony of the four creative Elements of Earth, Air, Fire, and Water.

The symbol tells a story in which the fifth Element of Spirit brings the Elements out of chaos and into balance. On the pentagram, Spirit is assigned to the upper point of the star. Each Element is assigned a point of its own. The entire star is enclosed within a circle, which represents the ritual and magickal circle of the Craft. The ritual circle is both a container and a barrier that collects and condenses power. The circle, having gates at each of the four quarters, symbolizes access to the outer planes from the inner. Put this all together and the pentagram makes a proclamation to all who behold it (on this plane and the next). It says that the Four Elements of Creation are at your command, and that you possess their cumulative power. It also proclaims that you are under its protection, shielded by energy, and can open the portal to other dimensions. To spirits, this is not a symbol but a reality of the concept in action (just like a cocked gun is not symbolic but a reality requiring response). They both command attention and state their purpose and power immediately. All traditional symbols of Witchcraft tell their stories and communicate their messages. Their stories are old and come from memory-chains formed by streams of consciousness. See Chapter Eight, "The Book of Shadows," for more information and sample symbols.

The need for a Mystery Tradition is rooted in the highest plane or dimension. Here exists what we cannot imagine about divinity and creation. This is sometimes called the Ultimate Plane, which is greater than we imagine at our present mental and spiritual evolution. Within this dimension, the "Perfect Ideal" exists in its purity without diminished expression or emanation. The Perfect Ideal is the Divine Blueprint for Creation in the hands of the Creator (see Glossary for more information).

The dimensions that exist within the Universe are active emanations, a communication of what is the Divine, creation, and the divine plan itself. The material dimension has the lowest vibration. The vibration is so low that energy becomes tangible as a "material" form. In the Material Realm, the perception of the Perfect Ideal is distorted due to dense conditions of the material world. It is like looking at a painting through a frosted glass door. Our discernment is distorted by our view.

Occultists of the past created techniques to raise their consciousness into higher planes, where they encountered beings from those planes. Some beings aided humankind to climb to a better viewpoint. Those humans able to rise through the dimensions became the great spiritual masters. Sometimes, this required leaving the physical body behind. In some occult societies, the pathway of ascension to higher planes is called the Ladder of Light (see Glossary).

For simplicity, the Ladder is depicted with seven rungs, each symbolizing one of the seven planes of existence. These planes are titled: Ultimate, Divine, Spiritual, Mental, Astral, Elemental, and Physical. Each rung on the Ladder of Light is a memory-chain association that brings the traveler from the lowest to the highest levels of perception. Access to and preservation of the Ladder of Light is essential to the Mystery Tradition.

Because the Ladder of Light is a construction of consciousness, it is vital that the mental and spiritual connections remain intact and integral. Any break or distortion can undo centuries of construction. This is why initiates of Mystery Traditions are strongly opposed to altering their teachings and practices. Abandoning the established connections can cause us to lose access to the Ladder of Light or dissolve one or more of its rungs that convey the Perfect Ideal. Restoring it can be quite a feat to undertake.

The Mystery Tradition and its memory-chain associations reside within the classic structure of ritual and theology. Under the category of ritual, we can include the following:

❖ **Ritual Altar:** The primary connection to the Perfect Ideal is through its manifestation in the sacred altar setup. The altar is like the keyboard on a computer, while the tools and paraphernalia are the keystrokes and command functions. Through the altar, we interface with the Divine Consciousness behind the ritual associations.

❖ **Elemental Forces:** The connection to the Divine Mind through its creative modes of expression. The Elemental Forces allow us to join in partnership with the divine formula of creation. In doing so, we re-unite our inner creative essence with its source. This temporary reunion places us in the stream of Divine Consciousness as it emanates from the Elemental Dimension.

❖ **Four Quarters:** The connection to the gateways of direction and communication. The quarters serve as portals that open to inner and outer levels of consciousness. These modes of consciousness touch upon spiritual dimensions, through which we can send and receive energy. These gateways are essential to the intent of ritual and magick as they convey the energy toward manifestation.

❖ **Guardians:** The connection to the ushering principles of higher consciousness, which grants access to the Ladder of Light. The Guardians serve as filters, directors, and safeguards that deal with energy. This includes energy sent outward from the circle and energy that streams towards the circle. These entities enforce the agreement of consciousness (see Glossary) to maintain the integrity and ethical foundation of the tradition and its members.

Under the category of Theology, we can include the following:

❖ **The Wheel of the Year:** The connection to the core cycle of divine expression of the waxing and waning forces within the material world. This is one of the Cycle of Return's key models, which is central to Witchcraft-based religions and practices.

The Wheel provides the internal and external modes of energy that are models for the soul to discern its own "seasons of the soul" during its material existence. This is accomplished through an unfolding vision of the Divine Consciousness in a wholeness of expression.

- ❖ **The Triformis Goddess:** The connection to the divine principles of life operating through youth, maturity, and old age. It is through the Triple Goddess that we find the inner reflection of our own cycles of evolution. These indicate our progress as souls and directionals that point to awaiting phases. The Triformis Goddess also connects us with the Three Great Realms: Overworld, Middleworld, and Underworld.

- ❖ **The Harvest Lord:** The connection to the divine principles of birth, life, death, and rebirth. This connection, like the Wheel of the Year, is related to the Triformis Goddess but is a more intimate cycle. Whereas the Wheel of the Year is the soul's journey through a higher cosmic pattern reflected within an earthly model, the Harvest Lord Cycle focuses on the Reincarnation Mysteries within the Wheel of Rebirth (see Glossary). By contrast, the Wheel of the Year unites the soul with Divine Consciousness as a whole, while the Harvest Lord Cycle directs the soul toward self-awareness as a part of the whole.

- ❖ **The Moon Goddess:** The connection to the divine expression of the feminine. This is the soul's awareness of the mystical nature. It is the memory of non-material existence and the longing of the soul to return home amidst the stars.

- ❖ **The Sun God:** The connection to the divine expression of the archetypal masculine. This is the soul's awareness of the Material Realm and its opportunities to teach and reveal how spiritual evolution is accomplished.

❖ **The Goddess and God Consort Pair:** The connection to the archetype of polarities within Divine Consciousness. This is the polarities of the divine feminine and masculine consciousness that provide a glimpse of the Divine Consciousness in its comprehensible expression. It is the soul's memory of wholeness before its isolation in a physical body assigned to a material dimension.

All the above (in both categories) are ritualized dramatizations and projections of the Mystery Tradition into various life-levels experienced in the material dimension.

By incorporating these elements into your tradition, you can create and sustain the necessary links to the Perfect Ideal. How you structure your tradition will not adversely affect these alignments if you incorporate them into a cohesive and practical system. The formula is most important.

The formula establishes a practical relationship between the initiate and the Divine Consciousness from which the memory-chain associations form the Ladder of Light. The function of the Mystery Tradition is to provide how the initiates can form reaction patterns, which result in spiritual development on the inner levels. The Mystery teachings and structure apply the effective stimulus to the required degree. This is measured out through the prescribed rituals and the cohesive formulation of the Mystery Tradition's theology. As noted earlier, this is one of the primary reasons why initiatory mystery traditions resist any changes to the established construction of its tradition.

Egregores

The concept of the *Egregore* (also known as a *Telesmic*) is important to the Mystery Tradition. An Egregore is a mental image, usually of a being, that is constructed on the Astral Plane. In the Mystery Tradition, it is created in such a way that draws archetypical energy. This allows the Divine Consciousness to pour into the Egregore, which then becomes sentient, like the concept of a soul dwelling in a physical body. While the soul may be living the life of John Smith this time around, it is not

John Smith nor is it *not* John Smith. It is, instead, a shared consciousness of two projections.

An Egregore is part human construction and part Divine Consciousness. From the perspective of the Mystery Traditions, the various gods are Egregore forms. The deities and entities associated with Witchcraft, from the perspective of the Mystery Tradition, are representations of consciousnesses not reachable by other means. By personifying them, humans can attain and access the levels of "actuality" instead of the envisioned or imagined. In other words, the initiate can make direct contact with the consciousness behind the projected image or pattern as it truly is on a higher dimension. Of course, the quality of such contact is in direct proportion to the spiritual evolution of the initiate.

One of the secrets of the Mystery teachings is that truth is found in falsities, or literally, "truth is found in the heart of a lie." To explain this, we need to look at old formulations. The structure of the ancient Mystery Traditions evolved through an effort to understand and map out the unknown. This involved the evolution of concepts related to forces, spirits, deities, and the unexplainable. When one model collapsed under new evidence or experience, it shifted to another and then to another until it maintained itself through the test of time. This is just like the methodology used in science.

In science, the scientist assumes their knowledge is true and accurate (although they may state that such and such is the "current belief"). Over the course of time, scientists have abandoned certain theories that proved untrue or not functional. The same thing is true of historians. These examples show that the methodology is accurate but not always the conclusions. We come close to the truth only when something is proven false. So, too, was the methodology of the ancients who founded the Mystery Tradition.

The initiate of the Mysteries understands that nothing is false or inaccurate unless a truth exists to render it so. Therefore, they know that the images and forms are not flawless. But the initiate also knows that they connect with what is empirical through the connection made to the consciousness that animates the form or image. Therefore, the initiate is not disturbed by thoughts of the existence or non-existence of the things of the Mystery Tradition. Instead, they rely upon the reality of the Divine Consciousness behind the forms and images, which connect the initiate with the actualities of the consciousness they represent.

Sacred Rites

Among the sacred rituals of the Craft, there are three most represented in literature. Two of them are lunar rites, including Drawing Down the Moon and the Rite of Cakes and Wine. In the Mystery Tradition, these rituals are deeper than what is commonly portrayed in most published books.

The third sacred ritual is known as the Great Rite. The Great Rite sometimes includes a sexual union, which is performed as part of the third degree initiation. In some cases, the Great Rite may be performed in conjunction with sex magick. The most common form of the Great Rite is reenacted symbolically with the wand (or athame) and chalice.

Let us now examine these rites as they appear in the Mystery Tradition.

The Rite of Cakes and Wine

This is part of the divine meal ritual, which takes place near the end of most rituals. It is intimately connected to the Harvest Lord and Earth Goddess Mysteries. The Rite of Cakes and Wine unite the inner divine spark of the ritualist with its source. This is accomplished using a ritual cake and a drink of wine, which are specially prepared for the rite.

The cake is usually made from grains, mostly barely, but wheat is often used instead. The grain is associated with myths of the Underworld and the Mysteries of the unknown. The mythos is established around the agricultural year, wherein the seed is planted in the darkness of the Earth and buried. There it remains, and from a mystical perspective, it receives the teachings of the Underworld. Afterwards, the seed breaks through to the light of the mortal world and imparts the teachings to the plant. New seeds arc produced and then harvested. The seeds are made into cakes, which contain the Inner Mysteries. They represent the body of the Slain Harvest Lord and, when eaten, they impart their secrets to the inner spirit of the person consuming the meal.

The wine is made from dark grapes growing in clusters that resemble the multi-breasted image of Diana of Ephesus. The grapes are associated with fertility and divine intoxication. The transformation of the grape into juice and the period of fermentation are associated with the menstrual cycle and the gestation period of pregnancy. In this regard, the wine symbolizes the magickal life blood of the

Goddess. When the mystical essence is consumed, it imparts the cyclical life essence and the properties of transformation to the person drinking the wine.

The Rite of Cakes and Wine is also known as the Divine Meal. Traditionally, this is presented to the initiate by the High Priestess and High Priest, who say:

"Through this cake and by this wine, may you come to know that which in you is of the eternal gods."

The initiate eats a portion of the cake and drinks a portion of the wine. Through this ritual act, the initiate unites with the Source of All Things on an inner and outer level. In this union, the divine spark (the indwelling soul of the initiate) joins in a moment of light with its creators.

Drawing Down the Moon

In modern Witchcraft, this ritual is designed to attract the consciousness of the Goddess into the mind, spirit, and body of a High Priestess or other person acting as the vessel during a Full Moon ritual. The older form of the rite involved drawing down the mystical force of the Moon's light to the Earth. This held a different significance, but ultimately connected with the same Divine Consciousness.

The most common purpose for this ritual is to receive an oracle. It is also used when serious problems arise, and the channeled consciousness of the Goddess is required. In either case, the vessel for the feminine Divine Consciousness needs to be experienced in receiving and handling this type of possession.

The basic technique involves attaining what occultists call the "nil state of consciousness." This involves emptying the mind so it becomes a still and quiet pool. Into this night-like darkness and quietness, the vessel visualizes an X and assumes the posture by raising and spreading their arms upwards and outwards. Their feet are also spread widely, which results in the body's formation of an X.

In the next step, the vessel visualizes the X again and mentally adds a V on top of it. This creates the ancient symbol of the chevron, which often appears in conjunction with symbolism and iconography in prehistoric art representing femininity. Once this symbol is fully visualized, the person slowly raises their chin upward, gently forcing

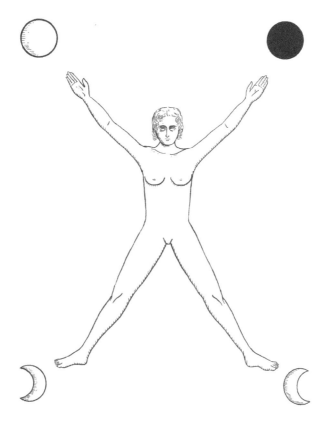

the head back. This signals that the vessel is ready for the High Priest or other practitioner, who kneel before them.

The High Priest or other practitioner raise the ritual wand and lightly presses the tip to the three sacred points on the body of the vessel. These points are the nipples and the groin, which collectively symbolize the nurturing and generative forces of the Goddess. It is from this power that all things issue forth and are sustained in the early portion of their manifestation. Therefore, it is through this principle that the Goddess possesses the vessel.

Once the purpose of the rite is completed, the vessel dissolves the connection. This is accomplished by the vessel, who once again takes up the X position and visualizes the Full Moon around their body. They then slowly lower their arms to their sides, visualizing the Moon waning. Finally, they draw their feet together as they complete the visualization of the Moon disappearing entirely. This places the vessel back in the inner darkness of the nil state of consciousness. All that is required at this stage is for the vessel to inhale and exhale deeply three times, open their eyes, and return fully conscious to the setting around them. A snack and drink should be given to the vessel at this time, as this helps them return to normalcy.

The coven scribe can keep record of such events, recording the date and what was conveyed by the Goddess through the vessel.

The Great Rite

A ritual where the participants invoke the nil consciousness, which is then temporarily filled with the downpouring of the divine feminine and masculine consciousness. This ritual is also known as the *Hieros Gamos* or Divine Marriage.

As noted earlier, the Great Rite is part of the traditional third degree initiation. In this context, the ritual weds the initiate with the divine polarity. In other words, a High Priest is "wedded" to the Goddess and a High Priestess is "wedded" to the God, though these binary dynamics are not necessary in contemporary practices. The wedding is, of course, metaphorical and denotes the level required to act as a representative of deity within a ritual setting. This is something a High Priestess and a High Priest may enact on occasion if all parties are willing and consenting to everything that the Great Rite entails.

The most common form of the Great Rite symbolically reenacts the union of divine polarities. This involves substituting the ritual chalice for the archetypal feminine polarity and the wand for the archetypal masculine polarity (some systems use the athame). The High Priestess raises the chalice, and the High Priest lowers the wand or athame into it.

Now that we have examined aspects that empower a tradition and provide spiritual and magickal growth, we can turn to a means of recording them for future use. In the next chapter, we will explore the Book of Shadows and look at various symbols used in the ritual and magickal art of Witchcraft.

The Book of
Shadows

The Book of Shadows is a classic component of traditional and mainstream Witchcraft. In some traditions, it is known as the "Black Book," which refers to folklore about signing your name in the devil's book, or a "personal grimoire." The earliest books were a record of rituals, beliefs, practices, and recipes. Sometime after the early 1980s, the Book of Shadows took on the form of a diary or personal journal. In many contemporary cases, this form now constitutes most Book of Shadows (particularly for solitary practitioners). For the purposes of this chapter, I will deal mainly with the traditional structure. I believe this will provide a good foundation for organizing your book. After looking this over, you can easily decide how traditional or informal you want your Book of Shadows to be.

Traditionally, the Book of Shadows was copied by new initiates. The book, while belonging to a High Priestess or High Priest, was available to coven members as part of their training. The High Priest or High Priestess would closely observe copying to guard against errors. Today, many of these books were not copied from a teacher's Book of Shadows but instead are self-creations (although they are often based upon published works).

In some oral traditions, the Book of Shadows originally did not possess any words because literacy was not widespread. It is said that the book contained instructional symbols and pictographs, which each student memorized. In this way, rituals and magickal technique were passed from teacher to student. The books were "read" and copied at night by candlelight or in front of the hearth. Shadows washed across the pages, and from this, the nickname "Book of Shadows" originated. (This is one of many tales regarding the origin of the name.)

The classic Book of Shadows begins with an opening page admonishing against any ill use of the book. If you wish to include this, then you can place words to this effect:

"This book is under the protection of the magick it weaves. Be forewarned that, if you should misuse it, all will turn back upon you thrice. In the name of the Goddess and God, so mote it be!"

For something with a gentle tone, you can use the following text:

"Harm ye none by the ways within,
not enemy nor closest kin.
The law is to live and let live,
you shall receive what you shall give."

For something more daunting, you may wish to use this text:

"Be it known unto all that this book is under the protection of the Old Ones who were from before time itself. If you misuse this book or steal this book, then shall all the arts you cherish turn against you. Then shall you be left to the mercy of the Dread Lords of the Outer Spaces."

Once you have written the text on the page, place the binding symbol (page 111, top) beneath the words in the center of the page.

Immediately following the opening page of text, draw the traditional pentagram seal (page 111, bottom) on its own page.

This seal bears the symbols of the following spirits from the top and moving clockwise: Abdia, Ballaton, Bellony, Halliy, and Halliza. In the center is the spirit Soluzen. These spirits have power and influence over the ritual and magickal arts and serve as protectors of the Book of Shadows.

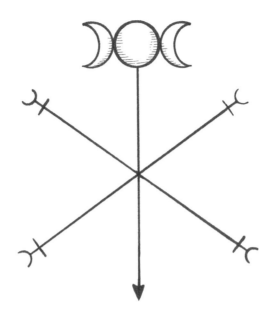

Once the symbols are drawn in your book, trace the pentagram with your athame. Begin by touching the top point of the star and tracing in a clockwise manner. End by touching the center. Each line of the pentagram corresponds with one of the verses. The final verse is recited when the athame is pressed to the center:

> *"Light and darkness bring the shadow's edge,*
> *oaths preserve the ancestral pledge.*
> *Whispers of Old Ones in the deep dark woods,*
> *voices known only to the wearers of hoods.*
> *Here are the secrets received in the night,*
> *kept now in this record of thrice sacred rite."*

Next, take your athame and trace the spirit symbols, speaking each name before you trace their corresponding symbol. Once all the names have been spoken, place the palms of both hands over the pentagram and say:

> *"Pen and ink to mark the rites,*
> *drawn from moonlight in the night.*
> *Guardian eyes that always look,*
> *protect all things within this book."*

You are now ready to write in your book your rituals and instructions for placing symbols, signs, and gestures of the Art.

The Book of Shadows in Order of Appearance

1. **The Tools of the Art:** In this section, place images and a list and description of the tools used in your tradition. Include any symbols or designs that are etched or painted on the tools. (These will also be included in another section of the book.) If there is any special lore associated with the tools, include this as well.

2. **Alphabet or Runic Script:** Books of Shadows in the mid-twentieth century contained a script known as Theban or the Witches' Alphabet. The inclusion of a mystical or secret alphabet is classic

within traditions that employ a grimoire. You may wish to use the Theban script or another system in your tradition.

3. **Ritual Signs and Gestures:** In this section, place drawings or photos of the ritual hand signs, body postures, or anything of this nature. These signs and gestures enhance communication and allow the mind to work on the mundane and mystical levels at the same time.

4. **Ritual Incense and Oils:** This section will include the types of oils and herbs used in your tradition. You may want to arrange them by magickal and ritual use and correspondences. This is also where oil and incense recipes live.

5. **How to Create Sacred Space:** In this section, place the preparation of a ritual setting, the method of casting a circle, and how the circle is dissolved after the rite is completed. Some traditions have different approaches to creating sacred space, such as "laying the compass" found in more recent traditions. You will find many references available online and in books related to "Traditional Witchcraft."

6. **Rites of Initiation:** This section will contain the rituals for dedication and the degree system used in your tradition. Also, include a reference list of supplies for each rite. This will save you time looking it up in another section. For an air of mystery, you may wish to add false instructions as a layer of secrecy. The correct rites may be passed down orally.

7. **Lunar Rites:** In this section, record lunar rituals for the Dark Moon, Waxing Moon, Full Moon, and Waning Moon. Also, record any special lore related to the Moon.

8. **Seasonal Rituals:** This section will contain all eight sabbat rituals and any other important celebrations specific to your tradition. Decide where in the Wheel of the Year you wish to begin the calendar and start with the ritual for that season. Keep the rituals in order of appearance, as this will make it easier to turn to the seasonal ritual you desire.

9. **Spells and Works of Magick:** In this section, record the spells and works of magick that have proven effective. You may wish to group them into categories for easy reference, such as love spells, prosperity sells, healing spells, spells of protection, curses, and so forth.

10. **Ritual and Magickal Correspondences:** This section will contain lists and charts of correspondences used in your rituals, spells, and works of magick. You may wish to group them into categories such as colors, stones, herbs, planets, animals, stars, chakras, and so on.

11. **Recipes:** Place in this section any recipes for cakes, cookies, drinks, and baked goods used for the celebrations in your tradition.

12. **Personal Journal:** This section can contain any personal information or reflections you want to record and pass on to others. This is your story and can be valuable to those who practice your tradition in the future.

The Traditional Tools

In Witchcraft, we commonly find the four traditional tools of Western occultism. These are the pentacle, wand, athame, and chalice. To enhance your Book of Shadows, you can add drawings or photos of the tools, accompanied by any symbols you wish to transcribe on them.

Symbols on the tools bring a special quality and provide an air of mystery or secrecy. Such things arouse an altered state of consciousness during ritual or magickal procedures. This is because symbols speak directly to both the subconscious and the conscious mind. In this regard, symbols are the language between the worlds.

The use of ritual tools, like those found in Witchcraft, is very ancient. One example appears in the Cult of Mithras. Here, we find the wand of command, the libation cup, a crescent-shaped knife, and a platter similar in function to a pentacle. Also included was the Sun sword, which, when added to the other tools, gives us a set allegedly like those of Gardnerian Wicca.

Another depiction of the four tools in an occult setting appears in the reconstructed card of the Magician from the fifteenth-century Italian tarot known as the Cary-Yale Visconti deck. The Magician stands before a table set with a pentacle, wand, chalice, and athame.

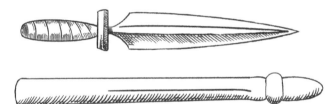

These elemental tools are available to the Magician for magick and ritual. Except for the chalice, these set of tools also appear together as ritual items in the Key of Solomon.

The four tools used in Witchcraft constitute a set of spiritual implements for religious and ritual purposes as well as mystical tools for magickal works. Some occultists assign certain virtues to them: the pentacle is the shield of valor, the wand is the lance of intuition, the athame is the sword of reason, and the chalice is the well of compassion. In such a view, the four tools are the weapons of the spiritual knight, which we noted in the Chapter Five, "Creating Rituals."

The following illustrations of the tools and their symbols can be used as a model for designing your own set.

- ❖ The Pentacle
- ❖ The Wand
- ❖ The Athame
- ❖ The Chalice

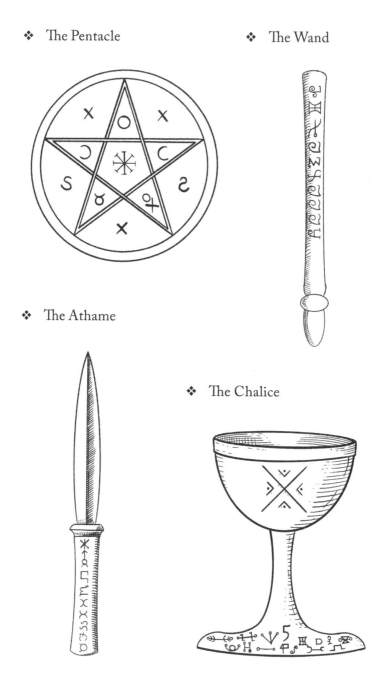

The Theban Script

Traditionally, many systems used an alphabet known as the Theban Script or "Witches' Alphabet." It was used to keep the Book of Shadows secret so prying eyes could not read the material. The use of secret alphabets was and is very common within secret societies.

The earliest known reference to the Theban alphabet appears in Cornelius Agrippa's sixteenth-century masterpiece, *Three Books of Occult Philosophy.* Agrippa is one of the greatest occult minds of his time. He lived in Italy from 1511–1518 and studied the writings of Marsilio Ficino and Giovanni Pico della Mirandola, who translated the great Hermetic texts of ancient Greece and Egypt.

According to occult tradition, the Theban alphabet originated in the ancient Greek city of Thebes, hence the name. Some people attribute its later popularity to the *Sworn Book of Honorius,* which is also known as "The Grimoire of Honorius."

A	B	C	D	E	F	G	H

I, J	K	L	M	N	O	P	Q

R	S	T	U, V, W	X	Y	Z

If suitable, you may wish to incorporate scripts or alphabets in accord with your tradition's cultural influences.

Ritual Signs and Gestures

It is more than likely that the earliest form of human communication, prior to words and sounds, was the use of hand gestures and body postures. In parts of North America, sign language was used between Native American tribes that spoke different languages, which shows a widespread knowledge of gestures as an independent form of communication. There can be no argument that sign language is vital for Deaf and non-verbal communities.

In occult tradition, the use of signs and gestures has a long history. They are designed to communicate in both realms during ritual and magickal work. In other words, such communication is directed towards the ritualists within the circle and the entities outside of the circle. If we think about the old saying "a picture is worth a thousand words," we can begin to understand the importance of signs and gestures. In this light, they can quickly convey entire concepts and communicate directions without uttering a single word. This helps maintain silence in a ritual setting, which enhances the air of mystery and sense of magick.

The following signs and gestures are the most common found in modern Witchcraft and come from a variety of occult sources.

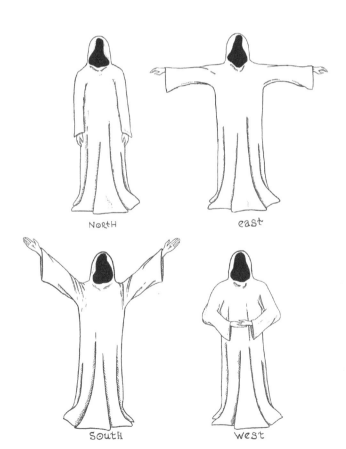

NORTH

east

SOUTH

west

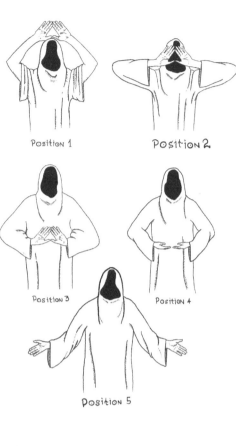

Position 1   Position 2

Position 3   Position 4

Position 5

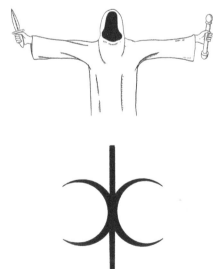

Symbols in Witchcraft

In Witchcraft, symbols can be used for a variety of purposes. They can be used as a script to define the use of a tool and mark it. They can also be used to denote a concept, convey a magickal principle, or simply indicate an association. The following symbols from the ancient grimoire *The Key of Solomon* are among the most common.

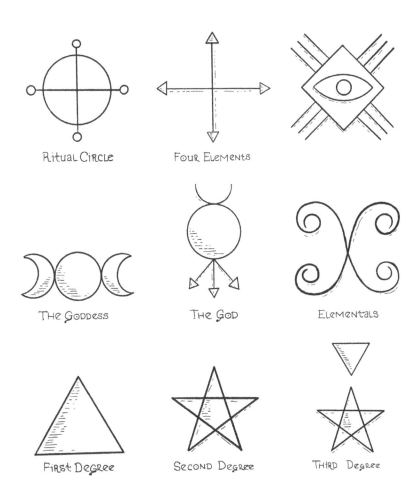

Ritual Circle   Four Elements

The Goddess   The God   Elementals

First Degree   Second Degree   Third Degree

XXX✕)OC✳S≤♃♀

Pentacle Symbols

Wand Symbols

athame Symbols

Chalice Symbols

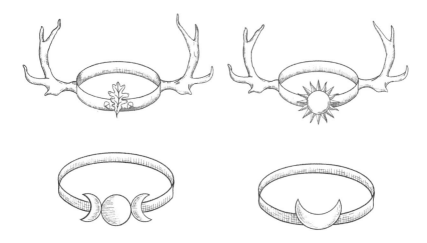

Ritual Altar and Circle Setup

As previously mentioned, the altar and ritual represent the mini universe of the ritualist. Both are constructed in accord with occult principles that reflect the Perfect Ideal from which creation of the Universe arose. The circle is set between the worlds, and the altar at its center fixes and holds it in place. The altar becomes the center of balance for the Four Elements that flank all four sides.

There are several different ways to set an altar. Your altar can be anything from a simple devotional place to a complex Ceremonial Magick altar. You may also want to research your tradition's own anthropological roots for inspiration. Deities and spirits may have their own preferences, and it is vital you include them. You will find it helpful to have at least some basics in place when it comes to most rituals. These include candles (to symbolize something and provide lighting), incense, four Elemental representations, a bowl of water and some salt, deity representations, and your ritual tools. On a mundane level, you will also want some matches on hand and something to snuff out the candles. A utility knife is also handy to have nearby.

In the Mystery Tradition, the altar is set with specific objects in a particular way. In essence, this puts into place the alignments that activate the vital states of consciousness. This makes the altar a type of battery that generates energy during the entire ritual.

Earlier in this chapter, we noted the black altar cloth, which symbolizes the darkness of procreation from which all things issue forth. This is included in the Mystery altar, which is also set with other symbolic objects. The illustration shows the basic setup, which can be embellished as needed in accord with the intent of the ritual or work of magick.

Note the presence of a candle in the center of the altar. Behind and off to each side are two other candles. Together, all three candles form a triangle, with the tip of the triangle closest to the front of the altar. This triangular configuration symbolizes the down-pouring of Divine Consciousness. The candle at this tip of the triangle is surrounded by four bowls, which are the Elemental representations.

The configuration of the Elemental bowls around the candle signifies the harmony of Earth, Air, Fire, and Water when brought into balance by the light of Spirit, which is the fifth Element. Here, you interface with the five streams of consciousness flowing from the Otherworld.

To the left of the Elemental bowls is salt water for purification of the ritual circle area. To the right of the Elemental bowls is a censer with smoking incense. The intent of the smoke is twofold: it serves as a medium in which non-material entities can reside in the Material Realm during the ritual, and it conveys the intent of the ritual as it rises and leaves the circle.

Returning for a moment to the triangle of candles, you will note that a skull figure is in the center. The skull symbolizes ancestral wisdom; it is what remains behind as generations disappear from the Material Realm. On top of the skull is a candle, which symbolizes the active connection to the Ancestral Group Mind when lighted.

Looking again at the illustration, you will notice a Goddess and God image next to the candles in the back of the altar. The Goddess image is set to the left and the God image is placed to the right. In Western occultism, theses placements represent the polarities of divinity in gender expression. The God polarity is active and electrical, while the Goddess polarity is receptive and magnetic. The directions of left and right are assigned the same traits.

At the center of the altar, the energy vortex appears and functions at its most intensity. Whatever is placed on the center of the altar becomes the point of alignment to the Elemental Realm. It also establishes a portal or gateway between the worlds and the inner planes. In the Mystery Tradition, Fire always occupies the center, as it did in the earliest of divine images, and in occult tradition, it establishes the presence of the fifth Element upon the altar.

Placing the ritual pentacle beneath the candle directly establishes an open connection between the material dimension and the non-material dimension. It mirrors "as above, so below." From this point, everything performed in the ritual (each vibration and emanation of energy) will be drawn to the center of the altar. From here, it will flow into the Elemental Portals. Once amplified by the Elements, the ritual intent will draw into the astral substance, where it will take on a representation. This is the principle of the thought-form described in Chapter Seven, "Initiation and Metaphysical Aspects of Witchcraft."

The symbolism incorporated into an altar setting is very important. In part, it will evoke and invoke certain alignments associated with the symbolism. Therefore, it is important to arrange the altar accordingly. The alignments you create will affect your ritual and your magick (for better or for worse).

The use of colors is vital to attract and direct mystical forces, and they serve as forms of communication in the same manner as any other symbolism. This is reflected in the black altar cloth, representing the darkness that existed before creation was generated through the Perfect Ideal. The center candle on the altar represents the Great Unmanifest at the center of nothingness. The two altar candles symbolize the Goddess and God, representing the first manifestations of definable consciousness that arise from the Source of All Things. The color of the Goddess candle is red, and the God candle is black. The meaning of these colors will become evident as we proceed.

A black candle is set on the head of the skull and is lighted for all rituals performed from the Autumn Equinox to the Vernal Equinox. A red candle is used from the Vernal Equinox to the Autumn Equinox. Black symbolizes the ancestral knowledge retained within the source, the Otherworld. Red symbolizes the ancestral knowledge that flows from the Otherworld to the world of mortals.

During the year, the skull's candle will match either the Goddess or God candle. Black represents the secret Shadow Realm, the deep dark forest, and the mystical journey that leads to the Otherworld. The God is the escort of the dead who aids in transition.

Red represents the lifeblood, the inner pulse that sustains and empowers. It runs through the Earth beneath the soil, for the Goddess is the Giver of Life. Red also symbolizes the place of life and renewal, which is reflected in the menstrual cycle. In the context of the skull figure, red symbolizes the ancient knowledge flowing into the world of the living from the source of its wellspring.

To better align with the ancestral memory, a small cauldron is placed in front of the skull. This represents the Moon Gate, which is the womb of the Goddess. Through the Goddess, all things are birthed from the Otherworld and return to her again. The cauldron leads to and from the ancestral knowledge. Because of this, it contains the magickal essence of transformation.

The remaining tools of the Craft are now placed on the altar with their corresponding quarter Element: the wand is set in the East portion of the altar, the athame occupies the South, and the chalice is set in the West. The pentacle has been previously set in the center beneath the candle. The altar itself is oriented to the East, meaning that the practitioner faces the East as they view it.

Now that we have looked at the basic layout for a Book of Shadows, we can consider compiling a list of correspondences. Let's turn to the next chapter and look at some foundational listings.

The Correspondences

No system or tradition is complete without ritual and magickal correspondences. The prepared correspondences make it easier to compile the necessary components to construct a ritual or spell. Whenever you need to design a ritual or spell, begin by including symbolic elements to empower and drive the ritual.

When creating your own spell or embellishing existing ones, it is important to consider any correspondences related to the work at hand. Go over the lists in this chapter and incorporate as much as possible. Consider the numerical value of the planet that rules over the spell's intent. For example, you might add seven roses to a spell for love, since seven is the number of the planet Venus, and roses are sacred to the goddess Venus.

Remember that colors, scents, and symbols are necessary to stimulate the senses of the spell-caster. This creates a vibration, which then causes a reaction within the subconscious mind and, in turn, within the etheric substance of the astral plane. As we know from the law of physics, every action causes a reaction. Likewise, it is too with the law of metaphysics.

Most rituals include a deity evocation, ritual tool, quarter direction, color, scent, symbolic totems, and a power object. These are basics to which you can add other enhancements. I encourage you to draw inspiration from your heritage or the cultures influencing your traditions. The following lists of correspondences can serve "as is" or as models to create what makes sense to your tradition.

Color Symbolism for Spellcasting

White: *Purification, protection*
Pink: *Love, friendship*
Yellow: *Drawing (pulling/compelling)*
Green: *Material success, abundance*
Red: *Passion, vigor, sexual energy*
Orange: *Concentration, psychic energy*
Purple: *Power over obstacles, magickal forces*
Brown: *Neutralizing*
Gold: *Drawing (when accompanied by other colors, all purpose)*
Blue: *Peace, spirituality, spiritual energy*
Dark Blue: *Depression*
Black: *Crossing, suppressing, ending*

Ritual Color Symbolism

White: *Purity, transmission*
Green: *Nature magick, love, receptive fertility*
Blue: *Peace, spiritual forces*
Red: *Life force, sexual energy, vitality, active fertility*
Brown: *Earth magick, neutralizing/grounding*
Yellow: *Mental energy*
Black: *Drawing, absorbing*

Elemental Correspondences

Earth
Tool: *Pentacle*
Direction: *North*
Elemental: *Gnomes*

Guardian: *Boreas*
Colors: *Yellow*
Associations: *Strength, fortitude*
Driving Force: *Power*
Polarity: *Receptive*

Air

Tool: *Wand or athame*
Direction: *East*
Elemental: *Slyphs*
Guardian: *Eurus*
Colors: *White, blue*
Associations: *Intellect, healing, liberation, inspiration*
Driving Force: *Persuasion*
Polarity: *Creative*

Fire

Tool: *Wand or athame*
Direction: *South*
Elemental: *Salamanders*
Guardian: *Notus*
Colors: *Red*
Associations: *Sexual energy, lifegiving, cleansing*
Driving Force: *Force*
Polarity: *Creative*

Water

Tool: *Chalice*
Direction: *West*
Elemental: *Undines*
Guardian: *Zephyrus*
Colors: *Green*
Associations: *Love, fertility, adaptability*
Driving Force: *Adaption*
Polarity: *Receptive*

Planetary Correspondences

Sun

Trees: *Laurel, birch, oak, ash, pine, walnut*
Stones: *Diamond, topaz, amber, carnelian, citrine, tiger's eye*
Herbs: *Peony, angelica, sunflower, saffron, cinnamon, laurel, wolfsbane*
Aromatics: *Cinnamon, laurel, olibanum*
Colors: *Gold, yellow*
Number: *Six*

Moon

Trees: *Willow, olive, palm, rowan*
Stones: *Moonstone, opal, crystal quartz, chalcedony, pearl, sapphire*
Herbs: *Selenotrope, hyssop, rosemary, watercress, moonflower, moonwort, garlic*
Aromatics: *Almond, jasmine, camphor, lotus*
Colors: *White*
Number: *Nine*

Mercury

Trees: *Hazel, myrtle*
Stones: *Chalcedony, citrine, agate, aventurine*
Herbs: *Fennel, mint, smallage, marjoram, parsley*
Aromatics: *Cinquefoil, fennel, aniseed*
Colors: *Violet*
Number: *Eight*

Venus

Trees: *Myrtle, ash, apple, alder, sycamore, elder*
Stones: *Emerald, green tourmaline, aquamarine, coral, jade, lapis, turquoise*
Herbs: *Lavender, vervain, valerian, coriander, laurel, lovage, foxglove*
Aromatics: *Myrtle, rose, ambergris*
Colors: *Green*
Number: *Seven*

Mars
> Trees: *Hickory, alder, holly, beech*
> Stones: *Bloodstone, ruby, jasper, garnet*
> Herbs: *Wolfsbane, hellebore, garlic, tobacco, capsicum*
> Aromatics: *Aloe, dragon's blood, tobacco*
> Colors: *Red*
> Number: *Five*

Jupiter
> Trees: *Pine, birch, mulberry, rowan*
> Stones: *Amethyst, chrysocolla, chrysoprase*
> Herbs: *Basil, mint, elecampane, henbane, betony, sage*
> Aromatics: *Nutmeg, juniper, basil*
> Colors: *Blue*
> Number: *Four*

Saturn
> Trees: *Elm, yew, alder, holly, beech*
> Stones: *Black onyx, jet, black jade, hematite*
> Herbs: *Dragon's wort, rue, cumin, hellebore, mandrake, aconite, hemlock*
> Aromatics: *Myrrh, poppy, asafetida*
> Colors: *Black*
> Number: *Three*

Numerological Correspondences

> **1:** *Primal, central, fortitude*
> **2:** *Polarity, balance, harmony*
> **3:** *Mystical, formational, uniting*
> **4:** *Ambition, innovative*
> **5:** *Action, friction, challenge*
> **6:** *Force, power, energy*
> **7:** *Completion, success*
> **8:** *Diversity, expansion, liberation*
> **9:** *Occult forces, veiled magick, the unrevealed*

Stone Correspondences

Amber: *Healing, luck, protection*
Agate: *Protection, healing, wealth*
Amethyst: *Dreaming, psychic natures, happiness*
Aventurine: *Money, luck, perception*
Bloodstone: *Healing, victory, courage, strength*
Carnelian: *Protection, vitality, health*
Chalcedony: *Peace, protection from nightmares*
Chrysoprase: *Happiness, success, friendship, luck*
Citrine: *Protection, psychic natures, dreaming*
Coral: *Protection, power, healing*
Crystal Quartz: *Protection, healing, psychic natures*
Diamond: *Loyalty, harmony, peace*
Emerald: *Love, money, mental powers*
Garnet: *Healing, strength, protection*
Hematite: *Grounding, divination*
Jade: *Healing, longevity, wisdom*
Jasper: *Protection, tenacity, protection*
Jet: *Protection, divination, shielding*
Lapis Lazuli: *Healing, love, protection*
Moonstone: *Divination, psychic natures, astral and dream control*
Onyx: *Protection, counter-magick, balancing sex drive*
Opal: *Astral projection, luck, power*
Pearl: *Love, wealth, good fortune*
Ruby: *Wealth, protection, power, vitality*
Sapphire: *Tranquility, defensive magick, health*
Tiger's Eye: *Money, protection, courage, energy*
Topaz: *Protection, healing, wealth, love*
Tourmaline: *Love, friendship, business, relationships*
Turquoise: *Protection, courage, money, friendship, love*

Tree Correspondences

Alder (*Alnus glutinasa*): *Oracular properties. In ancient lore, it is a guardian tree set at the gateway to the Otherworld.*

Apple (*Pyrus communis*): *Love and healing. It is also a Faery tree and, in ancient lore, a branch providing safe passage in and out of the Otherworld.*

Ash (*Fraxinus excelsior*): *Divinatory properties. It is also known as the "World Tree" and was a bridge between the Mortal Realm and the Otherworld in ancient lore.*

Beech (*Fagus sylvatica*): *Ancient knowledge and, in lore, favored by the Elven beings. The beech is also known as the "mother tree" and is associated with maternal mystique. The etymology of "beech" is traceable to the Anglo-Saxon word boc and the German word buch, which can be translated into the English word "book." In ancient times, thin slices of beech were used to make books.*

Birch (*Betula alba*): *Banishing evil spirits, purification, protection, and binding. In ancient lore, it is also associated with safe passage within the Otherworld.*

Elder (*Sambucus nigra*): *Faery doorways. In ancient lore, it granted the power of shapeshifting and possessed the power to transform.*

Elm (*Ulmus campestris*): *Gateways into the Otherworld. In ancient lore, it was associated with the Underworld as a type of bridge. The elm is considered especially sacred to the Elven beings, and some commentators claim that the name is an early form of the word "elf."*

Hawthorn (*Craetegus oxyacantha*): *Gateways as a guardian tree. Its blossoms herald the arrival of May and are associated with Faeries. In folk magick, the hawthorn is used to banish evil.*

Hazel (*Ilex aquifolium*): *Wisdom and occult knowledge. It is also a tree of general protection.*

Holly (*Corylus avellana*): *Regeneration in the presence of decline.*

Myrtle (*Myrtus communis*): *Love. In old folklore, it is sacred to Faery beings, who are said to live in myrtle trees.*

Oak (*Quercus robur*): *Oracular properties, protection. The oak symbolizes endurance and strength, and therefore holds the seasons of the year together.*

Pine (*Pinus sylvestris*): *Purification and cleansing.*
Rowan (*Sorbus aucuparia*): *Good fortune. In ancient lore, it was associated with life and death and was used in rites of passage to ensure renewal.*
Sycamore (*Acer pseudoplatanus*): *Nurturing and protection. Its seed pods were used in folk magick to ward off evil.*
Walnut (*Jugans nigra*): *Oracular properties. In ancient lore, Faery beings were said to be born in the walnut seed. In folk magick, the walnut bestows fertility to a couple that wants children.*
Willow (*Salix alba*): *Initiation and purification. In ancient lore, it was a gateway into the Underworld.*
Yew (*Taxus baccata*): *Death, rebirth, and transformation.*

Crafting the Patterns

Throughout the course of this book, we have demonstrated formulas and patterns that comprise modern Western Witchcraft. By now, you should have a working knowledge of these elements and the mechanisms through which they operate. In essence, you have been presented with the inner workings and the essential core of Witchcraft ritual. This will allow you to join the various aspects of Witchcraft ritual, religion, and philosophy into a complete and cohesive system of your own making.

To aid you in creating your own system of Witchcraft, let's look at the process of assembling the various aspects and elements. The first step is to think about your perception of the Divine. It is here that you will create your images of the Divine Source, which should reflect the archetypal feminine and masculine polarities. If you want to align your system with a specific culture, research the deity structure already in place. Focus on myths and legends to get a feel for how the ancient people viewed the role of the gods and goddesses. Look also for the lunar, solar, and stellar connections associated with a goddess or god figure. This will help you align the archetypal masculine and feminine connections. In your system, will the Moon be feminine and the Sun be masculine? For further information regarding deity concepts, review Chapters One ("The Enchanted Worldview") through Four ("Weaving the Wheel of the Year").

Once your deity structure is in place, outline the various worlds over which the deities exert influence. The most common will be a Heaven world where the deities dwell, and an Underworld or Otherworld in which the dead abide. Also, consider including a mystical realm with mythological beings, reincarnation, and magick. To complete this phase, think about adding the traditional doorways, including sacred wells, lakes, tree hollows, or mounds. For assistance in compiling this stage, review Chapters One ("The Enchanted Worldview"), Five ("Creating Rituals"), and Eight ("The Book of Shadows").

The next step is to establish connections to the mortal world, which will involve your deity structure and your understanding of other dimensions. It is here you will decide how the deities are involved and interact with the Earth. This phase also requires a view of how the other realms are connected. In other words, how do souls arrive in the material world, where do they go following the body's death, and how do they enter a non-material realm? This is where the importance of linking the Otherworld or Underworld comes into play. Review Chapters One ("The Enchanted Worldview") and Five ("Creating Rituals") for further information.

In Witchcraft, the role of Nature is vital, and in this regard, the eight seasonal sabbat festivals need to be set in place. Ideally, this structure will include the mythos of the Goddess and God, depicting their relationship throughout the year. This relationship expresses the aspects of each season that are experienced in life. Birth, life, death, and renewal are at the core of this mythos. When constructing your seasonal tale, select a starting point for the season of the year, which, in turn, will begin the story of the Goddess and God in your system. You will find foundational material in Chapters Three ("Finding Your Pantheon"), Four ("Weaving the Wheel of the Year"), and Six ("Ritual Patterns").

Another aspect centers on your view of spirits and guardian beings. Among the most common are the four Elemental Beings of Earth, Air, Fire, and Water. The Watchers are also important. They are typically associated with the directional quarters of the circle, but in some systems, they are also connected to the Elemental Forces. Therefore, you will want to consider the assignment of each Guardian and their associations. Review Chapters One ("The Enchanted Worldview"), Two ("Building Your Own Tradition"), Five ("Creating Rituals"), and Six ("Ritual Patterns") for further information.

Cosmology

You will find it very useful to establish a sound overview of your tradition's cosmology. The structure presented in this chapter is helpful, but you should also think of how this relates to your rituals. In this regard, I include religious, ceremonial, and magickal rites. This is the inner mechanism of your tradition, and everything will balance with and pivot upon whatever you establish.

All the tales, myths, and legends are part of our ancestors' cosmology. They reveal to us the perceptions, dreams, visions, and concepts once held by the ancients. Their cosmological views can provide a sound foundation to establish your tradition. Let's consider some of the fundamental rudiments.

Our ancestors no doubt looked upon the powerful force of Nature as the actions of supernatural beings. This seems evident in the assignment of gods and goddesses to thunder, volcanoes, earthquakes, and various types of storms. The fact that no one physically saw these gods and goddesses operate such forces points to the belief in a secret, hidden, or invisible realm. This later formed the foundation of mystical realms in myth and legend.

The light of the Sun, Moon, and stars must also have evoked a sense of mystery within our ancestors. One light produced heat and another did not. Instead, it changed its shape each month. The tiny stars were points of light scattered across the night sky. They did not produce heat nor change shape. On occasion, they appeared to fall from the sky. This placed the Sun, Moon, and stars in the realm between the world of humankind and the invisible realm of the gods. They were part of our world, yet not of our world.

Attempts were made to draw upon the forces of the Sun, Moon, and stars. From such attempts arose a tradition of mystical correspondences that reflect the powers ascribed to the celestial lights. Rituals were created to communicate with these astral bodies (or, more importantly, with whatever controlled them). One example is the etching of a large circle in the ground, which served as a ritual setting. The circle on the ground mimicked the circle in the sky (in this case, the Moon). To stand within the circle was to enter directly into the mystical realm above.

The Sun and Moon appeared to rise from below the Earth and later return beneath it, giving rise to the idea of a realm below. The idea that the Sun and Moon vanished into the Underworld only to return contributed to the concept of reincarnation. The entrance to the Underworld included the ocean, caves, wells, and lakes. A hidden world suggested inhabitants, which played a role in the concept of Faeries and other beings.

Communication with beings of the other worlds was intended to obtain favor and protection. This formed the basis of correspondences used in offerings, symbolism, evocations, and rituals. In effect, ritual is a means of communication with non-material realms and beings. The beings known as the Watchers are a good example.

When creating your view of the cosmos, think in terms of how you envision the role of other worlds. Try to see the world around you as your ancestors did. In other words, seek to invoke a primal consciousness demystified by scientific understandings. What and where are the connections between you and the worlds of existence? How will you connect and communicate with these realms and the beings within them? What do you want to attract and obtain? The answers will help you create something that keeps with the Momentum of the Past. They will also manifest what is most unique within you.

Ritual Structure

Most rites involved in Witchcraft connect with Nature or celestial bodies. The former includes the eight sabbats, and the latter involves the Sun and Moon. As the basis of ritual design timing, you will want to look at various correspondences that pertain to Nature and celestial elements. For the sabbats, sort them into the waxing and waning halves of the year.

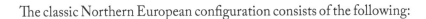

The classic Northern European configuration consists of the following:

❖ **Waxing:** Winter Solstice, Imbolc, Vernal Equinox, and Beltane
❖ **Waning:** Summer Solstice, Lughnasadh, Autumn Equinox, and Samhain

The classic Southern European configuration consists of the following:

❖ **Waxing:** Vernal Equinox, Beltane, Summer Solstice, and Lughnasadh
❖ **Waning:** Autumn Equinox, Samhain, Yule, and Imbolc

Remember that the waxing and waning periods pivot on the Winter and Summer Solstices in most Celtic systems, meaning that they begin or end on the solstice day. This is symbolized by the Oak King and Holly King, who battle for reign over the year. As noted in previous chapters, the Oak King represents the waxing forces of Nature, and the Holly King symbolizes the waning forces. In Southern European traditions, the waxing and waning periods of the year are marked by the equinoxes. The waxing period begins with the Vernal Equinox, symbolized by the stag figure. The waning period starts with the Autumn Equinox, represented by the wolf figure. Once you decide upon the waxing and waning configuration in your system, you can design the seasonal decoration theme for your Wheel of the Year rites.

The next phase of ritual design is deciding how to orient the sacred four directions and their Elemental natures. Here, you may consider the area in which you live. You will want to consider moisture, heat, landscape, and the prevailing winds. From this, you can make an association with Earth, Air, Fire, and Water as it presents itself in your region. Naturally, the directions of North, East, South, and West are not going to change with respect to region, but the Elemental assignment to a direction can be changed accordingly. Finally, decide where Earth, Air, Fire, and Water fit best with the four directions around you. You can, if you wish, choose to go with the classic occult assignments:

❖ **North:** Earth
❖ **East:** Air
❖ **South:** Fire
❖ **West:** Water

Once the four directions are in place within your system, you can focus on the correspondences relating to other realms of existence. For example, you may wish to assign the Realm of Death and the Departed to the Western quarter (where the Sun and the Moon return to the Underworld). You may connect the Eastern quarter with the evocation or invocation of Divinity (where the Sun and Moon rise). Heavenly worlds can be assigned above with the Celestial Realm, and hidden realms (such as the Faery Realm) can be aligned below. Much of this will depend upon your cosmology. Ultimately, it would be best to achieve continuity so there is no conflict between your correspondences and assignments. Look over everything and make sure it matches and works well together.

Parting Words

If you continue creating your own tradition, I hope this book has made the task more manageable. There is one thought I want to leave with you. You have the ancestral knowledge and wisdom of those who came before. This was passed to you just as the physical traits you possess are part of your ancestral heritage. Bound within the energy that maintains your DNA is the living essence of your ancestral consciousness. This calls to you and evokes your feelings about nationality and place of origin. This is what stirs within you when you visit your ancestral homeland. If you sincerely seek inner guidance while working to create your tradition, the essence of your system will be part of the past and the present, providing sound roots for future growth and survival.

In addition to your link to ancestral consciousness, you also possess the inner spark of the soul, which was generated from the Creators of the Universe. Your soul carries the memory of past lives and can possess strong ties to former lands, places, and people. In one form or another, you have existed since the beginning of time, even if only as part of something greater than yourself. There is much you already know, and it resides deep within you. I call this place the "Inner Cauldron."

In ancient myth and legend, we find talks of seeking the lost or hidden cauldron. It contains a mystical brew that bestows enlightenment. Even a tiny drop of this brew makes one wise beyond belief. The journey to find and retrieve the cauldron always takes the seeker to the Underworld or to a dark, secret dungeon. This is a metaphor for a personal journey deep within oneself. Here, one finds that which was lost or hidden. The mystical brew flavors the DNA spiral, which is a symbol of inward and outward movement. Here resides all that was ever known.

In some occult circles, it is believed that we do not ever create anything new; instead, we apply what we already know in various ways that appear new. In this light, the rituals, beliefs, and practices of Witchcraft are ancient memories that we express in contemporary ways. If so, this is a very comforting and reassuring thought as you craft your tradition. So, what's in your cauldron? Please share it with others through your creation.

APPENDIX I

Classic Witchcraft Myths

When Gardner's public works about Wiccan Witchcraft surfaced, this specific tradition of the Craft did not appear to have a creation myth. Several popular texts such as *The Charge of the Goddess* and *The Descent of the Goddess* were copied by many traditions. Although many other myths have appeared in writings, the adoption of a popular creation myth never transpired.

The closet we can come to a published creation myth that is not modern appears in Charles Leland's *Aradia, or the Gospel of the Witches*. In addition to this myth, I include three key texts that complete the mythos. You can use them as templates or examples when considering what mythos you desire for your tradition.

Before we begin with Leland's myth, I should point out that the name "Lucifer" appears in the text, and we should recall that Lucifer was a Roman god who was the herald of the Sun. He was identified with the planet Venus in its rising. The King James Bible names the Christian devil "Lucifer" based upon a misunderstanding (and therefore a mistranslation) of the Hebrew name *Hillel Ben Shakhar* in the book of Isaiah 14:12–17, which means "son of the morning star" and refers to the Babylonian king. The Latin translation of the Hebrew turned *Hillel Ben Shakhar* into *lux ferre,* which means "light-bearer." Another Latin rendering is *lucis fer,* which means "to carry light." St. Jerome used this translation to link the Roman god Lucifer to the villain in Isaiah.

How Diana Made the Stars and the Rain

"Diana was the first created before all creation; in her were all things; out of herself, the first darkness, she divided herself; into darkness and light she was divided. Lucifer, her brother and son, herself and her other half, was the light.

And when Diana saw that the light was so beautiful, the light which was her other half, her brother Lucifer, she yearned for it with exceeding great desire. Wishing to receive the light again into her darkness, to swallow it up in rapture, in delight, she trembled with desire. This desire was the Dawn.

But Lucifer, the light, fled from her, and would not yield to her wishes; he was the light which flies into the most distant parts of heaven, the mouse which flies before the cat.

Then Diana went to the fathers of the Beginning, to the mothers, the spirits who were before the first spirit, and lamented unto them that she could not prevail with Lucifer. And they praised her for her courage, they and told her that to rise she must fall; to become the chief of goddesses she must become a mortal.

And in the ages, in the course of time, when the world was made, Diana went on earth, as did Lucifer, who had fallen, and Diana taught magick and sorcery, whence came Witches and Faeries and goblins—all that is like man, yet not mortal.

And it came thus that Diana took the form of a cat. Her brother had a cat whom he loved beyond all creatures, and it slept every night on his bed, a cat beautiful beyond all other creatures, a Faerie: he did not know it.

Diana prevailed with the cat to change forms with her, so she lay with her brother, and in the darkness assumed her own form, and so by Lucifer became the mother of Aradia. But when in the morning he found that he lay by his sister, and that light had been conquered by darkness, Lucifer was extremely angry; but Diana sang to him a spell, a song of power, and he was silent, the song of the night which soothes to sleep; he could say nothing. So Diana with her wiles of Witchcraft so charmed him that he yielded to her love. This was the first fascination, she hummed the song, it was as the buzzing of bees (or a top spinning round), a spinning-wheel spinning life. She spun the lives of all men; all things were spun from the wheel of Diana. Lucifer turned the wheel.

Diana was not known to the Witches and spirits, the Faeries and elves who dwell in desert place, the goblins, as their mother; she hid herself in humility and was a mortal, but by her will she rose again above all. She had such passion for Witchcraft, and became so powerful therein, that her greatness could not be hidden.

And thus it came to pass one night, at the meeting of all the sorceresses and Faeries, she declared that she would darken the heavens and turn all the stars into mice.

All those who were present said—

'If thou canst do such a strange thing, having risen to such power, thou shalt be our queen.'

Diana went into the street; she took the bladder of an ox and a piece of Witch-money, which has an edge like a knife—with such money Witches cut the earth from men's foot-tracks—and she cut the earth, and with it and many mice she filled the bladder, and blew into the bladder till it burst.

And there came a great marvel, for the earth which was in the bladder became the round heaven above, and for three days there was a great rain; the mice became stars or rain. And having made the heaven and the stars and the rain, Diana became Queen of the Witches; she was the cat who ruled the star-mice, the heaven and the rain."[1]

The Myth of the Descent of the Goddess

"Our Lady and Goddess would solve all mysteries, even the Mystery of Death. And so, she journeyed to the Underworld in her boat upon the sacred River of Descent. Then, it came to pass that she entered before the first of the seven gates to the Underworld. And the Guardian challenged her, demanding one of her garments for passage, for nothing may be received except that something be given in return. And at each of the gates, the Goddess was required to pay the price of passage, for the Guardian spoke to her: 'Strip off your garments, and set aside your jewels, for nothing may you bring with you into this our realm.'

---

[1] Leland, Charles G. *Aradia, or Gospel of the Witches.* 1899.

So, the Goddess surrendered her jewels and her clothing to the Guardian and was bound as all living must be who seek to enter the Realm of Death and the Mighty Ones. At the first gate, she gave over her scepter; at the second, her crown; at the third, her necklace; at the fourth, her ring; at the fifth, her girdle; at the sixth, her sandals; and at the seventh, her gown. The Goddess stood naked and was presented before the Lord of Shadows, and such was her beauty that he himself knelt as she entered. He laid his crown and his sword at her feet, saying: 'Blessed are your feet which have brought you down this path.' Then he arose and said to the Goddess: 'Stay with me, I pray, and receive my touch upon your heart.'

And the Goddess replied to the Lord: 'But I love you not, for why do you cause all the things that I love and take delight in to fade and die?'

'My Lady,' replied the Lord, 'it is age and fate against which you speak. I am helpless, for age causes all things to whither, but when men die at the end of their time, I give them rest, peace, and strength. For a time, they dwell with the Moon and the spirits of the Moon; then may they return to the realm of the living. But you are so lovely, and I ask you to return not, but abide with me here.'

But she answered, 'No, for I do not love you.' Then the Lord said, 'If you refuse to embrace me, then you must kneel to death's scourge.' The Goddess answered him: 'If it is to be, then it is fate, and better so!' So, she knelt in submission before the hand of Death, and he scourged her with so tender a hand that she cried out, 'I know your pain and the pain of love!'

The Lord raised her to her feet and said, 'Blessed are you, my Queen and my Lady.' Then he gave to her the five kisses of initiation, saying: 'Only thus may you attain to knowledge and to joy.'

And he taught her all of his mysteries, and he gave her the necklace, which is the circle of rebirth. And she taught him her mysteries of the sacred cup, which is the cauldron of rebirth. They loved and joined in union with each other, and for a time, the Goddess dwelled in the realm of the Lord of Shadows.

For there are three mysteries in the life of humanity: Birth, Life, and Death (and love controls them all). To fulfill love, you must return again at the same time and place as those who loved before. And you must meet, recognize, remember, and love them anew. But to be reborn, you must die and be made ready for a new body. And to die, you must be born, but without love, you may not be born among your own.

But our Goddess is inclined to favor love and joy and happiness. She guards and cherishes her Hidden Children in this life and the next. In death, she reveals the way to her communion, and in life, she teaches them the magick of the Mystery of the Circle (which is set between the worlds of humans and of the gods)."²

The Legend of the Ascent of the Goddess

"Now the time came in the Hidden Realm of Shadows that [the Goddess] would bear the Child of [the Lord of Shadows]. And the Lords of the Four Corners came and beheld the newborn god. Then they spoke to [the Goddess] of the misery of the people who lived upon the World, and how they suffered in cold and in darkness. So [she] bid the Lords to carry Her son to the world, and so the people rejoiced for the Sun God had returned.

And it came to pass that [the Goddess] longed for the Light of the World, and for Her many children. So She journeyed to the World and was welcomed in great celebration.

Then [the Goddess] saw the splendor of the new god as He crossed the heavens, and she desired Him. But each night He returned to the Hidden Realm and could not see the beauty of the goddess in the night sky.

So one morning the goddess arose as the god came up from the Hidden Realm, and She bathed nude in the sacred lake [between the worlds]. Then the Lords of the Four Corners appeared to [the Sun God] and said: 'Behold the sweet beauty of the Goddess of the Earth.' And He looked upon Her and was struck with Her beauty so that He descended upon the earth in the form of a great stag.

'I have come to play beside your bath,' He said, but [the Goddess] gazed upon the stag and said: 'You are not a stag, but a god!' Then He answered: 'I am [Cern], God of the Forest. Yet as I stand upon the world I touch also the sky and I am Lupercus the sun, who banishes the Wolf Night. But beyond all of this I am [Tagni], the first born of all the Gods!'

[The Goddess] smiled and stepped forth from the water in all Her beauty. 'I am Fana, goddess of the forest, yet even as I stand before you

---

² Derived and revised from work by Doreen Valiente, based on Leland's *Aradia, or The Gospel of the Witches.*

I am [Diana], goddess of the moon. But beyond all this I am [Uni], first born of all Goddesses!'

And [Tagni] took Her by the hand and together they walked in the meadows and forests, telling their tales of ancient mysteries. They loved and were One and together they ruled over the World. Yet even in love, [Uni] knew that the god would soon cross over to the Hidden realm and Death would come to the World. Then must She descend and embrace the Dark Lord, and bear the fruit of their Union."[3]

The Charge of the Goddess

"Whenever you have need of anything, once in the month and better it be when the Moon is full, then shall you assemble in some secret place and adore the spirit of me, who am Queen of all Witches. There shall ye assemble, ye who are fain to learn all sorcery, yet have not won its deepest secrets; to these will I teach all things that are as yet unknown. And ye shall be free from slavery; and as a sign that ye be truly free, you shall be naked in your rites; and ye shall dance, sing, feast, make music and love, all in my praise. For mine is the ecstasy of the spirit, and mine also is joy on earth; for my law is love unto all beings. Keep pure your highest ideals; strive ever towards them, let nothing stop you or turn you aside. For mine is the secret door which opens upon the Land of Youth, and mine is the cup of the wine of life, and the Cauldron of Cerridwen, which is the Holy Vessel of Immortality. I am the gracious Goddess, who gives the gift of joy unto the heart of man. Upon earth, I give the knowledge of the spirit eternal; and beyond death, I give peace, and freedom, and reunion with those who have gone before. Nor do I demand sacrifice; for behold, I am the Mother of all living, and my love is poured out upon the earth.

I am the beauty of the green earth, and the white Moon among the stars, and the Mystery of the waters, and the desire of the heart of man. Call unto thy soul, arise, and come unto me. For I am the soul

---

[3]   Grimassi, Raven. *Hereditary Witchcraft: Secrets of the Old Religion.* Llewellyn, 1999.

of Nature, who gives life to the Universe. From me all things proceed, and unto me all things must return; and before my face, beloved of Gods and of men, let thine innermost divine self be enfolded in the rapture of the infinite. Let my worship be within the heart that rejoiceth; for behold, all acts of love and pleasure are my rituals. Therefore, let there be beauty and strength, power and compassion, honor and humility, mirth and reverence within you. And thou who thinketh to seek for me, know thy seeking and yearning shall avail thee not unless thou knoweth the Mystery; that if that which thy seekest thou findest not within thee, thou wilt never find it without thee. For behold, I have been with thee from the beginning; and I am that which is attained at the end of desire."[4]

---

[4]   This text is of unknown origin but was once attributed to Doreen Valiente.

APPENDIX II

Group Rituals

The following rituals are templates for your own rituals. They are complete, but you can easily add, remove, or alter their structure as desired. These rituals are formed upon time-proven themes and carry the energy of the Momentum of the Past. Therefore, it is suggested that you try to retain the general framework as you create your own rituals in keeping with your needs and desires. These basic themes are outlined in previous chapters dealing with the Goddess and God and the seasons within the Wheel of the Year.

Samhain

Items needed (other than the usual ritual items):
- ❖ 4 white candles for quarter points
- ❖ 1 red candle to symbolize the Goddess
- ❖ 1 black candle to symbolize the God
- ❖ 1 black candle for the skull
- ❖ 1 human skull (replica/symbol) placed on the altar
- ❖ 1 cauldron
- ❖ Winter incense blend
- ❖ Root of mandrake
- ❖ A small white candle for each person attending
- ❖ Dried leaves (oak leaves or pine needles)
- ❖ Personal offerings to the God

1. Cast the circle in the usual manner.

2. Light the candle on the skull. The High Priest moves to the West quarter and stands before the coven members as they assume the slain god posture. Coven members perform the Rite of Union gestures while facing the High Priest.

3. The High Priestess sounds altar bell thrice, saying:

   > *"We gather now at this appointed time to acknowledge the absence of our Lord and Lady; they who have departed into the Hidden Realms. The Great Horned God withdraws deep into the Sacred Forest, and the Wolf rules now in the wooded places. It is now the time of shadows and of decline. It is the time when spirits of the Otherworld return to the land of humankind. O' Ancient Gods of our ancestors, bless this sacred gathering, that we who worship in your ways may be protected from the coming powers."*

   Coven responds:

   > *"So mote it be!"*

4. The High Priestess stands at the West quarter, facing coven members, and recites the Myth of the *Descent of the Goddess* to the assembled coven:

   > *"Our Lady and Goddess would solve all mysteries, even the Mystery of Death. And so, she journeyed to the Underworld in her boat upon the sacred River of Descent. Then, it came to pass that she entered before the first of the seven gates to the Underworld. And the Guardian challenged her, demanding one of her garments for passage, for nothing may be received except that something be given in return. And at each of the gates, the Goddess was required to pay the price of passage, for the Guardian spoke to her: 'Strip off your garments, and set aside your jewels, for nothing may you bring with you into this our realm.'*
   > *So, the Goddess surrendered her jewels and her clothing to the Guardian and was bound as all living must be who seek to enter*

the Realm of Death and the Mighty Ones. At the first gate, she gave over her scepter; at the second, her crown; at the third, her necklace; at the fourth, her ring; at the fifth, her girdle; at the sixth, her sandals; and at the seventh, her gown. The Goddess stood naked and was presented before the Lord of Shadows, and such was her beauty that he himself knelt as she entered. He laid his crown and his sword at her feet, saying: 'Blessed are your feet which have brought you down this path.' Then he arose and said to the Goddess: 'Stay with me, I pray, and receive my touch upon your heart.'

And the Goddess replied to the Lord: 'But I love you not, for why do you cause all the things that I love and take delight in to fade and die?'

'My Lady,' replied the Lord, 'it is age and fate against which you speak. I am helpless, for age causes all things to whither, but when men die at the end of their time, I give them rest, peace, and strength. For a time, they dwell with the Moon and the spirits of the Moon; then may they return to the realm of the living. But you are so lovely, and I ask you to return not, but abide with me here.'

But she answered, 'No, for I do not love you.' Then the Lord said, 'If you refuse to embrace me, then you must kneel to death's scourge.' The Goddess answered him: 'If it is to be, then it is fate, and better so!" So, she knelt in submission before the hand of Death, and he scourged her with so tender a hand that she cried out, 'I know your pain and the pain of love!'

The Lord raised her to her feet and said, 'Blessed are you, my Queen and my Lady.' Then he gave to her the five kisses of initiation, saying: 'Only thus may you attain to knowledge and to joy.'

And he taught her all of his mysteries, and he gave her the necklace, which is the circle of rebirth. And she taught him her mysteries of the sacred cup, which is the cauldron of rebirth. They loved and joined in union with each other, and for a time, the Goddess dwelled in the realm of the Lord of Shadows.

For there are three mysteries in the life of humanity: Birth, Life, and Death (and love controls them all). To fulfill love, you must return again at the same time and place as those who loved before. And you must meet, recognize, remember, and love them anew. But to be reborn, you must die and be made ready for a new body. And to die, you must be born, but without love, you may not be born among your own.

But our Goddess is inclined to favor love and joy and happiness. She guards and cherishes her Hidden Children in this life and the next. In death, she reveals the way to her communion, and in life, she teaches them the magick of the Mystery of the Circle (which is set between the worlds of humans and of the gods)."

5. The High Priestess (at the West quarter) addresses coven members:

> *"Our Goddess dwells now in the Realm of the Lord of Shadows. The world grows cold and lifeless. But let us not sorrow for this harsh season, for all is as it must be. Therefore, let us draw close to the Lord of Shadows and embrace him. Let us find comfort in the knowledge of his essence. Blessed be all in the name of the God."*

Coven members respond:

> *"May the Lord of Shadows bless and protect us."*

6. The High Priest moves to the North and assumes the slain god posture.

7. The High Priestess moves to the North quarter and kneels. They touch the High Priest on the shoulders and groin with their left hand (tracing a triangle from their right shoulder, to left shoulder, then to groin, and back to right shoulder).

8. The High Priestess speaks:

> *"O' Ancient One, Lord of Shadows,*
> *Be present among us.*
> *For now is your time of power, O' mighty Horned One.*
> *Lord of our Passions and Desires,*
> *this night we do welcome you in love and trust.*
> *O' Ancient One, protect us from all things in the*
> *season of decline."*

9. The High Priestess lays their symbols and tools of rank at the High Priest's feet, saying:

"My Lord, I give my reign over to you, for
I know now the pains of love."

10. The High Priest takes up the symbols of the High Priestess and kisses the symbols, then places them down at the North quarter. The High Priest recites the *Charge of the God:*

"Hear you all, the words of the God. By the fallen temple stone or in a forgotten glen, there shall you gather, all who seek to know my secret mysteries. For I am He who guards and He who reveals all these things.

I am the Lord of Earth and sky, of rocky cliffs and forests deep and darkened. I was there when the world was new, and I taught you to hunt and to gather plants for food. Look within yourselves, for I am there. I am that strength upon which you draw in times of need. I am that which conquers fear. I am the hero and the fool. I am your longing to be free and your need to be bound.

In my love for you, I give up my life. I die but rise again. I prepare the path upon which you journey, going always on before you. For it is in becoming as you that you may become as me.

Hear the thunder, there am I. See the hawk and the raven soar, there am I. See the great wolf and the stag appear in the forest clearing, there am I. Close your eyes at the end of your days, and there am I, waiting by the temple stone."

11. The Maiden places the High Priestess's tools near the altar pentacle. They then lead the coven to assemble at the South quarter.

12. The High Priestess (in goddess posture at the altar) faces the coven and addresses them:

"The Wheel of the Year has turned, cycle unto cycle, time unto time. Behold now the Lady of Shadows. I have journeyed to the Hidden Realm to prepare a place for you. The harshness of the season I leave behind me; kindle for yourselves a fire of love

within, and I shall remember you and return to you. For you are the Keepers of the Flame, and to all who kindle the sacred flame, I shall never abandon. By the changing of the harsh season shall you know that I draw near again. And I shall return the greenness of plants and trees; then will you know that I have come."

Coven responds:

"We keep your sacred flame within us always,
and we tend it also on the sacred altar of our rites."

13. Each coven member now comes forward to the altar and receives a white candle. Members then move to the High Priestess who lights each candle from the "Goddess candle" on the altar.

14. The High Priestess kneels before the High Priest at the North quarter, lifting the chalice (filled with wine) to them. The High Priest charges the wine and places their wand (tip down) into the chalice.

15. The High Priestess raises the chalice and offers wine to the coven, saying:

"Accept now the essence of the God."

16. In response, each member goes to the High Priest at the North quarter, bearing the lighted candle that they received from the altar.

17. The High Priest addresses each member as they come one by one and stand before them:

"This is the light that you bore from the season before.
Accept now my essence."

18. The High Priest snuffs out the member's candle and bids the person to taste a small piece of mandrake root, which they first dips in the wine. Coven responds:

"Blessed be in the name of the God."

The person then tastes the root anointed with wine (mandrake is not chewed or ingested).

19. Coven members tread around the circle and back to the High Priest. All coven members embrace the High Priest with a hug. The coven reassembles at the South quarter.

20. The cauldron is brought to the West quarter and filled with dried leaves, lit, and set where it can be seen by all. Coven members individually place their offerings in front of it.

21. The High Priest then addresses the coven:

"Behold, the womb of the Goddess of Night, which is pregnant with the child of the coming year. O' symbol of the Mystery by which we return, we honor your essence and the magick that emanates from union with you."

Coven responds:

"We join our desires with the Seed of Light in the womb of the Goddess."

22. The High Priestess addresses the coven:

"Let us be secure in the protective power of the God. We shall not be in want, nor shall we suffer, for we are in his care. Let us therefore feast and celebrate, all in his praise."

Coven responds:

"Blessed be all in the name of the God. Lord of Shadows, protect us."

23. Coven assembles in a circle, standing along the perimeter of the ritual circle. Beginning with the High Priestess, coven members greet one another with the phrase "many blessings." Traditionally, embraces and kisses are shared among coven members.

24. Celebration of cakes and wine concludes the ritual.

25. Ritual circle is closed and candles are snuffed.

Yule (Winter Solstice)

Items needed (other than the usual ritual items):
- ❖ 4 white candles for quarter points
- ❖ 2 cauldrons
- ❖ 1 red candle to symbolize the Goddess
- ❖ 1 black candle to symbolize the God
- ❖ 1 black candle for the skull
- ❖ 1 small "Newborn God" candle (yellow or gold) for the "God-Flame"
- ❖ 1 human skull (replica/symbol) placed on the altar
- ❖ Winter incense blend
- ❖ Personal offerings to the God
- ❖ Anointing oil (solar blend)
- ❖ Evergreen wreath
- ❖ Small log of Oak
- ❖ Spring of evergreen for each coven member

1. Cast the ritual circle in the usual manner.

2. The High Priestess, at the altar, addresses the coven:

> *"We mark now, with this sacred gathering, the rebirth of the Sun God. It is the Great Mother who gives him birth. It is the Lord of Life born again. From the Union of our Lord and Lady, hidden in the Realm of Shadows, we receive now the Child of Promise!"*

Coven responds:

> *"O' bring to us the Child of Promise!"*

3. The High Priest stands at the East quarter in the god posture as the High Priestess addresses the four quarters. Coven members

perform the Rite of Union gestures to the God symbol as the quarters are addressed:

East

> *"We call forth now into the Portal of the Eastern Power. We call to the Ancient God, he who brought forth the light of day. We call upon the Ancient God, he who was beloved of our ancient tribes."*

Coven responds:

> *"We summon, stir, and call you forth!"*

South

> *"We call forth now into the Portal of the Southern Power. We call to the Ancient God, he who brought forth the warmth of day. We call upon the Ancient God, he who was beloved of our ancient tribes."*

Coven responds:

> *"We summon, stir, and call you forth!"*

West

> *"We call forth now into the Portal of the Western Power. We call to the Ancient God, he who brought forth the rain to cool the parched Earth. We call upon the Ancient God, he who was beloved of our ancient tribes."*

Coven responds:

> *"We summon, stir, and call you forth!"*

North

"We call forth now into the Portal of the Northern Power. We call to the Ancient God, he who marked the year with shadow and stone. We call upon the Ancient God, he who was beloved of our ancient tribes."

Coven responds:

"We summon, stir, and call you forth!"

4. The High Priest (in god posture) is addressed by the High Priestess:

    "My Lord, we greet you, O' Horned One, horned with the rays of the Sun, by whose blessings and grace shall life always be born again. Behold, your people are gathered! Bless them and the days before them! These gifts do we give you."

    Coven responds:

    "Blessed be all in the name of the God."

5. The cauldron is set before the High Priest, with the coven signing the gesture of manifestation as the High Priestess places an offering in front. Each member then places their offering while the other members maintain the ritual gesture. Once the last person has given an offering, the coven then assembles at the West quarter.

6. The High Priestess recites prayer at the altar:

    "O' most ancient provider,
    Lord of Light and Life,
    We pray you grow strong,
    that we may pass the winter in peace and fullness.
    Emanate your warmth and your love,

that the cold and harshness of winter
not dwindle your followers.
But instead, fill them with your divine light.
O' Ancient One, hear us!
Protect us and provide for us in the harshness of these times.
We give you adoration and place ourselves in your care.
Blessed be all in the God!"

Coven responds:

"Blessed be all!"

7. The High Priest now goes to each coven member, anoints them with the oil, and gives them a sprig of evergreen, saying:

"Blessed be in my care."

8. The High Priest and the High Priestess enact the myth of the season with four coven members as the rest observe the play, which takes place at the northeast. The Narrator says:

"Now, the time came, in the Hidden Realm of Shadows, that the Goddess would bear the Child of the Great Lord of Shadows. And the Lords of the Four Corners came and beheld the newborn God. So, it came to pass that the Great Lords were brought before the throne of the Shadowed One. And they spoke saying, 'Do we find you here in the Realm of Shadows, O' Lord of Light?' And the Great One replied, 'Yes, it is I. Now, you have truly seen my two faces.' Then, the Goddess spoke to the four Lords, saying 'Take my son, who is born of two lights, that he might bring new life to the world. For the Earth has grown cold and lifeless.' So, the Lords of the Four Corners departed to the world of men, bearing the new Lord of the Sun. And the people rejoiced for the Lord had come that all upon the Earth might be saved."

Ritualists now proceed with the drama play. The God candle is set inside the cauldron, which is placed at the East quarter.

I. The High Priestess takes the posture for giving birth, with the cauldron placed between their legs. The High Priest kneels in front of them and produces a flame (lighted candle) in the manner of delivering a baby. The Four Lords actors surround the High Priest and the High Priestess, slightly obscuring the view of the coven members (to induce an air of mystery).

II. Once born, the God-Flame is taken by the Lord of the East, who carries it to the East quarter. Here, the Lord presents the flame to coven members, saying:

"Hail, behold the newborn Sun."

Coven responds:

"Hail Shining One, Hail, Lord of the Sun."

Each Lord in turn (South, West, North) will perform the same act at the associated quarter with the same response.

III. The East Lord will tread the circle (from East quarter) to the North, taking the God-Flame from the North Lord and making one full pass around the circle again (holding up the God-Flame).

Upon returning to the North, the East Lord will raise the flame to this quarter and then to the assembled coven. The East Lord will then carry the God-Flame to the East and repeat the last act.

IV. The God-Flame is now carried to the altar and set upon it.

V. The High Priest addresses coven members:

"Let your spirits be joyful and your heart despair not. For on this sacred day is born he whose Light shall save the world. He has come forth from the Darkness and his Light has been seen in the East. He is Lord of Light and Life."

(The High Priest gestures the Horned God sign with hand, towards the God-Flame.)

"Behold the Sacred One, the Child of Promise! He who is born into the world, is slain for the world, and ever rises again!"

VI. The sacred evergreen wreath is brought out and placed before the altar. The small oak log is set in the center of the wreath. The God-Flame is then set on top of it (symbolic of the Lord of Light and the Lord of Vegetation, being as one and the same).

9. The High Priest addresses coven members, with palms held above the God-Flame:

"Behold the God whose life and light dwells within each of us. He is the Horned One, Lord of the Forest, the Hooded One, Lord of the Harvest, the Old One, and Lord of the Tribe. Let us therefore honor Him."

10. Coven members place gifts for each other before the sacred evergreen, in recognition of the divinity within each person. The ritual concludes with cakes and wine. Celebration of the season may continue within the circle or be taken to another location. Traditionally, bonfires are set either on hilltops or upon the beach. Coven members may leap the fire or simply toss items into the flames to "encourage the Light."

Imbolc

Items needed (in addition to standard altar items):

- ❖ 4 white candles for quarter points
- ❖ 1 red candle to symbolize the Goddess
- ❖ 1 black candle to symbolize the God
- ❖ 1 black candle for the skull
- ❖ 1 God-torch (candle for presentation)
- ❖ 1 human skull (replica/symbol) placed on the altar
- ❖ 1 cauldron
- ❖ Winter incense blend
- ❖ Personal offerings to the God
- ❖ Wolf skin cloak (or representation)
- ❖ Small fur or skin piece for charging chalice (traditionally wolf or goat)
- ❖ Small candle for each coven member

1. Circle is cast in the usual manner.

2. High Priest addresses coven members:

> *"We gather at this sacred time to give due praise and worship to the Lady of Fire and Lord of Ice. We mark now, at this appointed time, the young Sun God bound to winter's embrace and the Goddess who stands by the pool of fire, whose flames are the liberation through which the God can be freed."*

Coven responds:

> *"Hail, Lady of Fire! Hail, Lord of Ice!"*

3. The High Priestess lights a torch from the altar and treads the circle from the West quarter, returning West again. They then hold the torch up to the coven.

4. Coven members perform the Rite of Union gestures focused on the flame, as the Maiden addresses the coven:

> *"Behold the Lord of Light, he who mastered the twelve labors of the Great Lords. He who causes the world to rejoice in his rising. He whose light brings salvation to the Earth."*

Coven responds:

> *"Let his Wheel of the Year turn for us. Let the promise be fulfilled. Let the God be liberated."*

5. The High Priest moves to the East quarter and assumes the god posture. The High Priestess kneels in front of them and begins the invocation to the God.

> *"Hear me, Lord of Light.*
> *Hear the call of the Goddess,*
> *breathe the scent of perfume,*
> *receive the hot breath of the Goddess.*
> *Rise and swell, and release, release from winter's embrace!"*

Coven responds, calling out three times:

> *"Hear the call, breathe the flame, melt the ice!"*

6. The Guardian gives everyone a candle. Each member then moves to the North, pauses, and then proceeds to the South. There, each person lights their candle and then moves to the southeast to place an offering to the Sun God.

7. The High Priestess at the altar recites as members are circling:

> *"O' Ancient One,*
> *rayed in splendor and horned with power,*
> *be free and rise to embrace us,*

for without you we shall surely perish.
It is now the appointed time, and we offer you our worship.
Warm now the sleeping seeds that lie beneath the cool Earth,
within the womb of the Great Mother.
Comfort us and renew our strength!
Behold, this circle of your children;
we have lit the ancient fires and do faithfully serve you.
We await your emanation of warmth."

8. The High Priestess goes to the East and gives chalice of wine to the High Priest, who then charge it by wrapping chalice in fur piece and twisting it sunwise while visualizing the newly kindled Sun rise as they gaze into the wine.

9. The High Priest addresses coven members:

   "Behold the cool drink of immortality. For herein is the essence of life and the gift of life. Let your hearts now be joyful and come unto me and drink of the light of rejuvenation. Receive this into your blood and be fulfilled."

10. Coven members move to the High Priest and receive the wine, one at a time.

11. The High Priestess recites the final address:

    "Let us now give due praise and adoration unto the Lord of Light. For he is the symbol of the Mystery by which we are reborn again. Let us always rejoice in his rising, for by this we are joined to the essence of rejuvenation and rebirth."

    Coven responds:

    "Hail and adoration unto you, O' Lord of Light!"

12. Coven partakes in cakes and wine. Celebration continues as desired.

Ostara (Vernal Equinox)

Items needed (other than the usual ritual items):
- ❖ 4 white candles for quarter points
- ❖ 1 red candle to symbolize the Goddess
- ❖ 1 black candle to symbolize the God
- ❖ 1 red candle for the skull
- ❖ 1 human skull (replica/symbol) placed on the altar
- ❖ 1 cauldron
- ❖ 1 vase (filled with water)
- ❖ 1 reed
- ❖ 1 pouch of seeds tied around the High Priest's waist
- ❖ 1 large bag
- ❖ 1 candle to represent the Goddess's returning light
- ❖ Vernal incense blend
- ❖ Personal offerings to the Goddess
- ❖ Personal offerings to the God
- ❖ Scarf tied around the right thigh of the High Priestess
- ❖ Walnut shell

1. Circle is cast in the usual manner.

2. The High Priest addresses coven members:

> *"We mark now the beginning of the Ascent of our Lady from the Hidden Realm of Shadows. For this is the time of her desire for the light and life of the world. We mark the passing away of the shadow's hold and the hard embrace of winter's hand. We welcome the splendor of the new young God, rayed in power, Lord of the Sky."*

3. The Maiden holds up the vase with the reed in it, and the coven performs the Rite of Union.

4. The Maiden addresses coven members:

    "Now, it came to pass that the Goddess longed for the Light of the World and for her many children. And she departed from the Hidden Realm of Shadows in secret, leaving the Lord of Shadows in dark solitude."

5. The Maiden continues, as she recites the *Myth of Ascent*:

    "Now the time came in the Hidden Realm of Shadows that the Goddess would bear the child of the Lord of Shadows. And the Lords of the Four Corners came and beheld the newborn God. They spoke to the Goddess of the misery of the people who lived upon the world above, and how they suffered in cold and in darkness. So the Goddess bid the Lords to carry her son to the world, and so the people rejoiced for the Sun God had returned.

    And it came to pass that the Goddess longed for the Light of the world and for her many children. So she journeyed to the World and was welcomed in great celebration. Then the Goddess saw the splendor of the new God as he crossed the heavens, and she desired him. But each night he returned to the Hidden Realm and could not see the beauty of the Goddess in the night sky. So one morning the Goddess arose as the God came up from the Hidden Realm and she bathed nude in the sacred lake. Then the Lords of the Four Corners appeared to the Sun God and said:

    'Behold the sweet beauty of the Goddess of the Earth.' And he looked upon her from the heights and was struck with her beauty so that he descended upon the Earth and concealed himself as a reed near the bank of the lake.

    As the Goddess bathed in the lake she brushed against the reed, which was concealed among others. The Goddess immediately took hold of the reed and said: 'You are not a reed, but a god!' Then he answered, 'Yes, I am the Lord of the Reeds. Yet when I touch the sky I am the bright blessed Sun. But to be with thee I would remain a reed at thy bath.'

The Goddess smiled and stepped forth from the water in all her beauty. 'I am the Lady of the Lake. Yet when I touch the sky, I am the sacred light of the Moon. But to be with thee I would remain in the waters of this lake.'

And the God took her by the hand and together they walked in the meadows and forests telling their tales of ancient mysteries."

6. The High Priest moves to the East quarter and says:

"Where is my Lady?"

7. The High Priestess, beginning at the North, moves to each quarter with a lighted candle, and then, passing the North, stops at the East quarter.

8. The Maiden replies to the High Priest:

"O' Shadowed One, your Lady comes to us, and we welcome her with great rejoicing. All living things do know that she is near, and the world stirs with life again. Our Lady journeys now to meet us and her essence is upon the forest, field, and glen."

9. The High Priestess calls out:

"Hear me, for now I draw near! Hear me, all who sleep from winter's embrace, awaken unto rebirth, come forth now. Receive now my essence and be full of life and the desire for life."

10. The Maiden speaks to the High Priestess:

"O' Great Goddess of the Earth, return to us in your fair nature. You who are the lovely Maiden of Youth, Joy, and Love. Only you can break the spell of winter and enchant the Earth with your essence. Hail to the Great Goddess!"

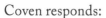

Coven responds:

"Hail, and praise to thee, Great Goddess!"

11. The High Priestess unties the scarf around their thigh, drops it to the ground, and then assumes the goddess posture.

Coven responds:

"Hail to the Great Goddess. All praise be to thee!"

12. Everyone then comes forward to the High Priestess and welcomes the Goddess by embracing them with a hug, and then kneeling to touch the High Priestess's feet with their hands (first the left foot and then the right).

13. Once everyone has participated, the Maiden kneels, picks up the scarf, and gives it to the High Priest. They then tie it to his cord of initiation, which is around their waist.

14. The High Priestess moves to the East quarter and assumes the goddess posture. Everyone comes forward and places an offering into the cauldron, which the Maiden sets before the High Priestess in the East. Prayers, requests, or blessings may be offered. When completed, the High Priestess moves to the West quarter.

15. The High Priest takes a lighted torch and treads the circle to all points thrice, beginning at the East. As they begin the third pass, four coven members (representing the Lords of the Four Quarters) stop them at the East quarter and present them to the High Priestess, who now stands at the West quarter.

16. A Lord addresses the High Priest:

"Behold the beauty of the Goddess, she who is the Lady of the Lake, she who is the fair light of the Moon in the dark sacred night."

17. The High Priest addresses the High Priestess:

> *"You are truly the beauty of all things.*
> *You are the Earth, the sky, and the beyond."*

18. A Lord addresses the High Priestess:

> *"Behold, the Power of the God. He who is Lord of the Reeds, he*
> *who is the bright Sun of the Blessed Day."*

19. The High Priestess addresses the High Priest:

> *"You are truly the power in all things.*
> *You are the Earth, the sky, and the beyond."*

20. The High Priestess and the High Priest embrace, and the coven repeats three times:

> *"Blessed be the plow, the seed, and the furrow."*

21. Coven then forms a circle. Traditionally, the coven members would exchange embraces and kisses at this stage of the rite. The High Priestess and the High Priest repeat three times:

> *"Blessed be the plow, the seed, and the furrow."*

22. As this takes place, the Maiden goes to the High Priest and unties the pouch of seeds and scarf from around their waist. They then take out three seeds and places them in the walnut shell, which they then spill onto the scarf. The rest of the seeds are poured into the cauldron.

23. The offerings are collected and placed within a bag. Coven members will later bury the seed pouch in a planting field

(for increase of crops) or will hang it from a tree within the woods (for an abundant hunt). The offerings will be scattered around the area.

24. The High Priestess gives blessings over the seeds within the cauldron, saying:

> *"Blessings upon these seeds, for without them, we ourselves would perish from this world. Blessed be the seed that goes into the Earth where deep secrets hide. There, shall you lie with the Elements and spring forth as flowered plant, concealing secrets strange. In the ear of grain, spirits of the field shall come to cast their light upon you and aid you in your growth. Through this, we shall be touched by that same race, and the Mysteries hidden within you shall we also obtain even unto the last of these seeds."*

25. The celebration concludes with wine and cakes, singing, and feasting.

Beltane

Items needed (other than the usual ritual items):
- 4 white candles for quarter points
- 2 green candles
- 1 red candle to symbolize the Goddess
- 1 black candle to symbolize the God
- 1 red candle for the skull
- 1 human skull (replica/symbol) placed on the altar
- Vernal incense blend
- Personal offerings to the God
- Crown wreath of flowers
- Antler crown
- Small candle for each member
- Twine
- Sword

1. Circle is cast in the usual manner.

2. The High Priest addresses coven members:

   "We gather at this joyous time of the courtship of our Lord and Lady. We rejoice in our queen, the Lady of the Green. We rejoice in our king, the Lord of the Green. Join the dance of the Lord and Lady."

3. Coven members recite three times:

   "Seed to sprout, sprout to leaf, leaf to bud, bud to flower, flower to fruit, fruit to seed."

4. The Maiden and the Guardian tie the green candles together with twine. The candles are then lighted at the East quarter.

5. At the North quarter, the High Priest calls down the Goddess upon the High Priestess (who assumes goddess posture), as the Maiden addresses the coven members:

   "By and by all things pass, season unto season, year unto year. The Beltane fire is kindled for our Lady of the Promised Return. We, her Hidden Children, do celebrate her tonight. Our Beltane fire burns for the young God who was bewitched by the beauty of the Goddess. And, in love, he bowed before her and would give his up place."

6. Coven members perform the Rite of Union to the High Priestess who stands in goddess posture.

7. The High Priest kneels before the High Priestess and lays down their sword, saying:

   "My Lady, I give all my power to you, for this is so ordained. And with love, I submit to you, and I give my reign over to your hands."

8. The High Priestess takes up the sword and recites a variation of the *Charge of the Goddess:*

> *"Whenever you have need of anything, once in the month when the Moon is full, then shall you come together at some deserted place or where there are woods and give worship to she who is your Queen.*
>
> *Come all together inside a circle, and secrets that are yet unknown shall be revealed. And your mind must be free and also your spirit, and as a sign that you are truly free, you shall be naked in your rites. And you shall rejoice and sing, making music and love. For this is the essence of spirit and the knowledge of joy.*
>
> *Be true to your own beliefs and keep to the Ways beyond all obstacles. For ours is the key to the Mysteries and the cycle of rebirth, which opens the way to the Womb of Enlightenment. I am the spirit of all the wise ones, and this is joy and peace and harmony.*
>
> *In life, your Queen reveals the knowledge of Spirit. And from death, she delivers you to peace. Give offerings to our mother. For she is the beauty of the green Earth, the white Moon among the stars, the Mystery which gives life, and she always calls us to come together in her name. Let her worship be the ways within your heart, for all acts of love and pleasure are like rituals to the Goddess. But to all who seek her, know that your seeking and yearning will reward you not, until you realize the secret. Because if that which you seek is not found within you, you will never find it from without. For she has been with you since you entered into the Ways, and she is that which awaits at your journey's end."*

9. The High Priestess moves to the East quarter, setting the sword before the altar as they assume the goddess posture. The High Priest gives address:

> *"Hail and adoration unto the Great Goddess! You who are the Great Star Goddess, Queen of Heaven, Lady of the Earth, we welcome you and rejoice in your presence."*

10. All coven members come forward and embrace the High Priestess. Traditionally, kisses would be shared. The coven members then assemble in the South quarter.

11. The Maiden takes a chalice of wine to the High Priestess at the East quarter. The Guardian takes the wand to the High Priest who is also at the East quarter.

12. The High Priestess lifts the chalice up to the High Priest. The High Priest lowers the wand into the chalice. Traditionally, the High Priest and the High Priestess would exchange a kiss.

13. The High Priest then leads the coven around the circle to the East quarter to receive the wine (the essence of the union of Goddess and God), which they all drink.

14. The High Priest takes the crown of flowers and places it upon the head of the High Priestess. Coven responds:

    "Hail, the Queen of May! Hail, the Lady of the Green!"

15. The High Priestess places the antler crown on the High Priest. Coven responds:

    "Hail, the King of May! Hail, the Lord of the Green!"

16. The Maiden and the Guardian lead the coven thrice around the circle in a dance. Coven members reassemble at the South quarter. The Maiden brings each member to the High Priestess and the High Priest at the East. Each person will receive a candle (token of the life force), which is lit from the Goddess candle on the altar, as the High Priestess and the High Priest say:

    "Bear now the light of my season and walk always in balance.
    May the power of the forces of light be with you."

Candles may be set aside for the duration of the rite.

17. The coven members form a circle along the ritual circle's perimeter, facing inward. Traditionally, kisses and embraces were shared.

18. Ritual celebration continues with cakes and wine and general merriment.

Litha (Summer Solstice)

Items needed (other than the usual ritual items):
- ❖ 4 white candles for quarter points
- ❖ 4 small bowls for libation (at quarters)
- ❖ 1 red candle to symbolize the Goddess
- ❖ 1 black candle to symbolize the God
- ❖ 1 red candle for the skull
- ❖ 1 human skull (replica/symbol) placed on the altar
- ❖ 1 cauldron
- ❖ Summer incense blend
- ❖ Personal offerings to the God
- ❖ Flowers for procession
- ❖ Symbol for God and Goddess
- ❖ Libation fluid (nectar/ambrosia)
- ❖ Offerings (one for other deities and another for Nature spirits)
- ❖ Fennel stalk (or wood staff)
- ❖ Sorghum stalk (or wood staff)

1. Cast circle in the usual manner, and then open a threshold at the Northeast.

2. Coven members form a line, making a corridor (at the Northeast) into the circle.

3. The High Priest and the High Priestess pass through the corridor into the circle. All members toss flowers about as the couple walks into the circle.

---

4. All enter the circle behind them, and then the threshold is sealed by the Guardian.

5. The High Priestess gives address at the altar to the coven members:

> *"We gather now on this sacred night of summer's eve and join ourselves to the powers and forces of this mystical season. On this night, the kindred gather, as do all the old spirits. And on this night, do they dance with the Lord of the Woods and the Lady of the Flowers in the meadows and deep woods."*

Coven responds:

> *"We sing to the Lady of Flowers, we sing to the Lord of the Woods, and we sing to the Old Ones who keep the ancient memories."*

6. Symbols of the God and Goddess are placed before the cauldron, which is set at the South quarter.

7. The High Priest addresses the coven:

> *"Here is the Divine Couple, whose union gives life to the world."*

Coven responds:

> *"Blessed be all in the God and Goddess."*

8. Coven performs the Rite of Union facing the deity symbols.

9. Coven members now come forward and place deity offerings in the cauldron at the South quarter.

10. Appointed members then go to each of the four quarters and pour a libation of nectar into the bowls.

11. All coven members now place nature spirit offerings at the four quarters.

12. The High Priestess speaks from the altar:

"O' spirits of the Elemental Forces, hear me, and receive our blessings. O' spirits of the Earth, O' Powers that Be, hear me and receive our blessings. Assist us on this sacred night to maintain the natural balance, which keeps vital the essence of the Earth. Let there always be clear, flowing water, freshness in the air, fertility within the soil, and abundant life within the world."

13. The High Priestess addresses the coven members:

"On this sacred night, we guard against the Forces of Darkness and against all distortion. We stand with the Forces of Light, protecting the harvest and the herds. We return what we have drawn through the seasons from the Earth. We renew our covenant with the Old Ones and cleanse the surrounding ether, wrapped around our community like a mist. As it was in the time of our beginning, so is it now, so shall it be."

Coven responds:

*"As it was in the time of our beginning,
so is it now, so shall it be."*

14. The High Priestess and the High Priest then direct a dramatic play depicting the struggle between the Forces of Light and Forces of Darkness. The fennel stalk represents the Powers of Light and the sorghum stalk represents the Powers of Darkness. Ritual combat begins at the East quarter and continues around the circle thrice, ending at the North. At its conclusion, the fennel stalk is raised in

victory and presented at each quarter. The coven members respond with cheers of approval.

15. The coven assembles in a circle to raise the cone of power. The High Priestess or the High Priest address the coven members as they prepare themselves:

> *"We form this cone of power to be a positive force, whereby we charge you, O' Sacred Ether of our world. Be free of all evil and negativity. We charge you for the good of all life within our world."*

16. Coven is then directed to raise the Cone of Power.[5]

17. Once formed, the High Priestess or the High Priest signal the release of power and directs the cone up into the ether of the community.

18. Coven chants three times:

> *"Up, out, and round about."*

19. End ritual with cakes and wine. Close circle and leave libation bowls out overnight for the nature spirits.

---

[5] Coven members form a circle around the High Priest or High Priestess (whichever is directing). The coven stands, while the director sits or kneels. The method may be performed with cords or blades. Coven members join hands and move in a clockwise circle around the director, quickening in pace. The chant should be simple, using a deity name or a word of power. When the signal to release is given, the members drop to the ground, and the director quickly rises and hurls the Cone upwards.

Lughnasadh

Items needed (other than the usual ritual items):
- ❖ 4 white candles for quarter points
- ❖ 1 red candle to symbolize the Goddess
- ❖ 1 black candle to symbolize the God
- ❖ 1 red candle for the skull
- ❖ 1 cauldron
- ❖ 1 human skull (replica/symbol) placed on the altar
- ❖ Summer incense blend
- ❖ Personal offerings to the God
- ❖ Offerings for the harvest

1. Circle is cast in the usual manner.

2. The High Priestess addresses the coven members:

> *"We gather now on this appointed day in anticipation of the coming harvest. Our Lady of the Fields is ripe with child, and by her side is our Lord of the Barley. We praise the Lord and Lady and give thanks for their gifts of great bounty!"*

Coven responds:

> *"Blessed be all, in the name of the Lord and Lady!"*

3. The coven members give offerings at the South, as the High Priestess says:

> *"Let us now go forth and give offerings to the great God and Goddess, and let us be thankful for all we have that is good in life. For the Great Ones provide for us, and we must always remember them and give due thanks and praise."*

4. Chanting or singing is performed during the offerings:

> *"May your fields be evergreen,*
> *and may abundance fill you to the seam,*

and may your life be all of what you dream,
and may the days ahead be evergreen.
May the spirits of the Earth and sky
raise each stock up strong, and firm, and high.
And may abundance fill you to the seam,
and may your fields be always evergreen."

5. The High Priest lights the cauldron at the South quarter and places a token of their needs or requests in the flames. Coven members come forth, one at a time, and do the same. Requests may be written on parchment or cloth and burned in the cauldron fire.

6. The High Priestess speaks at the altar as the High Priest pours sweet herb incense into the cauldron flames:

"I call out to you, O' Lady of the Fields and Lord of the Woods, and pray that you receive our wishes and desires as they rise up to you on the smoke of our incense. We ask that you grant our requests and bring them to fullness, just as you bring forth the fruit from the seed."

Coven members reply:

"By the Lady and by the Lord, so be it done."

7. The High Priestess addresses coven from the altar:

"Know that every action brings forth another and that these actions are linked through their nature. Therefore, whatsoever you send forth, so shall you receive. A farmer can harvest for himself no more than he plants. Therefore, let us consider what is good in our lives and what is full. Let us also consider what is fruitless and what is empty. And let us consider well the reasons for all these things."

8. The High Priest and the High Priestess bless the ritual cakes and wine. The High Priestess kneels with chalice of wine before the High Priest. The High Priest lowers their wand into the wine, saying:

> *"Herein is joined the essence of the Lady of the Field and the Lord of the Woods, wherein all things are renewed and made vital."*

9. The High Priest kneels before the High Priestess, holding up the ritual cakes to them. The High Priestess makes the Sign of Union with their hand over the ritual cakes, saying:

> *"Here is the substance of the union of the Lady of the Fields and Lord of the Woods, wherein all things are established and renewed."*

Coven responds:

> *"The two united bring forth the worlds."*

10. Coven members come one at a time to receive the cakes and wine.

11. As each one drinks the wine, the High Priest or the High Priestess says:

> *"Blessings to you, in the name of the Lady and the Lord."*

12. The coven members reassemble at the South quarter.

13. The High Priest holds up the wand, while the High Priestess holds up the chalice (or small cauldron). The High Priestess speaks:

> *"Blessed be the plow, the seed, and the furrow."*

Coven members repeat:

> *"Blessed be the plow, the seed, and the furrow."*

14. Coven members pair off and join hands (for odd numbers, you can rotate).

15. Member one of the pair (traditionally a female member) says to member two (traditionally a male member):

"Blessed be your strength."

16. Member two says to member one:

"Blessed be your magick."

17. Member one says to member two:

"Blessed be the plow."

18. Member two says to member one:

"Blessed be the furrow."

19. Member one says to member two:

"Blessed be the ripened grain."

20. Member two says to member one:

"Blessed be the vessels that nurture."

21. High Priestess and High Priest say in unison:

"Blessed be the plow, the seed, and the furrow."

22. Rituals concludes with song, dance, and general merriment.

Mabon (Autumn Equinox)

Items needed (other than the usual ritual items):
- ❖ 4 white candles for quarter points
- ❖ 1 red candle to symbolize the Goddess
- ❖ 1 black candle to symbolize the God
- ❖ 1 red candle for the skull
- ❖ 1 human skull (replica/symbol) placed on the altar
- ❖ 1 cauldron
- ❖ Autumn incense blend
- ❖ Personal offerings to the God
- ❖ Candle to represent the "God Flame"
- ❖ Wheat shaft
- ❖ Small cup or bowl (receiving vessel)
- ❖ Pouch of grain tied around the waist of the High Priest
- ❖ Loaf of bread
- ❖ Red cord to tie around God candle on altar
- ❖ Dried oak leaves
- ❖ Bowl for leaves

1. Circle is cast in the usual manner.

2. High priest at the altar says:

> *"We gather at this sacred time to rejoice for the abundance, which has come into the world. In this, we call out to the Lord of the Sheaf who falls now into Shadow and to our Lady of the Harvest.*
>
> *All life comes from her and all life to her returns. The time has come when all things have grown into their fullness and are gathered by hunter and fieldsman. As it was in the time of our beginning, so is it now, so shall it be."*

Coven responds:

> *"Hail the Lord of the Sheaf!*
> *Hail the Lady of the Harvest!"*

3. High Priest stands to the East and then moves West, bearing the "God-Flame" candle in one hand and the ritual wand in the other. High Priestess addresses them at the West (giving them a drink from the chalice filled with the "Wine of Farewell," which contains a shaft of wheat):

> *"Farewell, Lord of the Sheaf, who stands in the Light and within the Darkness. Farewell, Hidden God, who ever remains and ever departs to the Hidden Realm through the Gate of Shadows as the Ruler of the Heights and of the Depths. Farewell, Harvest Lord. Within you is the union of mortal and immortal. You dwell within the sacred seed, the seed of ripened grain, and the seed of flesh. You are hidden in the Earth and rise to touch the stars."*

Coven performs the Rite of Union to the High Priest in god posture, and then says:

> *"Blessed be all for the bounty."*

4. Coven members representing the receptive polarity go to each quarter (beginning North) and dance from quarter to quarter. When they come to the High Priest, they ritually seize them by the arms. The Maiden then takes their ritual wand in their hand and, with the other participating coven members, leads them back around each quarter, returning to the West.

   As the participating coven members surround them in a teasing manner, the Maiden unties the pouch of grain from around the High Priest's waist and places it in the vessel within the cauldron.

Immediately after this, the Maiden hands them a shaft of wheat and extinguishes the High Priest's God-Flame candle.

The High Priest slumps to the ground, assisted by the coven members who lower them.

5. High Priestess addresses coven members:

> *"The God has departed from his abode in the fields, for the season has come, and his shinning vitality withers in the cool winds. And death shall come to the world, for the winter draws near. The Lord of Light now becomes the Lord of Shadows."*

6. A vessel is brought out and placed in the West. Everyone comes forward one at a time and place some oak leaves within it. They then taste some of the grain placed beside the vessel.

7. The High Priestess recites a portion of the mythos:

> *"In the earliest times, our Lord and Lady lived in the ancient forest. Now, our Lady seduced the Lord and received the sacred seed from which all things spring forth.*
>
> *But our Lord knew not the secret which only the Goddess understood, for she had drawn the life from him. And the world was abundant with all manner of animal and that which grows from the Earth.*
>
> *Now, there came a time when all things grew to their fullness and were gathered by hunter and fieldsman alike. And in that time, was the God slain and drawn into the harvest."*

8. The High Priest is brought to the North. They are fully cloaked, and their hood is drawn up over their head (which is bowed down). Attendants representing the femininity polarity hold them on each side. The High Priestess leads the coven members from

the South, passing them twice. The coven members bow as they pass each time.

9. A chosen coven member will now perform the dance of the Descent of the Goddess, as the coven chants until the dance is complete.

10. The Hooded One assumes the god posture at the West quarter. The dancer stands before the Hooded One, and the sacred dialogue begins (assign speakers):

Goddess:

> *"I have come in search of thee.*
> *Is this where I begin?"*

God:

> *"Begin to seek me out, and I shall become as small as a seed,*
> *so you may but pass me by."*

Coven:

> *"Then we shall split the rind, crack the grain, and break the pod."*

God:

> *"But I shall hide beneath the Earth and lay so still*
> *that you may but pass me by."*

Goddess:

> *"Then I shall raise you up in praise*
> *and place upon you a mantle of green."*

God:

> *"But I shall hide within the Green and cover myself,*
> *and you may but pass me by."*

Coven:

> *"Then we shall tear the husk and pull the root*
> *and thresh the chaff."*

God:

> *"But I shall scatter and divide, and being so many,*
> *you may but pass me by."*

Coven:

> *"Then we shall gather you in, bind you whole,*
> *and make you one again."*

11. The Maiden comes forward to the altar, passing each quarter from the North, carrying the Sacred Loaf of Bread. The High Priest removes hood and resumes place among the coven (no longer impersonating the God).

12. The High Priestess addresses the coven members while holding the ritual dagger and pointing at the loaf upon the altar:

> *"Behold the Harvest Lord."*

Coven responds:

> *"Blessed be the Lord of the Harvest."*

13. The High Priestess cuts the loaf into pieces (one for each coven member).

14. Everyone then comes forward and receives a piece of the loaf. The High Priestess then says:

> *"Behold the Harvest Lord, the Lord of the Sheaf. Behold the Hidden Ones within: the Stag, the Hooded One, the King. Let us take him within us and be as one."*

15. Everyone eats a piece of the loaf but leaves a small portion to be buried in the field.

16. The High Priestess passes the chalice of wine and bids all to drink, then speaks:

> *"Behold, you are now as one, you are of the Royal Blood. That which was at the time of beginning, is now, and always shall be."*

Coven responds:

> *"As it was in the time of our beginning,*
> *so is it now, so shall it be.*
> *Blessed be all!"*

17. Celebration concludes with cakes and wine, music, and merriment.

APPENDIX III
Solitary Rituals

In this section, you will find solitary rites for the sabbats and the Full Moon. Solitary rites play a key role for the person who is not a coven member and for coven members who are alone due to traveling or other circumstances. Solitary rites also help provide ritual experience for the new Witch without the awkwardness of performing in front of other people.

The following ritual formats are somewhat different from the group rites in the previous chapter. This will help you see how different and yet related themes can work in various ways. As with the group rituals, use the following rites as a template to construct your own system.

In the following rituals, you will find references to certain objects. Most are easy to find in stores. Ideally, you should make them yourself for a stronger bond with the object, which can intensify the ritual experience. The more effort you put into the objects you bring to a ritual, the more power you will generate. Personal effort goes a long way toward the end results. This is as true in life as it is in ritual construction.

You will find that two things happen when you make your own ritual crafts. On one level, making your own decorations and ritual paraphernalia is an act of devotion to your deities and spirits. This will strengthen and enhance not only the ritual experience but also the experience of the religion.

On another level, making your ritual objects imbues them with your personal power. This creates intimate alignments that deepens your connection to the ritual theme and establishes stronger inner connections to the spirits and entities associated with any given ritual.

In the following rituals, a list of required items is provided. Look them over so that you know what is required ahead of time. This will also provide you with a list of projects you can undertake to make your ritual objects. Any well-stocked Craft store should have everything you need. You can also refer to the suggested reading list for other books on ritual and seasonal décor.

Samhain

Items needed:
- ❖ 2 black altar candles
- ❖ 2 offering plates
- ❖ 2 offering cups
- ❖ 1 red candle for skull image
- ❖ 1 skull representation
- ❖ 1 small cauldron
- ❖ 1 altar bell
- ❖ Seasonal altar decorations
- ❖ Offerings (see ritual text)
- ❖ Ritual tools (see ritual text)
- ❖ Parchment paper
- ❖ Pen
- ❖ Matches or lighter

The key themes of this season are Otherworld connection and creative potential. Both are related to the darkness of night (not the darkness of spirit). Therefore, you will want to use a symbol that connects to both. The traditional objects are the skull and the cauldron. The skull represents the spirits of the Otherworld (literally one's ancestors); it can be made of any substance. The cauldron represents the womb of generative life; it can be made of metal (preferred) or a heat resistant ceramic material.

On your altar, place two black candles at the opposite end from where you will be positioned. The candles should be several inches apart to your left and right. These candles serve as the sides of the doorway in the Otherworld. In the center of your altar, place the skull and secure a red candle on top. This will represent the living connection between you and the spirits on the other side. Red symbolizes the life force of blood.

In front of the skull, place a small cauldron. Ideally, the skull should be larger than the cauldron so that the skull is visible during the rite. Place a ritual bell to your right. The final item needed is a small plate and a cup. On the plate, you will want to place food offerings (fruit, cheese, and beans are preferred). In the cup, pour some water, wine, or mead. This offering, known as the "Meal of the Dead," appeases the spirits of the Otherworld. Place these items on the left side of the altar. This should leave some workspace directly in front of you.

On the altar, place offerings for the Goddess and God. Traditionally, this would be fruit, gourds, nuts, and red wine. These offerings will be given during the ritual in addition to those made to the ancestral spirits.

When you are ready, light the black candles from left to right. Ring the altar bell three times and then recite:

> *"I call to the God and Goddess to bless this ritual and protect all against harm on this sacred night. I call upon my guides and guardians to gather around and protect me from all misdeeds."*

Next, ring the bell three times, light the red candle on the skull, and say:

> *"In the name of the God and Goddess, I call to the spirits beyond the veil, between this world and the next. Come and partake of the offerings I freely give here upon this altar. Enter in peace and leave in peace."*

At this stage, take a piece of parchment paper and write a request. This should be something positive you would like to happen in the coming twelve months. The first time you perform this rite, keep the request simple and realistic. As a guide to some possible requests, intention is key: do not ask for money, ask for prosperity; do not ask for a specific lover, ask for a compatible one; do not ask for revenge or harm, ask for freedom from your enemies. The "Powers that Be" see further and with much greater wisdom than we do. Therefore, give the Universe some room to work and understand that success requires your full participation. In the Craft, there are no free rides, and you have no servants. Instead, you have faithful companions and powerful allies.

Once your request is written on the parchment paper, speak your wish out loud:

"In the name of the God and Goddess, I request...."

Then, fold the parchment paper three times and place it in the cauldron. Next, light a match, set the parchment on fire, and say:

"By the transforming power of fire, may these words become the manifestation of my desire. Spirits of the Otherworld, aid me from beyond. God and Goddess, bless my request and protect all from harm in the fulfillment of my desire."

When the parchment paper is consumed, gently blow the smoke with your breath directly toward the red candle. Next, increase the force of your exhalations until the red candle is blown out. Then, ring the bell three times and say:

"Spirits depart now in peace and return to your realm."

Gently blow the smoke from the red candle between the two black candles until there is no longer any smoke rising from either the cauldron or the red candle.

The final phase of the ritual turns now to giving offerings to the God and Goddess. Place your hands, palms facing up, on each side of the offering plate as a gesture of thanksgiving. Before making the offering, say:

"God and Goddess, I thank you for your presence in my life and for walking with me along my path. Please accept this offering as a token of my love."

Once the offering is made, you can remove, clean, and store your altar items. Take the ashes from the cauldron, find a private place outdoors, and blow the ashes to the East (or, if wind is present, turn your back to it). Imagine that the wind carrying your desire to be made manifest.

Yule (Winter Solstice)

Items needed:

- ❖ 3 red candles
- ❖ 2 green altar candles
- ❖ 1 orange votive candle
- ❖ 1 yellow or gold candle
- ❖ 1 evergreen wreath
- ❖ 1 small cauldron
- ❖ 1 altar bell
- ❖ 1 offering plate
- ❖ 1 offering cup
- ❖ Yule log
- ❖ Seasonal altar decorations
- ❖ Offerings (see ritual text)
- ❖ Ritual tools (see ritual text)
- ❖ Matches or lighter

The key themes of this season are rebirth and renewal. Both are related to the light of the Sun. Therefore, you will want a symbol that connects both concepts. The traditional objects are the evergreen wreath and the Yule log. The wreath represents the repeating cycle of life and the promise of survival, which is symbolized by the evergreen tree. The Yule log, traditionally oak or pine, represents the Sun and the Sun God. This is a symbolic remnant of tree worship from ancient times when people believed that the gods dwelled in trees.

On your altar, place two green candles at the opposite end from where you will be positioned. The candles should be several inches apart and to your left and right. These candles serve as the symbols of life in the material world and the spiritual world. Secure three red candles to the Yule log, symbolizing the vitality of the Evergreen God. In the center of your altar, place a yellow or gold candle in the middle opening of the wreath. This will represent the living connection between the Sun and the promise of renewal and rebirth.

In front of the wreath, place a small cauldron with an orange votive candle inside. The altar can be decorated with symbols, such as holly and mistletoe. Place a ritual bell on the right side of the altar. The final item needed is a small plate and a cup for offerings. Nuts, sweets, and wine or mead is traditional.

When you are ready, light the green candles from left to right. Ring the altar bell three times, and then recite:

> *"I call to the God and Goddess to bless this ritual*
> *on this sacred day of rebirth."*

Next, ring the bell three times, light the yellow or gold candle, and say:

> *"In the name of the God and Goddess, I call to the Spirit of the Sun,*
> *who is reborn this day. Come, partake of the offerings I freely give*
> *here upon this altar and remember your promise to return life in*
> *fullness. And through this, my life too will be renewed."*

At this stage, use the yellow or gold candle to light the votive candle in the cauldron and then recite:

> *"The fire of the Year God is passed into the Child of Promise. The*
> *Child of Light is born, the Child of Promise has come. In a new*
> *light shall I walk in the days to come."*

The final phase of the ritual turns now to giving offerings to the God and Goddess. Before presenting the offerings, say:

> *"God and Goddess, I thank you for your presence in my life and for*
> *awakening the new light of the coming seasons. Please accept this*
> *offering as a token of my love."*

Place your hands, palms facing up, on each side of the offering plate as a gesture of thanksgiving. Once the offering is made, you can remove, clean, and store the altar items (except for the votive candle). Allow the votive candle to burn out. Afterward, clean the cauldron and put it away.

Imbolc

Items needed:
- ❖ 12 white birthday candles
- ❖ 2 white altar candles
- ❖ 1 evergreen wreath (or hoop)
- ❖ 1 straw doll
- ❖ 1 small cauldron
- ❖ 1 altar bell
- ❖ 1 offering plate
- ❖ 1 offering cup
- ❖ Seasonal altar decorations
- ❖ Offerings (see ritual text)
- ❖ Ritual tools (see ritual text)
- ❖ Matches or lighter

The key themes of this season are purity and growth. Both are related to the light of the Sun. The traditional objects are the Sun wheel and the straw doll. The Sun wheel represents the growing cycle of life and the waxing light of the Sun. You can use a hoop or wreath to serve as the wheel and to secure the candles. The straw doll represents the young Sun God. This is a symbolic remnant of the Harvest Lord and Green Man imagery, which our ancestors believed lived in the trees and plants.

On your altar, place two white candles at the opposite end from where you will be positioned. The candles should be several inches apart to your left and right. These candles serve as the symbols of purification in the material world and the spiritual world. In the center of your altar, place the Sun wheel with twelve white birthday candles. This will represent the living connection between the Sun and waxing cycle of Nature. In front of the Sun wheel, place the straw doll.

The altar can be decorated with traditional symbols, such as pinecones and acorns. Place a ritual bell on the right side of the altar. The final item needed is a small plate for offerings of pumpkin seeds, nuts, and bread. A cup of milk is also traditional.

When you are ready, light the white altar candles from left to right. Ring the altar bell three times and then recite:

> *"I call to the God and Goddess to bless this ritual*
> *on this sacred day of purification and growth."*

Next, ring the bell three times, light the Sun wheel candles, and say:

> *"In the name of the God and Goddess, I call to the waxing spirit*
> *of the Sun. Come partake of the offerings I freely give here upon*
> *this altar. Grow in strength and purity. And through this, my life*
> *too is purified, and I am assured of growth in the coming seasons."*

Raise the straw doll up and pass it over the Sun wheel in a full circle (moving clockwise). Then, return it in front of the Sun wheel. The final phase of the ritual turns now to giving offerings to the God and Goddess. Before presenting the offerings, say:

> *"God and Goddess, I thank you for your presence in my life and*
> *for purifying the light within and without. May your blessings of*
> *growth and increase permeate the coming seasons. Please accept*
> *this offering as a token of my love."*

Place your hands, palms facing up, on each side of the offering plate as a gesture of thanksgiving. Once the offering is made, you can remove, clean, and store the altar items (except for the Sun wheel and straw doll). Allow the Sun wheel candles to burn out. When the candles have burned away, hang the straw doll in a window that faces East. Remove and put it away after sunrise. When planting your garden, you can dip the straw doll in water and anoint the seeds by shaking the wet doll over them.

Ostara (Vernal Equinox)

Items needed:
- ❖ 2 green altar candles
- ❖ 1 small red votive candle
- ❖ 1 raw egg (in shell)
- ❖ 1 small cauldron
- ❖ 1 altar bell
- ❖ 1 offering plate
- ❖ 1 offering cup
- ❖ Seasonal altar decorations
- ❖ Offerings (see ritual text)
- ❖ Ritual tools (see ritual text)
- ❖ Matches or lighter

The key themes of this season are regeneration and renewal. Both are related to the archetypal feminine or receptive principle in Nature. The traditional objects are the egg and the cauldron. The egg represents birth in the "breaking through" process, also reflected in the return of the Goddess from the Underworld. The cauldron is the womb of the Goddess, from which all things are born.

On your altar, place two green candles at the opposite end from where you will be positioned. The candles should be several inches apart to your left and right. These candles serve as symbols of renewed life. In the center of your altar, place the cauldron with the egg inside. This will represent the vessel of life (in the Underworld) returning through the vessel of regeneration.

In front of the cauldron, place a small red votive candle. The altar can be decorated with traditional symbols, such as flowers, hare images, seeds, and so forth. Leave room for a ritual bell and place it on the right side of the altar. The final item needed is a small plate and a cup for offerings. The traditional offerings are seeds, bulbs, colored ribbons, and colored eggs.

When you are ready, light the green candles from left to right. Ring the altar bell three times and then recite:

> *"I call to the God and Goddess to bless this ritual on this sacred day,*
> *which marks the return of life to the world."*

Next, ring the bell three times, light the red votive candle, and say:

> *"In the name of the God and Goddess, I call to the spirit of return and regeneration. Come, partake of the offerings I freely give here upon this altar. As you awaken the sleeping seeds, awaken also the seeds of the abilities I possess to accomplish my goals."*

At this stage, take the egg from the cauldron, hold it up, and recite:

> *"From the darkness beneath the Earth,*
> *the lifegiving vessel has returned. All is reborn, all is renewed."*

Set the egg on the altar where it will be safe. The final phase of the ritual now turns to giving offerings to the God and Goddess. Before presenting the offerings, say:

> *"God and Goddess, I thank you for your presence in my life and for the return of life in the coming seasons. Please accept this offering as a token of my love."*

Place your hands, palms facing up, on each side of the offering plate as a gesture of thanksgiving. Once the offering is made, you can remove, clean, and store your altar items (except for the egg).

Take the egg to your garden and crack it open on the ground. If you do not have a garden, use a pot of soil. As you pour the egg onto the soil, say:

> *"The land is renewed by the return of the Goddess,*
> *the vessel of life."*

Leave the egg undisturbed for twenty-four hours and then mix it in the soil. If using a pot of soil, bury the egg several inches deep and leave it untouched for three days.

Afterwards, remove the soil and save a handful for growing a potted plant (mixing this soil with some new soil).

Beltane

Items needed:
- ❖ 1 red altar candle
- ❖ 1 green altar candle
- ❖ 1 pink votive candle
- ❖ 1 mortar and pestle
- ❖ 1 small cauldron
- ❖ 1 altar bell
- ❖ 1 offering bowl
- ❖ 1 offering cup
- ❖ Seasonal altar decorations
- ❖ Offerings (see ritual text)
- ❖ Ritual tools (see ritual text)
- ❖ Matches or lighter

The key themes of this season are fertility and union, both related to the union of the polarities. The traditional object of this season is the mortar and pestle. The mortar and pestle are a unified symbol that require each other. Separated, their intended use is lost or greatly diminished.

On your altar, place a red and a green candle at the opposite end from where you will be positioned. The candles should be several inches apart to your left (green candle) and right (red candle). These candles serve as the symbols of the polarities. In the center of your altar, place the mortar and pestle side by side. Set a pink votive candle in front of the mortar and pestle.

The altar can be decorated with other traditional symbols, such as flowers and colored ribbons (red and white). Place a ritual bell on the right side of the altar. The final item needed is a small bowl for an offering of porridge, custard, or pudding. A cup of May wine is also traditional (essentially a white wine, chilled and mixed with some strawberries and a few woodruff leaves).

When you are ready, light the altar candles from left to right. Ring the altar bell three times, and then recite:

> *"I call to the God and Goddess to bless this ritual*
> *on this sacred day of fertility and unity."*

Next, ring the bell three times, light the pink candle, and say:

"In the name of the God and Goddess, I call to the essence of the feminine and masculine spirit. Come, partake of the offerings I freely give here upon this altar. Unite in creation and increase. And through this, my life too shall become fertile and fruitful in the coming seasons."

Place the pestle in the mortar and say:

"Phallus to womb, energy to formation.
Together, they create and generate the gift of life."

The final phase of the ritual turns now to giving offerings to the God and Goddess. Before presenting the offerings, say:

"God and Goddess, I thank you for your presence in my life and for the fertile and creative essence within and without. May your blessings of fertility and fruitfulness permeate the coming seasons. Please accept this offering as a token of my love."

Place your hands, palms facing up, on each side of the offering plate as a gesture of thanksgiving.

Once the offering is made, you can remove, clean, and store your altar items (except for the mortar and pestle). If you have any seeds to plant, place them in the mortar for blessings. You can also place an object in the mortar that symbolizes something you wish to increase or become fruitful: the key to a business, an investment statement, and so forth.

Litha (Summer Solstice)

Items needed:
- ❖ 2 green altar candles
- ❖ 1 green votive candle
- ❖ 1 red rose
- ❖ 1 leaf mask
- ❖ 1 small cauldron
- ❖ 1 altar bell
- ❖ 1 offering plate
- ❖ 1 offering cup
- ❖ Seasonal altar decorations
- ❖ Offerings (see ritual text)
- ❖ Ritual tools (see ritual text)
- ❖ Matches or lighter

The key themes of this season are ripeness and rapport. The traditional symbols are the red rose and the leaf mask. The rose represents the Goddess in the fullness and beauty of the blossom. The leaf mask symbolizes the God in one of his primal forms linked to the land and to the Sun. The fresh leaf can be of oak, holly, or ivy. Eyes, nose, and a mouth should be painted or cut out on the leaf.

On your altar, place two green candles at the opposite end from where you will be positioned. The candles should be several inches apart to your left and right. These candles serve as the symbols of ripeness and fullness. In the center of your altar, place the red rose and the leaf mask side by side. This will symbolize the union of the God and Goddess. Set a green votive candle in front of them.

The altar can be decorated with a variety of flowers, vervain, and St. John's Wort. Place a ritual bell on the right side of the altar. The final item needed is a small plate for offerings of fruit and vegetables. A cup of mead is also traditional.

When you are ready, light the altar candles from left to right. Ring the altar bell three times and then recite:

"I call to the God and Goddess to bless this ritual
on this sacred day of ripeness and union."

Next, ring the bell three times, light the green votive candle, and say:

"In the name of the God and Goddess, I call to the Spirit of Rapport that unites all polarities. Come, partake of the offerings I freely give here upon this altar. Join and become greater than the whole. And through this, my life too shall be abundant in the coming season."

The final phase of the ritual turns now to giving offerings to the God and Goddess. Before presenting the offerings, say:

"God and Goddess, I thank you for your presence in my life and for the gift of growth and increase. May your blessings permeate the coming season. Please accept this offering as a token of my love."

Place your hands, palms facing up, on each side of the offering plate as a gesture of thanksgiving. Once the offering is made, you can remove, clean, and store your altar items (except for the rose and leaf mask). In a private area outside, set the rose on the ground and place the leaf mask over it. Leave them undisturbed and do not retrieve them later.

Lughnasadh

Items needed:
- ❖ 2 green altar candles
- ❖ 1 yellow birthday candle
- ❖ 1 sheaf of wheat grain
- ❖ 1 cutting knife
- ❖ 1 corn doll
- ❖ 1 loaf of whole grain bread
- ❖ 1 small cauldron
- ❖ 1 altar bell
- ❖ 1 offering plate
- ❖ 1 offering cup
- ❖ Seasonal altar decorations
- ❖ Offerings (see ritual text)
- ❖ Ritual tools (see ritual text)
- ❖ Matches or lighter

The key themes of this season are harvest and abundance. The traditional objects are the sheaf, the blade, and the corn doll. The sheaf represents the abundant harvest, the blade is the reaper, and the corn doll is the spirit of the field. This is symbolic of the Harvest Lord figure.

On your altar, place two green candles at the opposite end from where you will be positioned. The candles should be several inches apart and to your left and right. These candles serve as the symbols of abundance and gain. In the center of your altar, place the sheaf, the blade, and the corn doll next to each other. In front of this, put a whole bread loaf (unsliced whole grain wheat is good). Place a yellow birthday candle in the center of the loaf.

The altar can be decorated with other symbols, such as seasonal berries and other fruit. Place a ritual bell on the right side of the altar. The final items needed are a small plate for offerings of oats, cornbread, or barley cakes and a cup of mead or glass of beer.

When you are ready, light the altar candles from left to right. Ring the altar bell three times and then recite:

> *"I call to the God and Goddess to bless this ritual*
> *on this sacred day of harvest and gain."*

Next, ring the bell three times, light the loaf candle, and say:

*"In the name of the God and Goddess, I call to the spirit of gathering
and abundance. Come, partake of the offerings I freely give here
upon this altar. Grant the fruits of all labor. And through this,
my life too shall be abundant and gainful in the coming seasons."*

Take the blade and lay the edge on the loaf. While you cut into the
bread, blow out the candle. Remove the candle and cut the bread into
three sections. Take one small piece of bread from each section and grab
a cup of mead or wine. Set them in front of you and recite:

"For there are three great Mysteries: Birth, Life, and Death."

Eat the three small portions of the bread and drink some of the mead
or wine. Next, recite:

*"May I grow in knowledge and wisdom
and may the Mysteries reveal themselves to me."*

The final phase of the ritual turns now to giving offerings to the God
and Goddess. Before presenting the offerings, say:

*"God and Goddess, I thank you for your presence in my life and for
the abundance you grant within and without. May your blessings
of harvest and gain permeate the coming seasons. Please accept this
offering as a token of my love."*

Place your hands, palms facing up, on each side of the offering plate
as a gesture of thanksgiving. Once the offering is made, you can remove,
clean, and store the altar items.

Pour the wine out upon the soil and toss the bread up into the air
and away from you. Do not retrieve them.

Mabon (Autumn Equinox)

Items needed:
- ❖ 2 black altar candles
- ❖ 1 black votive candle
- ❖ 1 small cauldron
- ❖ 1 dark mirror
- ❖ 1 altar bell
- ❖ 1 offering plate
- ❖ 1 offering cup
- ❖ Parchment paper
- ❖ Seasonal altar decorations
- ❖ Offerings (see ritual text)
- ❖ Ritual tools (see ritual text)
- ❖ Matches or lighter

The key themes of this season are internalization and introspection. The traditional objects are the cauldron and the dark mirror. The cauldron represents the entrance to the Underworld, and the dark mirror symbolizes looking inward. For a simple dark mirror, you can apply black paint to the underside of a clear piece of glass.

On your altar, place two black candles at the opposite end from where you will be positioned. The candles should be several inches apart to your left and right. These candles serve as the symbols of the Otherworld. In the center of your altar, place the cauldron and mirror. Set a black votive candle in front of them.

The altar can be decorated with other traditional symbols such as dried leaves and gourds. Place a ritual bell on the right side of the altar. The final items needed are a small plate for offerings of cereal grains and a cup of dark red wine or juice.

When you are ready, light the altar candles from left to right. Ring the altar bell three times and then recite:

> *"I call to the God and Goddess to bless this ritual*
> *on this sacred day of entering into the shadows."*

Next, ring the bell three times, light the votive candle, and say:

"In the name of the God and Goddess, I call to the spirit of quiet shadowed places. Come, partake of the offerings I freely give here upon this altar. Grant the inner vision and the clarity of discernment. And through this, may I gain enlightenment in the places of darkness."

On a piece of parchment paper, write a situation in your life that needs reassessment or greater discernment. You can also write down what you want to be rid of in your life, such as smoking or some other addiction. When completed, speak your intention, fold the parchment three times, and drop it into the cauldron. Finally, place the dark mirror over the cauldron like a lid.

The final phase of the ritual turns now to giving offerings to the God and Goddess. Before presenting the offerings, say:

"God and Goddess, I thank you for your presence in my life and for the shadows and dark periods that help me change and grow. May your blessings of peaceful withdrawal and contemplative solitude permeate the coming season. Please accept this offering as a token of my love."

Place your hands, palms facing up, on each side of the offering plate as a gesture of thanksgiving. Once the offering is made, you can remove, clean, and store the altar items. Take the piece of parchment, soak it in water for a few minutes, and then bury it several inches deep in soil.

Full Moon Ritual

Items needed:

- ❖ 3 cookies or small cakes
- ❖ 1 altar cloth (black, if possible, to represent procreation)
- ❖ 1 offering plate
- ❖ 1 bowl of water (add three pinches of salt to water and stir)
- ❖ Cup or chalice
- ❖ Incense of your choice (jasmine or wisteria is good)
- ❖ Wine or fruit juice
- ❖ Ritual tools (see ritual text)

Prepare an altar with a cloth and two white altar candles. Between these candles, place your deity images or totems that you selected to represent each deity (Goddess on the left, God on the right). Place a cup or chalice on the altar along with an athame. Place a bowl of water on the altar where it is easily reached.

Decorate your altar with seasonal flowers and other corresponding symbols. Set a plate of sweet cookies or cakes on the altar. Pour some wine into the cup and light the incense. Then, anoint your forehead, solar plexus, and stomach with the salted water for purification. Following this, extinguish all artificial lights and light the altar candles. You are now ready to begin.

Stand before the altar, look up at the Moon, and say:

> *"On this sacred night of the Lady, beneath the Full Moon, which she has placed among the stars, I give veneration. I join on this night with all who gather in the name of the Goddess."*

Hold your palms out (facing away from you) and form a triangle by touching the index fingers and thumbs of both hands. Enclose the Moon in the triangle opening between your fingers and recite:

> *"Hail and adoration unto you, O' Great Lady. Hail, Goddess of the Moon and the night! You have been since before the beginning and caused all things to appear. Giver and Sustainer of Life, adoration unto you."*

Lower your hands (releasing the triangle) and dip the fingers of your left hand into the bowl of water. Then, anoint your forehead and recite:

"My Lady, I pray thee, impart to me thy illumination."

Anoint your eyes and recite:

*"Enlighten me that I may perceive more clearly
all my endeavors."*

Anoint your heart area and recite:

"And illuminate my soul, imparting thy essence of purity."

Anoint your stomach and groin by brushing down your fingers from the navel and then present both palms upward to the Moon as you recite:

*"I reveal my inner self to thee and ask that all be cleansed
and purified within."*

Place an offering of flowers to the Goddess between your ritual tools and recite:

"O' Great Lady, think yet even for a moment upon this worshipper. Beneath the Sun do people toil, go about, and attend to all worldly affairs. But beneath the Moon, your children dream, awaken, and draw their power. Therefore, bless me, O' Great Lady, and impart to me your mystic light, in which I find my powers. Bless me, O' Lady of the Moon."

Hold the chalice of wine up to the Moon and recite:

"O' Ancient Wanderer of the Dark Heavens, Mystery of the Mysteries, emanate your sacred essence upon me as I wait below at this appointed time. Enlighten my inner mind and spirit, as do you lighten the darkness of night."

Drink from the chalice and place it back on the altar.

Place the cookies or small cakes on the pentacle and make sure there is still some wine in the cup or chalice. Trace a crescent with your wand over the cakes and wine and recite:

> *"Blessings upon this meal, which is as my own body. For without such sustenance, I would perish from this world. Blessings upon the grain, which as seed went into the Earth where deep secrets hide. And there did it dance with the Elements and spring forth as a flowered plant, concealing secrets strange. When you were in the ear of grain, spirits of the field came to cast their light upon you and aid you in your growth. Thus, through you shall I be touched by that same race, and, with the Mysteries hidden within you, I shall obtain even unto the last of these grains."*

Trace a crescent over the wine with your athame and recite:

> *"By virtue of this sacred blade,*
> *be this wine the vital essence of the Great Goddess."*

Trace a crescent over the cakes with your wand and recite:

> *"By virtue of this sacred wand,*
> *be this cake the vital substance of the Great God."*

Lift the pentacle and the chalice, look up at the Moon, and recite:

> *"Through these cakes and by this wine, may the Goddess and God bless me and give me inner strength and vision. May I come to know that which is of the eternal gods within me. May this blessing be so, in the name of the Lord and Lady."*

Eat a portion of the meal and drink some wine. Leave some for libations at the close of the ritual. The wine will be poured out on the soil, and the cakes will be tossed up to the Moon.

Sit now before the altar, look up at the Moon, and visualize it as the Goddess appearing to you in a sphere of light. Kiss the palm of your left hand and extend it up to her. Then say:

"O' Bright Lady, Queen of all the Wise Ones, hear my adoration. Hear my voice as I speak your praises. Receive my words as they rise heavenward when the Full Moon shines and fills the heavens with your beauty. I come before you and reach my hand up to you. As the Full Moon shines upon me, give me all your blessings.

O' Great Goddess of the Moon, Goddess of the Mysteries of the Moon, teach me secrets yet revealed, ancient rites of invocation, for I believe the Witches' creed. And when I seek for knowledge, I seek and find you above all others.

Give me power, O' Most Secret Lady, and protect me from my enemies. When my body lies resting nightly, speak to my inner spirit, teach me all your holy Mysteries. I believe your ancient promise that all who seek your holy presence will receive your wisdom.

Behold, O' Ancient Goddess, I have come beneath the Full Moon at this appointed time. Now, the Full Moon shines upon me. Hear me and recall your ancient promise. Let your glory shine about me. Bless me, O' Gracious Queen of Heaven. In your name, so be it done."

Before completing the ritual, a work of magick or spellcasting may be performed. When you are finished, remove, clean, and store your altar items. Offer libations to the Earth and Moon, pouring out remaining fluids and tossing whatever remains of the cookies or cakes up toward the Moon. The rite of the Full Moon is thereby completed.

Glossary

Agreement of Consciousness: An established set of concepts, teachings, and methods that are a point of agreement. In this regard, the matter is understood within context and relationship. In a stricter sense, an agreement of consciousness refers to pre-established and accepted norms and definitions that form the basis of understanding.

Cone of Power: An energy vortex generated by ritualists within a magickal or ritual circle. It is envisioned as a swirling cone of energy that forms above the ritualists. The most common means of generating a cone of power is through dancing. Other methods include drumming, trance, and altered states of consciousness.

Crone of the Cottage: A legendary figure in folkloric and magickal traditions. In her tales, the Crone was taken by the Faery when she was young. She lived with them for many years, and when she returned to the mortal world, so much time had passed that everyone she knew had perished long ago. The Crone lives alone in a cabin deep in the woods and serves as a go-between for Faeries and humankind. Through this, she makes contact possible, which can lead to mentorship by the Faery beings.

Group Mind: The collective thoughts and energy of a group that join in a common cause. This forms "one mind" with many parts that act together in harmony and agreement. The sum of the group mind is greater than that of its parts.

Ladder of Light: A series of concepts formed together for the purpose of connecting realms of existence and levels of consciousness. This is envisioned as a ladder made of light, which can be climbed up to the higher realms of spiritual vibration or down into the lower realms of ancestral vibration.

Memory-chain Associations: A series of connective pathways, leapfrogging back to the original source. Each idea is linked to an earlier idea that reflected yet another earlier idea of the source from which it came. By tracing backwards, we arrive at the source and unite with the purity of the concept.

Momentum of the Past: A current of energy generated by the ancestral group mind, which flows from the past to the present. It is passed through bloodlines and is an occult counterpart of our genetic patterns.

Nil Consciousness: Clearing the mind of all thoughts and perceptions. When "nothingness" prevails within the mind, the consciousness of the soul and the personality is bypassed, and we are connected for a moment to the Perfect Ideal. This informs the subconscious mind and plants the seed of enlightenment into the conscious mind.

Otherworld: The non-material realm of myth and legend where hidden and mystical realms exist with beings like the Elven and Faery. In some myths, this is the realm where mortals find rest, healing, and renewal (whether living or dead).

Perfect Ideal: The original design of creation and its purpose. This exists undiluted and undistorted. It is the mind of the Source of All Things, conceiving the universe and the purpose of everything within it.

Walker in the Woods: A spirit or entity attached to a place of power or a sacred grove. It serves as both a guardian and a preserver. The Walker can be contacted for information.

Wheel of Rebirth: An occult concept in which the soul is drawn back into material existence. This is caused by dense energies attached to the soul from previous lives. These are manifestations of negative feelings, fears, regrets, and traumas. The attachment of dense energy makes non-material existence impossible, and so the soul sinks back into the world of matter to be born again.

Suggested Reading List

Ritual

Ashcroft-Nowicki, Dolores. *First Steps in Ritual.* Aquarian Press, 1982.

Gray, William. *Seasonal Occult Rituals.* Aquarian Press, 1970.

—. *Inner Traditions of Magic.* Samuel Weiser, 1970.

—. *Magical Ritual Methods.* Helios Book Service, 1971.

—. *Western Inner Workings.* Samuel Weiser, 1983.

Magick

Bardon, Franz. *Initiation in Hermetics.* Dieter Ruggeberg, 1971.

Butler, W.E. *The Magician: His Training and Work.* Wilshire Book Company, 1976.

Gray, William. *Temple Magic.* Llewellyn Publications, 1988.

Denning, Melita, and Osborne Phillips. *Magical States of Consciousness.* Llewellyn Publications, 1985.

Cicero, Chic, and Sandra Cicero. *Creating Magical Tools.* Llewellyn Publications, 1999.

Mystery Traditions

Harris, Mike. *Awen, The Quest of the Celtic Mysteries.* Sun Chalice Books, 1999.

Stewart, R.J. *The Underworld Initiation.* Aquarian Press, 1985.

Grimassi, Raven. *Witchcraft, A Mystery Tradition.* Crossed Crow Books, 2024.

Spence, Lewis. *The Mysteries of Britain: The Secret Rites and Traditions of Ancient Britain Restored.* Newcastle Publishing, 1993.

Traditional Wicca

Gardner, Gerald. *Witchcraft Today.* Citadel Press, 1973.

—. *The Meaning of Witchcraft.* Samuel Weiser, 1976.

Valiente, Doreen, and Evan Jones. *Witchcraft, A Tradition Renewed.* Phoenix Publications, 1980.
Crowther, Patricia, and Arnold Crowther. *The Witches Speak.* Samuel Weiser, 1976.
—. *The Secrets of Ancient Witchcraft with the Witches Tarot.* University Books, 1974.
Buckland, Ray. *Witchcraft from the Inside.* Llewellyn Publications, 1995.
Ryall, Rhiannon. *West Country Wicca: A Journal of the Old Religion.* Phoenix, 1989.

Pagan Religion
Baring, Anne, and Jules Cashford. *The Myth of the Goddess: Evolution of an Image.* Arkana, 1993.
Millis, Ludo. *The Pagan Middle Ages.* Boydell Press, 1998.
Gooch, Stan. *Cities of Dreams: When Women Ruled the Earth.* Inner Traditions, 1995.
—. *The Dream Culture of the Neanderthals.* Inner Traditions, 2006.
MacMullen, Ramsay. *Christianity and Paganism in the Fourth to Eighth Centuries.* Yale University Press, 1997.
Frazer, James. *The Golden Bough: A Study in Magic and Religion.* MacMillan Co., 1922.

Gods and Goddesses
MacKillop, James. *Dictionary of Celtic Mythology.* Oxford University Press, 1998.
Murray, Alexander S. *Who's Who in Mythology.* Crescent Books, 1988.
Seznec, Jean. *The Survival of the Pagan Gods.* Princeton University Press, 1981.
Stewart, R.J. *Celtic Gods, Celtic Goddesses.* Blandford, 1990.

Ritual Items and Practices
Campanelli, Pauline, and Dan Campanelli. *Wheel of the Year: Living the Magical Life.* Llewellyn Publications, 1997.
—. *Pagan Rites of Passage.* Llewellyn Publications, 1998.

Bibliography

Alba, De-Anna. *The Cauldron of Change: Myths, Mysteries and Magick of the Goddess.* Delphi Press, 1993.

Baring, Anne and Jules Cashford. *The Myth of the Goddess: Evolution of an Image.* Arkana Books, 1993.

Bord, Janet and Colin Bord. *The Secret Country.* Paladin Book, 1980.

—. *Earth Rites.* Granada Publishing, 1982.

Bourne, Lois. *Witch Amongst Us: The Autobiography of a Witch.* Robert Hale, 1995.

Butler, W.E. *Practical Magic and the Western Mystery Tradition.* Thoth Publications, 2002.

—. *The Magician: His Training and Work.* Wilshire Book Co., 1969.

Chappell, Helen. *The Waxing Moon.* Links Books, 1974.

Crowley, Vivianne. *Wicca, The Old Religion in the New Age.* Aquarian Press, 1989.

Crowther, Patricia and Arnold Crowther. *The Secrets of Ancient Witchcraft with the Witches Tarot.* University Books, 1974.

Davies, Morganna and Aradia Lynch. *Keepers of the Flame: Interviews with Elders of Traditional Witchcraft in America.* Olympian Press, 2001.

Elworthy, Frederick. *Horns of Honour.* John Murray, 1900.

Farran, David. *Living With Magic: Witchcraft and Sorcery as a New Way of Living, Loving and Expanding Our Consciousness.* Simon and Schuster, 1974.

Fortune, Dion. *The Esoteric Orders and Their Work.* Aquarian Press, 1982.

Frazer, James. *The Golden Bough: A Study in Magic and Religion.* MacMillan Co., 1922.

Gardner, Gerald. *Witchcraft Today.* Citadel Press, 1973.

—. *The Meaning of Witchcraft.* Samuel Weiser, 1976.

Graves, Robert. *The White Goddess.* Farrar, Straus and Giroux, 1974.

Gray, William. *Seasonal Occult Rituals.* Aquarian Press, 1970.

—. *Inner Traditions of Magic*. Samuel Weiser, 1970.

—. *Magical Ritual Methods*. Helios Book Service, 1971.

—. *Western Inner Workings*. Samuel Weiser, 1983.

Grimassi, Raven. *Hereditary Witchcraft: Secrets of the Old Religion*. Llewellyn, 1999.

—. *Wiccan Mysteries*. Crossed Crow Books, 2023.

—. *The Witches' Craft*. Crossed Crow Books, 2024.

—. *Witchcraft, A Mystery Tradition*. Crossed Crow Books, 2024.

Good, John Mason, Olinthus Gregory, and Newton Bosworth. *Pantologia: A New Cyclopaedia*. G Kearsley; J Walker; J Stockdale, 1813.

Hartley, Christine. *The Western Mystery Tradition*. Aquarian Press, 1986.

Huson, Paul. *Mastering Witchcraft*. Putnam, 1970.

Kondratiev, Alexei. *The Apple Branch: A Path to Celtic Ritual*. Citadel Press, 1981.

Lang, Andrew. *Myth, Ritual and Religion, Volumes 1 and 2*. Random House, 1996.

Leek, Sybil. *The Diary of a Witch*. Signet Books, 1968.

—. *The Complete Art of Witchcraft*. Signet Books, 1971.

Leland, Charles G. *Aradia, or Gospel of the Witches*. 1899.

Matthews, John, and Caitlin Matthews. *Walkers Between the Worlds: The Western Mysteries from Shaman to Magus*. Inner Traditions, 2003.

Millis, Ludo. *The Pagan Middle Ages*. Boydell Press, 1998.

Murray, Grace A. *Ancient Rituals and Ceremonies*. Alston Rivers Ltd., 1929.

Paine, Lauran. *Witchcraft and the Mysteries*. Robert Hale and Company, 1975.

Regardie, Israel. *The Tree of Life: A Study in Magic*. Samuel Weiser, 1971.

—. *Ceremonial Magic: A Guide to the Mechanisms of Ritual*. Aquarian Press, 1980.

Sagan, Carl and Ann Druyan. *Shadows of Forgotten Ancestors*. Ballantine Books, 1992.

Seznec, Jean. *The Survival of the Pagan Gods*. Princeton University Press, 1981.

Sheba, Lady. *The Grimoire of Lady Sheba*. Llewellyn Publications, 1974.

Stewart, R.J. *The Living World of Faery*. Mercury Publishing, 1999.

Valiente, Doreen. *Witchcraft for Tomorrow*. St. Martin's Press, 1978.

Valiente, Doreen, and Evan Jones. *Witchcraft, A Tradition Renewed*. Phoenix Publications, 1980.

Wind, Edgar. *Pagan Mysteries in the Renaissance*. Yale University Press, 1958.